BOOKS BY

Rick R. Reed

====================

Obsessed

Penance

A Face Without a Heart

Twisted: Tales of Obsession and Terror

IM

In the Blood

Rick R. Reed

Quest Books

Nederland, Texas

ISBN 1-932300-90-1
978-1-932300-90-2

First Printing 2007

9 8 7 6 5 4 3 2 1

Cover design by Donna Pawlowski

Published by:

Regal Crest Enterprises, LLC
4700 Hwy 365, Suite A, PMB 210
Port Arthur, Texas 7764

Find us on the World Wide Web at
http://www.regalcrest.biz

Printed in the United States of America

Acknowledgments

As always, gratitude toward Cathy LeNoir, not only for publishing my work, but for her dedication to seeing that great gay and lesbian writing finds a voice and a home. Thanks also to Lea Schizas and Sylverre, for their sharp editorial insights; to Donna Pawlowski for her always-beautiful cover designs; and to everyone who craves immortality, in all its forms...everywhere.

For my son, Nicholas
I hope I inspire you as much as you do me

Chapter
One

ELISE GRONEMAN STARES out the window, stomach roiling. What she has is like stage fright. She gets it every night, before she ventures out of her tiny Rogers Park studio apartment on Chicago's far north side. It's always been amazing to her that just a few minutes walk to the north is the suburb of Evanston and a different world; there, the streets are tree-lined and clean, the homes palatial, the condos upscale, the restaurants grand, and the stores exclusive. Affluence and culture preside. Yet here, on Greenview Street, one encounters abject poverty, crime, the detritus of urban desperation: tiny brightly-colored baggies, fast food wrappers, condoms, empty alcohol bottles, even pieces of clothing. The sidewalks are cracked, the grassy areas choked with weeds and garbage. Here in Rogers Park, the normal folks, the ones who travel on the el to work downtown every morning, stay inside, so as not to mingle with people like Elise, or the man outside her window right now, who's screaming, "What the fuck do I care what you do, bitch? It ain't no skin off my ass." Elise glances out and sees the man is alone. A boy cruises by on a bicycle that's too small for him. The bike is stolen; either that, or he's a runner for some small time dealer, delivering and making collections. Sometimes, there aren't many options for moving up the ladder.

But this neighborhood is all Elise can afford, and, unless she picks up more clientele soon, she may even be crowded out of this hovel she begrudgingly calls home. Once, she shared the place with someone else, but those days, for better or worse, are long behind her.

Elise moves closer to the window, attempting to obliterate memory by the simple act of staring outside. Dusk has fallen and the sky belies the earthbound life before her. The sun is setting, the sky deep violet, filtering down to tangerine and pink near the horizon. If she keeps her eyes trained on the riot of color and shape to the east, she can almost forget where she is.

But the denizens of Greenview Street make sure she stays reminded. They stroll the night in an attempt to escape the heat, the hot, moist air pressing in, smothering. They call to one another, using words she had barely heard, let alone used, back in Shaker Heights, Ohio, where she had grown up: *nigga, motherfucka, homey.* Fuck used as an adjective, verb, and ejaculation (but rarely, ironically, utilized in a sexual context). Snatches of music filter out from apartment windows. Cruising vehicles pass by, bass thumping hard enough to cause the glass in her windows to vibrate. She has picked up names of artists like Bow Wow, Def Soul, and Trick Daddy as she walks the streets. Elise puts a hand to the screen, testing the air. Will there ever be a breeze again? She wonders if her neighbors would recognize any of the names attached to the music she loves, names like Vivaldi, Smetana, Bach. Other music fills the street: arguments and professions of love shouted with equal force. Headlights illuminate the darkening night, which is also lit by the flare of a match here, neon there, and sodium vapor overall. The world glows orange, filling up not only the streets of the city, but the sky, blotting out the stars.

East of her churn the cold waters of Lake Michigan, and Elise imagines its foam-flecked waves lapping at the shores. She'd like to pad down to the beach at the end of Birchwood Street, kick off her sandals and run across the sand and into the water, its cold obliterating and refreshing. She wishes she had the freedom, but east is not her path. Her way lies south, to Howard Street, purveyor of pawnshops and prostitution.

Her destination.

Elise turns to survey her cramped apartment. Near the ceiling, industrial green paint peels from the walls to reveal other coats of grimy paint no color describes. Metal-frame twin bed, sheets twisted and gray, damp from sweat and humidity. Next to that, Salvation Army-issue scarred oak table, small, with the remains of this night's meal, a few apple peelings, a knife, and a glass half filled with pale tea, darkening in the dying light.

It's a place no one would ever call home. Elise's apartment is utilitarian, a place to work, to sleep, to eat. It's little more than shelter.

The only sign of human habitation is her work: huge canvases mounted on easels, bits of heavy paper taped to her drawing board. Much of her work is done in charcoal and pencil, but the palette of grays and black remain constant, whether it's a sketch or a completed painting. Her subject matter, too, is always the same, although the variety of choices she has to explore is endless. Elise likes to draw intensely detailed renderings of crime and accident scenes, aping the cold, clinical detachment one might find in a book of crime scene photographs. Here is a woman, slumped beside a corduroy recliner, a gunshot ripping away half of her head (the blood black in Elise's rendering), beside her, a half-eaten chicken leg and the Tempo section of the *Chicago Tribune*, folded neatly and splattered with her gore. There's a man lying beside a highway, the cars a fast-moving blurred river. His head has been severed from his body. On the wall she has masking-taped a nightmare in quick, staccato slashes: a young woman strangled and left to lie in the pristine environment of an upscale public washroom, clean, shiny ceramic tile, untarnished metal stalls. Another woman, looking bored, checks her lipstick in the mirror. Near Elise's floor is a small, intricately detailed drawing done in charcoal: two lovers lie in a bed of gore, the aftermath, one presumes, of discovery of their union by a jealous lover. The woman has a sheet discreetly covering her up to the neck. The man lies splayed out in a paroxysm of agony. And why not? His offending penis has been slashed from his body. Is that it on the floor beside the bed, a smudge of black, nearly shapeless?

Where is all the color? Elise herself wonders as she dresses for the evening. Color has been leeched out of her world; it is getting increasingly difficult to be able to remember what color was like and thus, increasingly difficult to duplicate its varied hues on paper or canvas. Color, it seems, is but a hazy memory out of her past.

Enough of art analysis, she thinks. It's her *days* she has designated to her art. Nighttime is when she prepares for her other job, the occupation that keeps a roof over her head. The job which perhaps is responsible for stealing the color from her vision.

Enough! Enough! Enough! she thinks. *Put the introspection behind you.* It's time now, time to become a creature of the night, an animal doing what it must to provide its own sustenance.

She rummages in the apartment's lone closet, pulling out one of her "uniforms," clothing that helps identify her occupation as much a mechanic's jumpsuit, or a waitress's ruffled apron and polyester dress.

Tonight, she dons a short black skirt bisected by a wide zipper ending in a big silver loop. Over her head, she pulls a white T-shirt, tying it just above her waist. In combination with the low-riding skirt, it perfectly frames her navel. Elise pulls the skin apart and plucks out a piece of lint. She completes her ensemble with dark seamed stockings and spike heels. These are the tools of the trade as much as the brushes, sticks of charcoal, and pencils littering her space.

Elise flips back her long whiskey-colored hair, and leans close to the mirror. She lines her lips with a shade of brown, then fills in with glossy crimson. Cheapens her green eyes with thick black kohl. Elise pulls her hair back, away from her damp neck, and up, pinning it all together with a silver barrette adorned with the smiling face of a skull. Pentagram earrings. Tonight a witch, creature of the night.

Then she turns, hand on doorknob. The night awaits: exhaust fumes, traffic, the chirping of cicadas.

MARIA, TERENCE, AND Edward sit in a circle, facing one another. Atop the mantel, an army of candles, blood red pillars, votives, tapers, flickering, banishing the shadows to the corners, barely. The gloom is palpable, a fourth presence. But here is a trio who prefers the darkness, a threesome preternaturally attuned to it.

Edward, as always, has one eye on the paintings covering the wall. His vision reacts to their presence, even in the dim. His favorites stand out. There's an original etching by Van Gogh hung next to a portrait of Terence done years ago by a bag lady who used to sell her paintings on the steps of the Art Institute for a pittance. Even while living on the streets, Lee Godie's work was being collected by museums and important collectors. This one of Terence, commissioned on a bright, moonlit night in 1969, would probably sell these days for around $5,000. Terence had paid ten dollars for it. Further down, a Picasso (in his blue period) painting of a boxy woman contrasts with a drawing of a scream, giant, done in shades of magenta, black and yellow...a siren. Edward likes the paintings that have distilled emotion and movement into simple colors and lines. More paintings and sculptures choke the room, making of it a gallery, a warehouse, anything but what it is supposed to be—a living room. *No room in this house,* Edward thinks, *is a living room.* He does not grin at this play on words.

For Terence, the art is mostly a backdrop, a witness to an evening ritual and to his stunning presence. Terence has always been his own canvas, and the artwork he admires most. He holds a glass cylinder topped with a glass bowl. He has filled the bowl with a sticky mass, a brownish-green bud, sticky and redolent with a pungent aroma. He tamps the bud in firmly with his thumb, leaving just enough room to allow it to ignite and burn. His long, flat palm covers the cylinder's opening at one end as he brings it to his lips. A flame shoots up from a sterling silver lighter and Terence lights the bowl of marijuana. The bud glows orange, drawing Edward's gaze; it's a beacon in the darkness. Smoke rolls into the cylinder, gray and ephemeral. Terence removes his hand from the end of the cylinder and his mouth becomes a vacuum; the smoke disappears.

He passes it to Maria. "To hedonism! To art!"

Maria rolls her eyes. "Save the hyperbole for someone who gives a shit." She takes the glass cylinder and lighter from him. Where Terence's mouth and hand had been, the glass is icy cold.

ELISE PACES HOWARD Street. Her face, lit by street lights from the parking lot across the way, reveals apprehension and longing in yellow. She toys with an earring, examines the bottom of her shoe. Behind her a 7-11 and an adult bookstore compete for not-so-conspicuous consumption. The 7-11 offers Big Gulps. *So does the adult bookstore,* Elise thinks.

Her heart pounds faster. There is more sweat at her hairline, dribbling down her back like the crawly legs of insects, than even the humid night could provoke. Even though she has been doing this "work" for at least two years, she never gets over the fear. Never gets over the shame. Never gets past wondering if she will end up another crime statistic, another hard-to-identify young woman discovered in morning mist in an alley, or stuffed into a Dumpster. She did a drawing once of a woman in spike heels, lying in an alley with a plastic bag over her head, its bottom knotted tightly around her throat. She called it "Pessimistic Self Portrait." Thoughts like these cause her to shiver, in spite of the heat. Thoughts like these make her long for the solace of her tiny apartment, despite the mice whispering through the walls, and the cockroaches scattering when she turns on a light in the middle of the night.

Right now, it feels like one of those mice gnaws at the inside of her stomach. She breathes deeply, trying to focus her attention on the traffic cruising by. Which will slow to look? Which will cause her to move forward from her post in front of the store, a smile brave and totally false, plastered across her features? These initial movements, before any words are exchanged, are where the deal is truly struck. The eloquent meeting of the eyes between the wanted and the wanter is where decisions are made. Elise's slow walk to the idling car, the negotiations: nothing more than busy work, after-the-fact necessities. In spite of her anxiety, the motions of this work have become stale and as routine as the filing and photocopying her more conventional sisters do downtown, in some Loop office.

Elise smoothes her skirt, stiffening as a gang of Hispanic boys charges up the street. They call to each other in Spanish, tossing a basketball back and forth. There are at least eight of them, their youth raucous and threatening. They haven't seen her yet, but soon will, and Elise knows what's coming from past experience: the whistles and catcalls, the unintelligible sexual come-ons in Spanish they will all laugh at.

And she is a woman alone. No matter that she is plying a trade almost as old as mankind itself. Never mind that she is a criminal in this commerce.

These boys could take what she seeks to sell.

Take and destroy.

Elise prays they will surmise she has a pimp, leave her alone. Running in these heels is a fantasy, and a gangbang is not what she has in mind for tonight.

The boys press closer and Elise strains to understand the quick, staccato rhythm of the Spanish. But only the most basic words filter to Elise, not enough to make sense. Their laughter is evil, predatory.

The boys surge close, their heat and aggression a warning scent.

Elise moves on.

MARIA SETS THE glass cylinder on the floor. She closes her eyes, and beneath the delicate, blue-veined lids, her eyes flutter. Movement stops and she exhales; a plume of blue smoke jets upward into the darkness, tinged just a bit brighter where dull light shines in through leaded glass. "That's it; there's no more left in the bowl."

The two men nod. Edward rises and moves to the rheostat on the wall. Recessed lighting disperses the room's shadows and brings the paintings to brilliant life. Sculptures formed from granite, marble, and metal move in the sudden light. The three's eyes glaze at the drama the paintings and sculptures present: the liquid flow of color, images conflicting, jumping from canvas and paper, rock or metal become bone, flesh. It is the ingestion of THC that causes their sudden fascination, but it's also the sudden riot of color and form the light reveals.

It excites them. They see mockery in this art, love, too...sex, death, and betrayal. Violence. Serenity. The art sharpens their focus and brings them closer to what they will hunt, the population they were once part of: humanity.

They see it all. Theirs is a special sensitivity, approaching empathy.

This is an old ritual.

It attunes them to the night...and the hunt.

ELISE HAS FOUND solace under the Howard Street el tracks, under a street lamp's pool of light. Trains rumble overhead; she barely hears herself breathe. She wants to vanish, to become silent and invisible. *If I had any guts at all,* she thinks, *I'd go into the station, pay the fare, walk upstairs, and fling myself on the tracks just before the next rapidly approaching train.* Think of the excitement, the clamor, the shouts, and the cries. Picture the blood dripping down from the tracks onto the sidewalk and street below. Windshield wipers swishing away blood. *And I would be a part of none of it. I would exist only in memory.*

But whose?

Her own memory she would like to extinguish, have an operation to excise that part of her brain that stores what happens to her. There would be a kind of comfort in awakening each day and not remembering what happened before, starting life over every day. It seems there would be more possibilities. But that option has already been explored too much by Hollywood screenwriters and seldom happens in reality.

Besides, she is a nameless entity now, a utilitarian tool, waiting to be used. This other job allows her to disconnect, in a way. It frees her from worrying about where the idea for her next drawing or painting will come. It frees her from wondering if the only thing she has a passion for is anything she's really good at. If she deserves, one day, to make a living from it.

An el train rumbles by above, the brakes squealing as the muffled voice of a conductor announces, "Howard Street, change here for Evanston/Wilmette trains. Howard Street."

There's a rush of people behind her as passengers descend the stairs from the platform. Elise casts her gaze downward when the stares come...in an instant, contempt, desire, and indifference. They know her and they don't. In some ways, she's used to the looks, the leers, and the sneers. In others, she will never get used to it. She can never stop being the good Jewish girl from Shaker Heights. She thinks of her mother, to whom she has not spoken in two years, and imagines her shock if she could see her daughter now, the clothes she wears and the blatant advertising the shoes, shirt, and skirt convey. What would her mother do? Try to strong-arm her into coming home? Arrange for a deprogramming?

"Excuse me, miss."

A wheedling voice. Elise tries not to jump. Before her is a man, shifting his weight from one foot to the other. Seersucker suit, frayed around the edges; dirty, colorless hair hanging limp across a creased forehead. Black plastic-frame glasses. The glare on the lenses makes it impossible for Elise to discern color or intention in the eyes beneath.

"What?"

The man slides his hand around in the sweat on his forehead. Thin, pale lips like worms break into a grin. "You sellin' it?"

What is this? Elise wonders. *Chicago vice? He's got quite a disguise. The nerd routine, perhaps it's worked before...*

"Well?" The man moves even more restlessly, toying with buttons, mopping the sweat that pops up in frantic beads from his forehead.

"I don't know what you mean."

"You know," he says like a whining child. "Come on."

Elise shakes her head. One of his shoes, a scuffed Hush Puppy, has a hole in it. His baby toe, pink and crowned with a dirty nail, pokes out.

Is this character for real?

"I can't help you, *sir.*" Elise puts mocking emphasis on this last word. "Unless I know what it is you want."

"You," he stammers, "I want you."

"Well, you can't have me." There's something too odd about this one, something too bizarre. Besides, if he can't afford even a pair of shoes, how could he afford her?

"Even if I pay?" Words tremble. His shirt collar darkens with perspiration.

Elise looks him up and down, considering.

Something better will come along. Elise's stomach churns at the thought of this man above her.

Still, the rent will be due in a few days. She has closed her eyes to others before.

No. Even a streetwalker has to have some standards. "Get lost," she whispers to the guy. "I couldn't. Not even for a million bucks."

Even though nothing has blocked the glow from the streetlight, a shadow darkens the man's face before he turns and hurries away. And

Elise shivers. In this commerce, even the most innocent-looking prospect can be a latter-day Jack the Ripper. By refusing, one never knows whom one is pissing off. She's dealt with outraged rejects before...and in spite of his look of harmless geekiness, this one could have a switchblade in his pocket, the strength of a strangler in his hands.

THE NIGHT IS alive. Humidity and heat press in, heightening the smells and feel of living, breathing flesh. They are restlessly attuned to the smell of prey. Criteria: Which one is weak enough? Which one has a healthy supply of blood, one that will not pollute their evening repast with disease or drugs that have the power to set their systems on edge and cause them to turn and thrash in their daylight slumber?

They have moved north, to Roger's Park. Here Terence, Maria, and Edward can mingle with the detritus Lake Michigan and the city has washed up: the homeless, the runaways, drug addicts (crack, coke, meth, and heroin their most popular choices) and those who seek to addict others. Hunger.

Prostitutes.

The ones no one asks questions about. The ones few notice missing and fewer still care about. These people are especially drawn to their looks, their casual affluence, and the lure of easy money. These are the ones that go missing for days with no one wondering who they are, the ones the authorities don't spend much time searching for. The three of them prefer the lonely, the alone, the ones who arouse no suspicion upon their departures.

In their clothing, their looks, the images they have chosen to project, the three all are bait. Lures. The twinkling of an eye, a smile, an outstretched hand: all are nothing more than razor-sharp steel, ready to hook the unwary.

Maria sees her first: a whore. Long hair and tight clothes. Stiletto heels and black rubber bracelets climbing up one arm. She stands alone, watching the traffic go by, her eyes staring restlessly into the glass shielding each driver. She tries to appear streetwise and tough, but there's a vulnerability to her stance, a little too much hunger in her eyes to make the act convincing.

She's desperate.

She's perfect.

Maria moves back into the shadows, pulling her companions with her. They are sandwiched between a convenience store and a movie theater, long ago abandoned, a home for nothing more than pigeons and trash. With Jimmy Choo spike heels, she kicks aside a fearless pigeon and a Popeye's chicken box.

"Look." She nods toward the whore. All three pairs of eyes train in on the woman across the street. Her beauty draws them, or at least what once could be referred to as beauty, her looks are sliding downhill; she looks beyond tired, a rose whose petals are velvety, but blackened and drooping. What really sets their mouths to watering is her vulnerability. Easy pickings are always the best. Why cast a line into an ocean when you can shoot into a barrel?

At once, each of the three is more aware of the woman than she could ever realize. She is like something small, a rabbit nibbling on grass as a hunter is positioning it in the crosshairs of his rifle. Even from their vantage point across the street, they feel the heat emanating from her body, drifting over to them in shimmering waves. They see it as no one else can: a crimson aura surrounds her body, pulsing in the heat. Her scent, sour body odor not masked at all by cheap cologne, rides the heat like a magic carpet. It smells of fresh game, clean, yet musky. Heavy. The blood pulsing in the whore's veins reveals itself; almost audible, the tide of it, as the heart pounds out a beat. She is alive, glimmering with life.

Appetizing.

It's almost too much. A feast of the senses; a cornucopia. Corpuscles of fat floating in the most delicious blood, thick and viscous, with a sharp metallic tang. It excites all sorts of hunger. Maria turns to Terence and wraps her arms around him, her mouth devouring his, tongue exploring the dryness within, sliding over his teeth. Edward presses himself into Maria from behind, thrusting against her, feeling the taut flesh and bone outlined beneath the satin of her dress. Tight between the two men, Maria throws back her head, grinding herself back and forth, pushing their insistent hardness against her. She sighs, imagining someone walking by, deigning to join this impromptu orgy. If someone should, they would never emerge from the shadows again. This trio has always had a problem dealing with the curious, but no problem with swiftly extinguishing that curiosity...forever.

Cold flesh touches cold flesh. Eyes close. Each whispers and moans proclamations of lust and desire. Edward nuzzles the ice skin just below Maria's hairline in back, biting, biting harder until the skin breaks, exploring the small barren openings his teeth have made with his tongue. Maria arches her back, and stops.

"Now, we should go to her now." Maria pulls away from the panting men, lust brightening their eyes, even here in the shadows. "Terence, you approach her."

Terence doesn't need further encouragement. He loves this part of the hunt. Breaking away, Terence waits for the passing cars and dashes across the street. He knows exactly how he looks, the blond hair shining in the artificial neon brightness of the night, the high cheekbones and full lips. The costume of tight leather and pewter latex. A whore's dream: money and beauty, too.

The whore is about to light a cigarette. An opportunity. Terence brings out his silver lighter and hurries to her, flame erect, before she can raise the cheap plastic disposable in her hand. He meets her eyes as the flame transfers some of its glow to the tip of her cigarette.

"Thanks." She exhales twin streams of smoke through her nostrils, and appraises him, taking in the leather and latex, wondering perhaps what someone like him is doing in her part of town. She draws in hard on the cigarette, cheeks collapsing. Thin tusks of blue gray smoke rise. She burns.

"Hot tonight." Terence smiles and looks around him, as if for the source of the heat.

The whore smiles, shakes her head. "You gotta do better than that for an opening line." She laughs. "Ah, but the way you look, what do you need lines for?" She cocks her head, suddenly the coquette.

"Flatterer." Terence touches the whore's bare shoulder.

She flinches, shrugging his hand away. "Baby, you're cold. How'd you manage that?"

Terence thinks for a moment. "Just got out of air conditioning."

The whore looks around, trying to locate the building from which Terence has emerged.

More conversation. Cheap words mouthed to get to the real purpose. Finally, the whore cuts short the compliments and inanities about the weather and cuts to the chase, not knowing that the chase began a while back.

"What do you get into?" Her eyes flicker, moving down Terence's body like liquid. Her voice has a broad, Midwestern twang: flat A's, sharp and nasal.

"There are three of us."

"Group scene." The whore nods. "Been there. There's no group rate, though. It'll cost each of you the same as if you came to me individually."

"So that's all right with you?"

"Anything's all right, so long as it's worth my while." She takes one more drag off the cigarette, drops it to the pavement, and grinds it under her toe. "I assume you got a place. Otherwise, it's extra. There's a motel on Sheridan."

"No need for that. We have a car nearby. Come with us?"

"What kinda car?"

"A black Mercedes."

Eyes light up. "Let's go."

The Mercedes idles at a corner, just steps away from Lake Michigan. It's quieter here, away from the bustle of Howard Street. Once in a while, someone strolls down to the lakefront, or a figure passes across a lighted window. Otherwise, here so close to the lake, it's deserted.

"Shit! Why you wanna make me walk so far in these shoes? Couldn't you have had one of your friends come and pick us up? Jesus, don't you have a cell?" The whore bends down and pulls off the black spike heels and grips them angrily in one hand, continuing in a tight little barefoot canter. "You're gonna have to give me some money for new hose."

"Sorry," Terence says, not bothering to explain, but there is a reason: Maria always plans ahead; she's cautious. The car will be close to the lake, away from the bright lights and bustle. This way, there will be fewer witnesses. Even whores, sometimes, have friends. There have been times when they had taken the wrong person. There was trouble, and they had to flee. Terence and Maria have lived all over the world, nomads with the stench of death following them, too cunning to be caught, but unable to stay, and feed, in one place for too long.

"Not to worry, my dear. Our vehicle is just ahead." Terence nods at the Mercedes, black, shimmering, and reflecting the moon. There's a low hum, the song of solid German engineering. The windows are black.

"Nice car." She giggles, running a red fingernail across the trunk.

Terence opens the back door for her. She slides in; Terence follows, closing the door behind them with a muffled *thunk*.

The whore settles in, grinning and leaning back into the leather. It takes her a second to notice Maria in the front seat. "Ah," she says, "we got a lady here."

Maria turns. "I hope that's not a problem."

"Problem? Honey, it's a bonus." The whore smiles at Maria, engaging her with her eyes. She tries to keep their gazes locked. Maybe that way, Maria won't notice the crooked teeth and the slash across her right cheek, the smooth white scar.

"This is Maria."

The whore offers her hand. Maria makes a kissing expression in its direction but does not touch it. "I'm very pleased." Maria gestures toward Edward, sitting next to her. "And this is Edward."

Edward turns and gives a small wave. His face is tight, revealing nothing.

The car pulls away from the curb, makes a U-turn, and heads south on Sheridan Road.

Back at the vampires' house, the mood is one of anticipation: a party on the cusp of bursting into revelry. Terence, purveyor, escorts the whore to a bedroom done entirely in red: red satin settees, heavy red drapery, blood red velvet, flocked wallpaper.

The whore giggles at the sight of the room's interior. "God! It's like a womb." She paces, fingering the heavy draperies. "Or a bordello."

The three say nothing. Terence leads her to the bed and pulls her down next to him. Wordlessly, they begin shedding their clothes. The air fills with the whispers of satin, creaks of leather, the thud of shoes hitting the floor. Terence implores the whore to keep her stilettos on, though. "You look so hot with those on...and nothing else," he tells her. The three take their places, wordlessly concurring. Maria sits on the floor at her feet, and Edward remains in a corner near the door, watching, eyes brilliant in the flickering of the candles.

Now, Terence strokes the woman, cupping and holding her breasts. He stares into her eyes while pinching harder on her nipples, almost as though searching for an indication of pain.

"Your hand's so cold."

"Warm it."

The whore gasps and stiffens as Terence's hand dives between her thighs. "I don't understand..." There is something wrong. This coldness is unnatural. The whore thinks this leathery cold flesh feels dead. But that can't be. They're horny. They want a three-way. Dead people don't wander around at night, picking up streetwalkers. She knows; she's seen enough dead people. None of them managed to worm a cold hand between her thighs. But still, the feel of the cold flesh pressing inside her makes her feel nauseous. If she didn't need the money, maybe she would get up, saying something like, "Sorry folks, this isn't my scene. I'll find my way out." But she knows it's not that simple. Once you commit to a scene, putting things in reverse is very difficult. Sometimes, it's easier to just go through with it. Still, this cold flesh is *really* creepy.

She whimpers and shifts slightly to free herself from Terence's cold probing fingers. Fear is making her own skin icy.

Maria, attuned to the fear in her eyes, rises and moves to a walnut armoire. She extracts several one hundred dollar bills and scatters them over the whore. They flutter down over her body.

"Warmer?" Maria's voice is throaty. Deep as a man's, yet in no way masculine. She knows how to speak the whore's language.

"*Yesss,*" the whore hisses, staring at all the money. She spreads her legs to give Terence better access. Maria kneels at the whore's feet and removes a stiletto heel. She takes the whore's great toe in her mouth and sucks it. The whore closes her eyes as Terence moves to kiss her. She stiffens at the feel of his tongue: dry, rough, and again, icy cold. But she makes herself kiss back, trying to ignore the repulsion she feels. They're all beautiful, but not one of them is desirable. She forces herself to think about the money, scattered around her. *Christ,* she thinks, *there has to be at least a thou...*

Terence pushes her hand down on his sex. It feels like ice.

The woman stiffens. In spite of all the money, in spite of everything, she doesn't know if she can do this. She doesn't know if there is a place in her mind that's far away enough to distance herself from the revulsion and the horror. She sits up abruptly, pulling her foot away from Maria. "Why are you all so cold? I don't get it." Her heart races. Perhaps she can grab a few of the bills and make a break for it. Something is not right here. Something she doesn't want to think about too closely, for fear she'll lose her mind. But something instinctive in her is telling her she needs to get away. Even if it would mean running into the street stark naked and screaming...

And Edward is there to calm her. "Have some of this." He hands her a lighter and the glass cylinder, its bowl filled with a fat bud of marijuana glistening with resin. She looks down at it in surprise, looks back up at Edward, not sure whether to be grateful or wary.

The whore's chest heaves. All three sense her dichotomy: dread and desire wrapped into one conflicting package, each emotion pulling with its own force. They are old hands at dealing with this kind of war. They are confident in its outcome.

The whore takes the pipe and fires up the bowl. The cylinder fills with smoke, becoming opaque. Clarity returns in seconds as the woman sucks down the smoke. "Damn," she whispers. "Where'd you find shit like this?" Already, she feels as though she is speaking from within a long tunnel.

No reply. Terence takes the woman's hand and forces her to put the pipe back to her mouth. She giggles. "Okay, okay."

After three hits, the woman has forgotten her fear, has stopped wondering why her three companions for the evening have such cold flesh and empty eyes, pale skin smooth like polished stone. Standing naked, the whore surrenders to their touch—all over, hands moving faster and faster, exploring. She closes her eyes, no longer aware who is twisting her nipples to an area where pain and pleasure mesh, no longer aware whose fingers are exploring her sex, her ass. The pot has filled her with a warm stupidity. She can think of only one thing at a time and that is how good these three pairs of hands feel on a body that is growing hotter and hotter with their chilled caresses. Juices run down her thighs, viscous, fragrant. Three tongues lapping make it almost impossible for the whore to stand. Dragging the three with her like sucking leeches, the whore moves to the fireplace and lies on the red and black patterned rug before it. She spreads her legs wide, pushing at them to enter her more deeply, to continue to bring out this wondrous pleasure she has never felt.

And then, the whore is sitting astride Terence, cock like an icicle buried deep. Edward squats behind and above her, pelvis arched out to thrust more deeply into her ass, and Maria presses the whore's face into her own cold but yielding sex lips. Vaguely, through the fog of sensual pleasure and drugged stupidity, the whore remembers reading that the devil's penis feels like ice. She shuts her eyes and grinds down harder on this pillar of ice muscle inside her. It feels good, damn it. It feels good. She reaches out with her tongue, lapping at Maria's sex, tasting her, burying her face in the silken black hair that frames Maria's moist lips, digging her tongue deep inside.

The whore sees this tableau in her mind's eye, almost as if she is at once removed from it and deep within it, the center. She cries out, not knowing how she can stay conscious under the weight of such pleasure.

And then they are biting.

And at first, it's all right, the tiny nips and nibbles nothing more than an extension of their lust, making it better and better. She's endured nibbles and even harder bites in the name of pleasure. Seldom has she let anyone actually break her flesh...and seldom has anyone wanted to. She winces as their teeth penetrate. "Ow!" She laughs. "Watch it, there! I don't go in for the rough stuff. Not too rough, anyway." She bats at them with an ineffectual hand.

But then the bites become harder and harder and the whore awakens from the haze of the marijuana as the teeth, suddenly razor-like and distinctly not human, pierce and rend her flesh. "Oh, God," she whimpers, muscles contracting at the pain like hot needles boring into her. She wants to scream, but feels paralyzed. Her voice dies in her throat as she looks down and sees Maria tear a hunk of flesh from her inner thigh, the skin, muscle, and blood hanging from her teeth. The whore lies convulsing, struggling as the bites penetrate deeper, ripping and shredding, faster and faster, on her breasts, her stomach, her thighs, her ass, all the tender areas. Piercing and penetrating. Sucking sounds filter up to her dull hearing.

Before everything goes dark, she sees: Terence and Edward biting down into her breasts, their mouths ringed with blood. Terence's gaze meets hers. He smiles, fangs bright in a sea of crimson. One drop of her blood drips from his chin. And then, with a grunt, he lowers his head again, and rips her nipple off with his teeth. He teases the nipple with his teeth, playing with it, and then suddenly it's gone.

The whore closes her eyes, shuddering and surrendering. She does not have enough sense to wonder why the cold bodies have suddenly become hot.

THE FACE ABOVE Elise's is little more than a mask, white shapes in all the right places, backlit by the streetlight filtering in through the van's windows. It's how she gets through it, her commerce. She makes her clients inhuman, things that thrust, grunt, and groan above her. As much as she can, Elise goes elsewhere.

The man pants, squeezing her breast with one hand as he thrusts within her. Elise lies with her arms at her sides. Immobile, she tries to discern the color of the shag carpeting that covers the interior of the van, making it cave-like and muffling the man's grunts. "That's it, baby. Fuck me hard. Harder. Ooooo...you got such a big cock. Shove it in deep. Make mama feel good." Elise repeats the words, hoping their crudeness will have the desired effect: to end this little session as quickly as possible. She doesn't even have to put much emotion behind these porno-quality speeches. Just saying "fuck" and "cock" and "pussy" is often enough to drive them over the edge. And then they will be disgusted with themselves and her and want to dump her as quickly as possible. That's just fine with Elise.

He stops and stiffens. He stares down at her. Elise bites her lips, tasting blood, as he comes.

In an instant, he has pulled out of her. He tugs off the condom and flings it on the floor. He is breathing heavily, and his hairy back is matted with sweat. He crawls to where his pants lie and digs in the pockets.

"Here." Tossing two twenties on her chest, he leans back and lights a cigarette, the acrid burn of the match filling the air. He settles against the carpeted wall, panting still. He smokes for a moment, then looks over at her. "Don't you have somewhere else you gotta go?" He laughs, but there's no mirth in it. "Another date?"

The act has taken no more than ten minutes, yet the man glistens with sweat, his fat hairy belly covered with slick. Elise feels soiled, but scoops up the damp money from her breasts and sits up.

She struggles into her clothes; zippers catch, nylons run, her shirt gets stuck as she pulls it over her head. Sheepishly, she grins at the man, her lover, her partner in sin and crime.

He glares at her.

"That was nice," she says with little emotion and even less veracity.

"Just get the fuck out."

Elise scrambles backward, like an animal out of a hole, from the van. The night surrounds her. Cold. Forty bucks.

THE THREE LIE together on the bed. The carcass lies alone, by the fire. It has been almost completely drained of blood and much of its flesh has been ripped from the bone. It is barely recognizable as human. In the early morning, before day's cruel light intrudes, they will rip the carcass further apart and will feed it to the fire. The smell of roasting meat will send them off to sweet dreams.

Edward moves close to Terence and snuggles against him. When he encounters no resistance, he puts his head on Terence's chest.

Terence turns away. "Get the fuck off, fancy man."

"Sorry," Edward whispers into the darkness, turning his back away from Terence.

"You should know by now I'm not into that."

But you once were. At least when you wanted me. Edward thinks about the night they met and the promise. He didn't know how quickly the promise would be met.

And then reneged on.

Chapter
Two

1954

THE TIGER'S EYE was on Eighth Street, between Fifth and Sixth Avenues, in the heart of Greenwich Village. It was a little bar, scarcely more than a long, dark hallway, almost a basement tunnel. Passersby would completely miss it, unless they were among the few who frequented the place. Those wise to its existence entered it through a heavy oak door, veneered with a drab coat of chipped and peeling paint. They'd take a few steps down a small flight of stairs — and be assaulted by the smell of beer, cigarette smoke, and a faint ammonia tang, which the discerning knew better than to think too much about.

And then there was the interior of The Tiger's Eye. Along one brick and mortar wall, there was a row of high tables and stools; along the other was the bar itself, an ancient, heavy wooden affair that rose almost organically up out of the creaking floorboards. How anyone might have ever been able to maneuver the massive thing inside these narrow confines to begin with would forever remain an unsolvable mystery. That no one would ever be able to maneuver it out again was a certainty. The bar had no stools along its length; for comfort, patrons could lift a foot to the brass rail that ran the length of the bar. Cobwebs hung heavy in the corners of a peeling painted black tin ceiling. Music came from a Wurlitzer juke, the only bright spot in an ocean of gloom. The selections on the Wurlitzer were all jazz: Art Blakley, Miles Davis, Sam Rivers, Anita O'Day, Dinah Washington, and Cannonball Adderly.

A grimy mirror that was losing its grasp on reflection hung above the rows of third-rate bottles of bourbon, vodka, and gin. More exotic liquors found a home elsewhere. There was a tap with three choices of beer (Black Label, Genesee, and Hamms), and a cooler with chilled brown bottles of Budweiser and green ones of Rolling Rock. Nothing fancy.

The bar had become a sort of home to Greenwich Village artists, poets, and writers. If you came into The Tiger's Eye's dank interior, you might hear a lively conversation going on about the worth of painters such as Lee Kasner or Philip Guston. You might hear a withering disagreement of critical assessments made by Clement Greenberg in *The*

Nation. Beat poetry, the future of American art... You might also hear the husky music of men propositioning men, or sighs and moans coming from within the red-painted stall of the restroom at the rear of the bar.

The Tiger's Eye was not a place where established artists and writers hung out. Jackson Pollock or Willem de Kooning would not have been glimpsed there, although they may have been nearby, perhaps in a cab with Peggy Guggenheim heading up to her Art of This Century Gallery on West Fifty-Seventh.

But those who aspired to be the next Pollock or de Kooning took advantage of the cheap price of spirits and the "starving artist" ambiance afforded by The Tiger's Eye.

Edward Tanguy was one of those artists. For Edward, The Tiger's Eye afforded an escape from his tiny studio apartment (and workspace) on Horatio Street. He could walk there, nurse a beer or two all evening, engage in conversation with other patrons, which might or might not inspire him to work, and perhaps catch the eye of a handsome stranger. This last was a rare occurrence, usually accompanied by racking guilt the morning after and a determination to "throw himself completely" into his art.

Edward was tired. He had worked all day trying to create something that would move him from being the "crazy guy who fancies himself an artist" who lived at the back of a four-story walk-up inhabited mostly by drunks, heroin addicts, women of easy virtue, rats, and cockroaches to being "that crazy artist who fancies himself alive." Edward still had primary colored paint under his fingernails. A smear of green on his forehead was partially obscured by his blondish brown hair, which hung like dirty corn silk. His skin was pasty from too many long nights at The Tiger's Eye and too many days spent inside his one-room apartment, whose only light, save for the 60-watt bulb that hung from an uncovered ceiling socket, emerged from a gritty window that faced the side of another building. But the ashen pallor of his skin lit up his eyes, a shockingly pale green, flecked with yellow. Edward's wideset eyes, ringed in black, gave his face a startling beauty and magnetism. Without those eyes, Edward might have simply melted into the crowds of similarly dressed poor New Yorkers, culturally aware young men who dressed themselves in worn berets, tattered jeans, and cotton print shirts. Edward wore paint-spattered jeans, ripped at the knees, black Converse sneakers, and a rumpled plaid cotton shirt. He forewent the beret; he didn't want to look *that* affected.

Edward was actually sipping whiskey that cool September night, a rarity. He couldn't usually afford anything more than beer, and tonight was no exception. But it had been such a hard day. His body ached from his efforts to distinguish himself, to transform himself from someone who aspired to being a painter, to one who actually was. He wanted to free himself from the bondage of necessities such as short-order cooking, selling encyclopedias, cab driving, apartment cleaning, or message delivering. The aches along his rib cage and the bruises on his limbs came from Edward's style of painting, which was to smear his entire body with various colors and fling himself at over-sized canvases, contorting, rolling, and turning his body to create, he hoped, an electric fusion of color and movement, a way to record something important about himself *at that moment* that no one had ever seen.

Today, his work had littered the floor of his apartment (a wooden plank floor almost black from neglect and from not having seen the underside of a mop in generations): three canvases, all of them riots of color that traced the movements of a small man, ambitious and a dreamer. There were only small paths from his front door to his bed (a mattress on the floor), his bathroom (a toilet and small claw-footed tub occupying one corner of his kitchen), and to the grimy window, which would never close all the way.

When evening came, and the apartment grew dim, and the sounds outside of cab horns, newspaper vendors hawking that day's news, and the cries of passersby became intolerable, Edward dressed himself, stopped at the newsstand on the corner for a pack of Luckies, and headed over to The Tiger's Eye.

Alcohol and maybe, if he was lucky, the warmth of another man's arms might act as a balm to the soreness in his muscles and the drain of his hard day's work. If he could procure that balm, Edward thought, it would be worth losing the little bit of money he still had left from his last temporary job working as a clerk in a paint store on West 14th.

He leaned against the bar, smoking, listening to Charlie Parker's plaintive sax, and watching a guy at the end of the bar. The guy was dressed all in black, wearing sunglasses in spite of the gloom of The Tiger's Eye. Little, tiny, round gold-rimmed sunglasses that made it look like he had holes where his eyes should be. The effect was chilling, scary...and it drew Edward in a dangerous way, repellent and gripping at the same time. His face, like Edward's own, was pale, but defined by sharp angles, good jaw line, and strong chin. Blond hair fell in soft waves to his shoulders. There was something stirring, strange, and beautiful about this character, something that made him stand apart from the other men and the few women in the bar, all roughly the same age as Edward, all sporting the same look of studied bohemian dishevelment.

Edward had been watching him for the past hour or so, his stare growing more obvious as the beer and whiskey emboldened him. There wasn't enough alcohol in the bar, however, to provide Edward with enough courage to actually approach the man and initiate a conversation. Trolling for men, his method was always the same: watch and wait. If his pointed eye contact yielded no results, Edward would go home alone. Since the bar was dark and smoke-obscured, not allowing the casual observer to take in the allure of Edward's emerald eyes, he often traveled back to his Horatio Street walkup by himself, accompanied only by the stench of stale beer and smoke on his clothes.

But tonight, Edward wasn't sure he would be making that walk alone. Even though it was impossible to tell what the man was thinking behind those odd, old-fashioned glasses, there was an almost palpable connection. Edward could feel it. The sensation was akin to the prickle he got when he knew someone was watching him, even if his back was turned. The stranger's face was turned toward him, and Edward was positive their gazes were engaged, even if a shield of black glass prevented him from confirming it.

Almost. He was almost to the point where impatience and desire collided, at the point where he would disregard his own fear and let hunger usurp it. He was almost there: where he'd break his own rule and approach the man. What would he say? What would be clever enough to amuse this stranger?

Unfortunately, Edward's expressiveness was confined to canvas and oil paint. He sipped his whiskey and lit another Lucky. What was the point? As acute as his desire was, there was no arguing with his shyness. He would never have the courage to drop a line as simple as, "Hey there, what brings you out tonight?" Edward figured no matter what he said, it would come out sounding stupid. He could already feel the hot flush of shame on his face as he imagined the stranger looking at him with amusement and then distaste, his glance withering enough to send Edward away, stumbling, self-confidence knocked down another notch.

"So what brings you out on this rainy night?"

Edward swallowed and didn't turn for a moment. He looked to the place where the stranger had been standing and saw it was vacant, which could lead to only one conclusion...

Edward turned, and there he was, close enough to touch. Edward looked the man up and down, taking in the thin frame that seemed anything but frail: a coiled-up energy (again, the danger) seemed to pulse within him. His body had a steeliness not apparent from across the room. Edward took another sip of his whiskey and lit another cigarette, ploys to give him time to think.

Fuck it, though, there was no clever answer to a question like what brought him out this night. The idea, Edward supposed, was not to act as a prelude to witty banter, but to initiate conversation so the two of them could meet. *God, Edward, you're stupid. Just answer the man before he walks away, questioning his taste.*

"Just needed a little drink." Edward smiled and raised his glass, which was empty. He felt a line of sweat trickle down his spine. "A little drink never hurt anyone, right?"

The man edged closer. There was a faint, bitter aroma to his person, like old smoke, but not from cigarettes. It took a moment for Edward to place the smell: marijuana. He'd been to enough East Village parties to recognize the scent that made Edward think of the incense priests burned at Mass (his altar boy days from Summitville, Pennsylvania rushed back).

"Oh, I don't know about that." The man smiled. "It depends on a little drink of what and who's doing the drinking to determine if there's harm, or at least the potential of it."

The guy was as strange as he looked. His voice had a mellow, deep timbre to it, drawing Edward further in, making the music in the background (was it Anita O'Day?) fade, along with the voices in the bar. What the hell was he talking about?

Edward ran a hand through his hair. "Not sure what you mean."

And then the man touched him, which surprised Edward. Just reached out and ran a hand across his cheek, almost a corporeal whisper. In that instant, Edward felt the network of bones and cartilage in the hand; the dry, leathery skin was oddly cool. Again, Edward felt a bizarre marriage of repulsion and lust in his gut.

"I just mean that, no matter what decisions we make, once made, they're fraught with danger or delight, or both. So, is it simply the need for a drink that brings you out tonight? I presume a bottle could be purchased for home consumption just as easily, and probably much more affordably, on a cost-per-drink basis."

"You have a point there." Edward scratched his head. "What brought me out?" Edward took a deep breath. "Maybe it was the need to meet someone like you." Edward was immediately grateful for the bar's darkness, concealing the blush that radiated upward from his chest, completely enveloping his face. He knew if he couldn't find more intelligent things to say, he would be spending yet another night alone.

The man laughed, a husky chuckle that made Edward shiver. He squeezed Edward's shoulder. "Well, then, it appears you made the right decision."

"Yeah...meeting someone and getting a break from my work."

"Which is?"

"I paint."

"Ah. An artist. I love artists. I could eat up an artist's soul." Again, the chuckle.

"Well, I hope I'm an artist. All I can say for sure is that I'm a painter. Anyone can be a painter. It takes something more to be an artist."

"What are you looking for, then? Outside validation? Don't you know you're an artist? How else can you go on working unless you have confidence in yourself?"

Edward stared at the bar, uncertain how to respond. He knew he was an artist. He was just attempting to be pithy with the wordplay and the meanings behind painter and artist. He should have just told the guy he was a house painter. It would have been easier. "I don't know. I guess I was stupid saying that."

"Not stupid. Realistic. I like that." The man took off his glasses and Edward felt a dizzying sensation. Romantic and over-the-top as it sounded, he felt like he was falling into an abyss. The stranger's irises, if possible, were even blacker than the glass which moments ago had sheathed them. "My name is Terence."

"Edward."

Terence squeezed Edward's hand. His touch was like ice. It was off-putting and at the same time, alluring. "Your hand is so cold. Did you just come inside?"

"I did not. I'm just a cool cat." Terence laughed.

"Now who's the one saying stupid things?"

"Barkeep? Can you bring us another round?" Terence waved a five-dollar bill in the air, reaching over Edward, who could smell something sweet and cloying beneath the bitter aroma of grass. "You'd like another one, wouldn't you? Or am I being presumptuous?"

"If you're buying, I'm drinking. A boy has to take his pleasures where he finds them."

"Indeed."

Once the bartender, a handsome blond man whose features were marred by the addition of too much mascara ringing his blue eyes, had set their new drinks before them, Terence squeezed Edward's shoulder. "So, tell me about your art."

"Do you really want to know?" Edward sipped. He didn't want to sound pretentious. He hated artists that were all the time talking, talking, talking. Art should speak for itself. And if the two of them ever made it back to his apartment, maybe his art would speak for him.

"You need a dose of self-confidence, young man. Artists have to be self-promoters, if they want to get anywhere. It's a hard reality. So, what do you paint? What medium? What are you trying to get across?"

"You ask too many questions." With trembling hands, Edward lit yet another cigarette. He knew that, soon, his throat would feel sore and scorched. He rubbed the back of his neck. "I paint myself." Edward chuckled. "In more ways than one."

Terence raised his eyebrows.

"Y'see, I smear paint on myself and then I apply myself to the canvas. I move. I apply more color, different color...and move. I roll. I twist. I wave my arms around, swing my legs."

"So, you're your own brush."

"I suppose you could think of it that way. But I'm my own subject, you know? I'm hoping to say something about myself with my work, to capture something essential about me that people can see and connect with."

Terence nodded, his dark gaze never moving from Edward's face. "You know Mark Rothko's work?"

Edward's eyes lit up. His shyness continued to ebb. "I love Rothko! There's something he said that sticks with me; it sums up what my work is all about. He said...”

Terence cut in. “He said something like, ‘Art is not about experience. It is itself the experience.’”

Edward was awed. The statement, slightly paraphrased, had been his credo since he had moved to New York five years ago, after making the decision that he would do whatever it took to live his life as a painter. “That’s exactly right. I’m shocked that you know that.”

And at that moment, the combination of Terence’s fine-boned, yet strong, features and his passion for art sparked something in Edward. Some would call it love. At least for the rest of the night, and for perhaps much longer, Edward knew he would do whatever this man asked.

IT WAS RAINING. When Edward had walked the dozen or so blocks from his apartment to The Tiger’s Eye, there was a mist in the air, chilling it and muffling sound. It was almost like a fog. But now, as he emerged from the bar with Terence behind him, a downpour of King Learish proportions had blown up. Thunder rumbled and roared. Lightning lit up the sky, leaving the smell of ozone as an afterthought. And the rain poured, hissing, seeming louder in the lull between thunderclaps.

Terence stopped and grabbed Edward by the shoulders at the corner of Sixth and Christopher Street. He smiled, not enough to show his teeth, just enough to look kind of slow and sexy, one corner of his mouth turning up more than the other. “Indulge me in a little romantic purple prose.”

“Okay.” Edward looked out of the corner of his eyes to see if they had witnesses. But the storm had driven most potential observers indoors; those who remained outside didn’t have sense enough to be outraged, amused, or confused by the sight of one man embracing another.

“Don’t worry. No one’s watching.”

Edward let himself fall into Terence’s gaze. He must ask him if he could do a portrait. Even though his work wasn’t representational, he still had the skills he had honed as an art student at Carnegie Mellon. He could dabble in realism.

“Come on, allow me this moment.” Terence gently guided Edward’s face to his own by his chin. “We have to use this line, it’s so brilliant!, in the first chapter of our ‘how we met’ story.”

“Okay...”

“It was a dark and stormy night.”

Edward rolled his eyes. Terence looked offended for just a second and then the moment broke, along with a thunderclap overhead. The two men collapsed against each other, howling with laughter. Terence took the opportunity to pull Edward closer, to brush a kiss along his neck. Edward didn't mind.

He looked up at Terence, smiled. "God! We need to get you inside. You'll catch your death."

Terence said nothing, and if Edward witnessed the glimmer of a wry smile whisper across his features, he said nothing about it. "Why don't we hail one of those horseless carriages to take us to our destination."

"Because I can't afford it and this is more memorable. Now, it was a dark and stormy night. Thunder roared overhead...

"The angels were bowling..."

Terence took Edward's hand and they hurried through the night, while taxi headlights threw harsh illumination on their drenched figures.

Outside his building, Edward felt a flush of shame at the seedy walk up and its rusting fire escape, upon which laundry-minded neighbors had hung wash, which would now need a second dry cycle. He noticed his building through Terence's eyes and saw how obvious its flaws were: the boarded-up window on the third floor, the graffiti marring its ground floor, and the cans and bottles littering the front sidewalk. What would Terence think when they entered the grimy vestibule, with its chipped green paint, broken tile, and millennia-old odors of cooked cabbage and perspiration?

"I assume it's dry."

"I'm afraid it's not much."

"God! I'm sorry. Let's get inside."

Edward fumbled with his keys, dropping them once before he finally got the one that matched up with the lock on the front door. As he was opening the door, he quipped, "Just think of what you're smelling as the rarified air of despair."

Terence grinned. "Just move it. We need to get upstairs. I need another drink."

Once in the apartment, Edward lit candles. The overhead bulb would not do. And besides, candles were more romantic and economical (he couldn't help but think of the practical, now that he had spent his last five dollars on well whiskey).

"I don't have much to drink." Edward rummaged around in the refrigerator, but its interior was empty and the action was more for show rather than any actual results. "Water?"

"I'm fine." Terence had taken off his shoes and sat down on Edward's mattress. He patted a spot next to him. "Why don't you come here and sit down beside me?"

"Said the spider to the fly?"

Terence raised his eyebrows and laughed. The laugh was a bit too loud and a bit too shrill, causing hackles to rise on Edward's neck. He shook his head, shivering. *Stop it now*, he told himself, *you're being stupid.*

But bad things can sometimes happen to boys who bring stranger's home. Fear is never stupid.

Perhaps Edward would have paid more heed to his inner voices if his mind hadn't been fogged by lust and liquor. The spot next to Terence looked very inviting indeed, in spite of his hesitation. He ambled over to Terence and the bed, concentrating on walking in a straight line. *I am not drunk,* he thought, *I am merely feeling good. There's a difference.*

He sat down hard enough next to Terence to feel the wooden floor beneath the mattress painfully on his ass.

"Careful, there." Terence grabbed his shoulder to keep Edward upright.

Edward let out a big sigh and turned to look into Terence's eyes. "You know, all night long, I wanted to meet you."

"And I you."

"You were the best lookin' fella in the place."

Terence nodded. "Next to you, my friend."

"Aw, get outta here." Edward swallowed. The room was spinning. This wasn't going at all the way he thought. He felt nauseous, the tiny bit of food and the alarming amount of alcohol he had consumed that day churning in his stomach. He couldn't throw up. He just couldn't. He'd lose the guy for sure. But as his face began to feel clammier, hot and cold intermingling, he began to think that being alone might not be such a bad idea.

And what if he did throw up? He didn't even have a bathroom. The toilet was in full view across the room.

He hadn't even given the guy a show of his art.

Edward stood, swaying. "Don't feel so good." Spittle ran down his chin. He wiped it away with the back of his hand.

He would not kneel and vomit into a stained toilet bowel in his first encounter with this handsome stranger. He hurried to the window, struggled to get it up high enough to allow his head to emerge, and vomited down four stories, retching until nothing came out by yellow bile.

"Feeling better?" Terence was next to him, rubbing his shoulder.

Edward's face was slick with sweat, but his stomach felt more settled and he was seeing things, whether he wanted to or not, with renewed clarity. "I am so sorry."

"Don't worry about it. It has its own beauty." Terence reached out with his finger, slid it along some of the vomit that had landed on the sill, and took it into his mouth.

Edward took a step back, tasting bile at the back of his throat.

Terence cocked his head. "What? It's you. I'm tasting you."

"Maybe tonight isn't such a good idea."

"But I want to see your art."

"Another time for sure. I just don't feel so good anymore."

Terence knelt by the windowsill and licked more of Edward's bile up. He looked up and smiled. His teeth were very tiny and very sharp. It almost seemed as if he hadn't moved from the kneeling position when suddenly he was holding Edward in his arms, close enough that Edward could smell gastric acid on his breath.

"I have something that will make you feel a lot better."

Edward shook his head. "Honey, if you're talking about sex, I..."

"Not sex. This." Terence held out a small pipe, carved from burled walnut and ebony. Into the bowl of the pipe was etched a grinning skull. Terence touched the springy, mossy bud within. "This will settle that queasy tummy and make you forget *all* your troubles." Terence pressed the pipe into Edward's hand. "Go on, take it."

Edward grasped the little pipe. Already the pungent aroma of marijuana, green and bitter, drifted up. In fact, the idea of a little smoke did seem soothing. He positioned the pipe in his hand and raised it to his lips.

From within a pants pocket, Terence fished out a silver lighter. "Now just suck," he whispered, bringing the flame closer and closer to Edward's face. "You do know how to suck, don't you?"

Edward shut his eyes and prepared to draw in.

Chapter
Three

EACH LINE HAS to be perfect. Elise steps back to survey the drawing before her, taped to a board on an easel. To give the parchment paper more of an aged patina, she has stained it with coffee. She sighs, trying to concentrate on form and function rather than the emotions the drawing arouses. *Maybe that's a good thing*, she thinks, *maybe the fact the piece elicits a visceral reaction even in me means something. Perhaps my striving is getting me somewhere.* Still, is this vague feeling of dread somewhere she wants to be?

There he is, the man from the night before, the one in the van. He had been middle-aged, overweight, a pale featureless face, doughy. But Elise has transformed him with charcoal. Dark squiggly lines have made of him an insect: the eyes blind black orbs, a cavity for a nose, black pincers almost mobile at the corner of thin lips. Delicate wings sprout from his back, segmented, bifurcated, transparent. Elise has made her perspective from below, so the man/creature looms above, menacing yet distant.

She has a flash of him in memory: grunting as he thrust into her, his face clammy with sweat, eyebrows furrowed in concentration, lips parted to emit stale breath, exerted. What should have been pleasure looked much closer to disgust.

Elise picks up a tube of black acrylic paint. She creates a border, thick, like piping, around her drawing. The framing device works, confining and highlighting the creature. Elise stares at the drawing for a while. Her lower lip quivers. And then, sobbing, she smears the ink, obliterating and erasing what has taken her all day to create.

It is too good. Too good for him.

She turns her back to the easel and stares outside, where the sky glows purple. Dusk signals the end of one workday and the beginning of another, when a different kind of discipline and diligence will be required. The night is waiting outside for her, like a suitor on a doorstep.

And, she supposes, so are the creatures inhabiting the night. The starved and the starving, conning themselves into believing she has something that will remove the hunger, that will sustain them. She trembles at the thought of how she will deal, yet again, with their rage when they realize she offers only the most temporary respite and that, in the end, offers them nothing.

But she needs these creatures. Needs them for her own sustenance and, more importantly, for their essence. It is their essence that allows her to continue to create.

THE VAMPIRES DO not always travel together. They sometimes hunt alone. Even though their insatiable hunger unites them, sometimes it's more efficient to work alone. They even form relationships and have experiences that do not include the others.

This is one of those nights. Terence heads north on his 1953 Harley FL Panhead. He has restored the bike to its original glory and there is nothing that makes him feel freer than to be astride this roaring beast, especially when the night is clear. A glowing silver moon shimmers above the rolling waters of Lake Michigan and the promise of the hunt is fresh and new. He feels powerful as the bike roars, spitting out exhaust, noisily shifting, and cutting strategically between lanes to claim an always-constant pole position. He is powerful with anticipation, secure in his ability to lure, seduce, and kill.

The feeding is all the sweeter when it's not shared, when victory is his alone to claim. Sometimes he wonders if he wouldn't be better off solo.

Wind slithers through his hair. The glow of the moon makes his skin bleached bone, marble, alabaster. He has dressed himself from head to toe in leather, and it creaks satisfyingly with every movement.

His destination is Howard Street. Perhaps he will strike gold again. As he rounds the corner from Lake Shore Drive onto Hollywood, he remembers the whore from last night and the heat of her blood as it pumped into his mouth like a copper ejaculation, the intense gaminess of her flesh as he ripped it away. The scent of the blood and the rent flesh. Terence's cock squirms inside tight jeans. Heading north once again, now up Sheridan Road, Terence feels anticipation: an electric current, pulsing.

There will be another perfect one. Waiting just for him. Waiting for a fall.

Terence twists the throttle, revving the engine, and swerves left to claim the open space in the lane.

ELISE PULLS THE door closed behind her, not bothering to lock it. After all, what is there to take? Her art? Who among these filthy minions would appreciate it? Where could it be fenced? Her other belongings? They could be found anywhere, discarded with the trash.

And what if someone is lying in wait when she comes home, ready to slit her throat? Elise shakes her head. She could never be so fortunate.

Tonight, she has dressed herself in a simple red satin sheath that drops to mid-thigh. The red and the dress's Mandarin collar give it an Asian feel; sometimes that works. Even though her hair is auburn and her eyes are green, and her skin tells a tale of Scotland, there are those for whom the simplest visual cues can create an alternate reality. What does she care if they think of her as a geisha? A Thai streetwalker? Their money pays the rent just the same.

She turns the corner and stops. Her eyes closed, she breathes in. The scene is predictable, but still she hates the prospect, hates having to deal with all of this, wants to crawl into a hole and never come out again.

Howard Street swarms with people. Friday night: the cars roll by like insects, headlights glowing like hundreds of pairs of eyes. Exhaust fumes perfume the air. Profanity and greetings compete with car horns and mufflers.

Elise takes her place near the 7-11, hoping she won't be chased away tonight by marauding youths or vice cops. In a way, she can't wait until the evening is over and she can slide down the black fishnet stockings and kick off her red satin stiletto heels. At least there will be the comfort of not having to wear these stupid clothes, so obvious they're laughable, but no one's laughing. The passersby either ignore her, shooting her looks of distaste "why are you fouling my neighborhood?" or leer at her with lust, not bothering to conceal their salacious interest. Why bother? She isn't worthy of discretion, out here selling it as she is. Elise braces herself for the catcalls and whistles, the verbal filth showered on her like a cascade of excrement.

Only moments pass before a motorcycle's rumble drowns out all other sound.

The engine cuts and for just a second, it's as if all the sound in the street cuts as well. Elise turns.

A man, impossibly beautiful, is astride the motorcycle. Leather and chains, boots. Not the type of man she would fancy in her other life. (*And what life is that?* Elise wonders, realizing suddenly this *is* her life and perhaps there is no other; that the "other" there once was has shrunk away to almost nothing...and that little is perhaps irretrievable.) He looks her up and down, his gaze frank. A smile, or a smirk, plays around the corners of his full lips.

He must fancy himself quite the prize. Cheekbones sharp and defined, skin almost too smooth to be real, white in the light from the moon. *Poseur.*

Elise turns away; this is not the sort of trade she deals in. No, Elise is a lower class of street trade, in spite of her youth and beauty. It's the role she has directed herself in for years now. Giving herself as a gift to worthless, ugly men somehow seems right. She doesn't quite know why, and doesn't choose to explore why she abases herself this way.

Perhaps she won't like the answer.

A gloved hand, fingers cut away, caresses her shoulder. Elise shrugs the hand away and whirls to face the stranger. Her eyes spark. He grins. Warily, she smiles back.

"I'm not certain you're in the right part of town," Elise says.

"I'm not certain you know what you're talking about. I know where I am, and it's right where I choose to be, sweetheart." His deep, resonating timbre distinguishes itself from the sounds of urban night. "How much?"

Elise shakes her head, her laughter mocking, derisive. "Again: I'm not so sure. You get right to the point, don't you? Hasn't anyone taught you the rules? Or were you too busy playing macho on your motorcycle?"

"The games I like to play are a bit more sophisticated than you can imagine which is why I do get right to the point. Now, how much?"

Elise pulls hair from her neck, where it's stuck with the glue of her sweat. Vice? Will it matter if she asks him? Contrary to popular belief, cops aren't all angels of veracity. They lied to her before, when she was just starting out and relied on the rumor that, if asked, an officer of the law must divulge his occupation.

So what point would there be in asking? She could name a price for a specific sexual act and could be run in, end up cooling herself in a cell with other streetwise sisters for a few hours while the arrest is processed and then get sprung out into another humid night. Or, she could ask him to prove he isn't a representative of the Chicago police force, vice division. He could respond with something clever, eyes growing wide, something like, "Me? You gotta be kidding. Now, why would you ask a thing like that?"

Just get it over with. She's been run in before. An inconvenience. The arrests stop no one. In her desire to hasten the bust, Elise blurts, "Fifty dollars for a blow job, a hundred and up for more. Depends on what you're into. Anal's extra, but I'll do it if the price is right."

He doesn't blink. Reaching into the pocket of his motorcycle jacket, he pulls out a wad of bills. Elise recognizes a hundred on the outside of the roll. He tucks it into her cleavage. "Got someplace we can go?"

The money between her breasts is enough to free her for several nights. Yet, they still haven't discussed what it is he wants. What if he's into heavy S&M? Elise looks at him out of the corner of her eye, taking in all the leather; his deathly white pallor speaks of parties in dungeons. In spite of being a cheap whore, a streetwalker, she hasn't really walked on the wild side all that much. She knows all about bondage, whips, cigarette burning, tit torture, and all the rest, but she's a vanilla kind of prostitute. Straight-up sex. She can manage a little water sports here and there, or maybe even getting a little rough, but the more extreme end of the spectrum she leaves to her sisters. And yet, she can feel the stiff crispness of the currency between her breasts. She wants the money. But going this far could be leading her into a realm where it will be hard to escape. Suddenly, she finds herself wishing for a scared Loyola boy who just wants to get sucked off in an alley.

The stranger's touch on her shoulder is cool, but insistent. "Do you have a place where we might get more comfortable or not?"

Elise breathes in, deep. The time for decisions is now. She takes the man's hand, meets his gaze, and smiles, the curtain rising on her show. "This way. It isn't far." She leads him east, toward Greenview and the place she calls home. She pulls him along, hurrying him, the click of her heels insistent on the hot pavement. She wants to get him home, get him done, and get it over with.

"My name's Terence." His grip on her hand is firm and cool. He has no trouble keeping up.

She hopes she will have no trouble keeping up with *him*.

"Mine's Midnight," Elise murmurs, glancing at him out of the corner of her eye. Wondering, will this be the time she regrets breaking her own rule and letting a john into her own home? Will this be her Mr. Goodbar, with strangling hands or a switchblade in his pocket? In spite of her earlier cavalier attitude toward her own murder, there is still a compulsion to live, a will to survive. Feeling threatened makes her realize that, no matter how desperate an existence she has, she still wants to keep it. It is her own.

She squeezes his hand and slows a little. "So, we haven't really talked about it."

"Yes?"

"What are you into?"

"I just like plain old sucking and fucking. I trust that doesn't disappoint you."

"Not at all."

And Elise picks up the pace once more. His response is small comfort.

Once back in her studio, she doesn't want to turn on any lights. Spare as it is, it's still her home. It holds memories (once upon a time, things were different: it was brighter, crowded, not exactly happy, but still there were happy times...early on). It holds her art, and grim as that has become, it's still a piece of herself, a substantial piece that she doesn't want to share with a trick. She doesn't want to share this world with anyone, not yet, not in any personal capacity anyway. Perhaps one day things will change and she will spend her evenings at gallery shows of her art, appropriately modest and dressed in black, but those dreams of glory hardly seem within her reach. Not now, with a horny trick at her back.

The moonlight streams in, making the short passage across the room easier. The moon gives everything a grayish cast, making of the easels, drawing board, and few pieces of furniture nothing more than dark shapes. As they move across the room, she is stepping out of her dress, kicking off her heels. She sits on the bed and pulls off her stockings in one fluid motion; she's had practice. Naked, she leans back on the bed, draws in air, and lets out a slow, quivering breath. *Never let them see you're afraid; never let them feel your anxiety. If you do, they sometimes pounce, smelling your weakness.* Recklessly, she tosses her hair back and puts on her most alluring smile, hoping its bravado isn't lost in the shadows. She parts her legs and touches herself. The move is calculated to look like she can't help herself; in reality, she hopes the digital stimulation will get the juices flowing.

She touches, flicks a tongue out of the corner of her mouth, stares. Provocatively, she hopes; she's learned that the whore's first rule is to get 'em excited, get 'em overly excited. That way, you get rid of them sooner. You learn to welcome the "afterglow": his remorse and desire to get away. She pats the bed beside her.

"What about light? Surely, you have some candles around." Terence stands above her, and suddenly fear grips Elise. The dark shape of him, the smell of the leather, the chain around his neck, the thicker one around his waist. She has put herself in this submissive position carelessly, and now she wonders how vulnerable she is and what will happen to her. It would be so easy, he is, after all, a big man, for him to just reach down and hit her, pummel her face, strangle her. She shivers. Such scenes happen all over the place every night. She should never have brought him here. She will become, she just knows it, another grim statistic.

Her lackadaisical attitude about life crumbles as her heartbeat picks up, thudding. A line of sweat forms at her hairline and her muscles flex, taut.

"We don't need any light." Her voice comes out, hoarse from fear, a croak. She thinks for a moment and then mumbles, unconvincingly, "The electricity's out."

"I think we do. And I'm paying. I call the shots." He shifts his weight from one foot to the other. "I think you're lying about the electricity being out."

"No!" Elise shrieks and runs toward him. "No." She takes his arm and pulls it back. "I've got to have the darkness. Please." Elise tenses. "This is my place. I..." Before she has a chance to say anything further, he is moving toward the door, where the switch for the overhead light is.

He reaches out, and Elise tries not to flinch at the coldness when he caresses her face, long fingernails sliding across her cheek like the tender touch of a switchblade applied lovingly. She continues to meet his gaze, supplicant and pleading. She doesn't want him to see her art. It would be more of a violation than if he fucked her up the ass.

"All right. If it's so important to you."

When Terence reaches into his pocket, Elise expects a gun or knife, but all he has withdrawn is a small wooden pipe. It's burled walnut and black, a skull carved into the bowl. It's kind of beautiful, really, and, for just a moment, Elise forgets her trepidation, forgets what's taking place here. The craftsmanship and the old wood, burnished to a dull glow, fascinate her artist's eye. She then notices there's a bud in its bowl. She breathes in, taking in the aroma of the resin.

It's been years since she's gotten high, partying days left behind long ago. College, art school, memories of another life. But the idea doesn't seem so bad...perhaps the smoke will obscure the experience, cloud and befuddle her brain, allow her to get through this, anesthetized.

"Go ahead." Terence hands her the pipe and silver lighter.

Elise fires up the bowl. In the flame, the hunger in Terence's eyes is startling: more than lust, it encompasses and embodies him. Elise draws the smoke into her lungs quickly, holding it as she returns the pipe.

What has it been? Minutes? Hours? Elise has no idea. This isn't the way it's supposed to go. She is supposed to save all of her feelings for her art. These men are just a means to an end. She shouldn't be feeling any kind of pleasure, or any emotion, really, with her tricks, they who are nothing more than commerce.

Yet her legs feel weighted, glued to the floor as the chill of his lips and tongue move up and down her thighs, exposing and caressing. Somehow, she has let go and buried her hands in his thick blond hair as he kneels before her, supplicant and instrument of a pleasure so intense Elise cannot consciously describe it. Her head lolls back and, for the first time, she hears herself sighing and whimpering. It's almost as if she has stepped outside herself and these cries of pleasure, so intense, are coming from someone else.

His tongue moves up and inside her and for now, nothing else exists. Elise closes her eyes, panting as shudders and waves of pleasure claim intellect and body. She yearns for more, yearns for him to be inside her. She would pay *him*. *Please*, she thinks, *please, now...*

Suddenly, he withdraws, and she cries out, synapses tingling, craving, yearning. Mute, she watches as he undresses, the leather and chains falling to her filthy floor in a heap, clinking and thudding, becoming a burrowing animal in the shadows. His naked body reminds her of Michelangelo's *David*, and it reinforces her knowledge of what the sculptor was expressing, something about the perfection of the human form, about rising above the physical and approaching the ethereal. Elise reaches out, fingertips tingling, wanting to cry out, "Come to me," but unable to form words with her thick tongue.

And then he is moving across the room.

And then the room is flooded with yellow light.

Elise closes her eyes, something from underneath a rock exposed suddenly, cruelly. All her work. "No," she whimpers. She is unable to move, unable to do anything more than just lie there, a vessel waiting to be filled. She hates herself. But her brain is clouded, the drug and desire twisting inside her, creatures that have taken on lives of their own, overpowering her.

Jealous. His lover's gaze is no longer on her, but on her creations, boring into them, penetrating them instead of her.

She watches, mute and paralyzed, as he takes in her drawings and paintings, one by one, opening them with his eyes, seeing everything Elise has said in the last few years with her dark vision. She tries to get up, but slumps back down, wishing for once she could gather up all of her art and destroy it. She would trade it all for just a few moments in his arms, their bodies joined like one organism.

His cock is stiff, jerking as he absorbs the art. Elise crumples to the floor. What he has paid her is not enough. In the midst of her lust-filled delirium are the stirrings of rage and betrayal. No matter if she didn't feel ready to share her art with the world, it was still *hers*, her essence, maybe even her soul. How dare he?

"You're a genius." The words filter down as if played at slow speed, heard through a tunnel. What need has she for praise? Angrily, she watches him devour her art, stealing it. He touches the paper upon which she has drawn with reverence, touching himself with the other hand.

"You see. You really see," he whispers, and turns to gaze down at her.

And then he is gone. Wind rushes in through the open door, lifting her drawings, the paper rattling in the breeze. And Elise lies alone, naked and betrayed on the floor, where a cockroach, sensing her heat, skitters across her thigh.

TERENCE BLAZES THROUGH the night, Harley roaring between his legs, wind whipping his hair behind him. His teeth are clenched as he tries to sort out the emotions caroming through him, crashing like cymbals. Is it rage he feels? He grips the throttle so tightly it's as if his knuckles will burst through the skin. The world whizzing by is a blur, incomprehensible.

All he can see is Midnight's art. He remembers leaning against her peeling, colorless walls, finishing the pipe, letting the THC do its work: sharpening his focus, bringing her art to life. What horrifying vision. Terence swears the art has let him see the woman's soul, dark, her own, no way to possess it. The bleak drawings, black and gray, layers of shadows, speak of the void in which she lives: the animal lusts, the chains confining her, earthbound...her need for survival. The woman speaks with a knowledge he had thought no human possessed.

And the woman herself: reddish-brown hair, fright in her eyes as he stood above her, blood heat pulsing through her veins. He remembers it all, even in the lightless void of her apartment. The temptation to devour it then was nearly unbearable, filling every fiber of his being with need so intense it virtually erased his reality. By devouring it, literally, teeth gnashing, saliva making of the paper upon which she has drawn her visions nothing more than graying pulp, he might perhaps begin to touch what she can do in her humanity, with feelings that have long since become alien to him, to all three of them, to the entire race of beings he calls brothers and sisters. By ingesting her art, perhaps he could begin to feel what makes her human, in a way similar to the manner in which he feels things as blood from his victims' pumps down his throat and fills his veins and brain with their memories and experiences, with core images of what makes them alive. The temptation was a fierce, burning desire.

But he stopped.

He could not destroy her, not the vision she had splattered or drawn with precise detail on paper, on canvas.

And yet the red aura surrounding her called to him with the voice of a siren. Calls still with a fire so intense it could destroy him. The flames are a peripheral orange blur, caught by dangling threads of consciousness. But if he took this woman's lifeblood, he would take also her abilities to create things he could now only dream of fashioning himself. For once, Terence, purveyor of pleasure and pain, the greediest of his little three-pronged family, has shown some restraint, demonstrated respect for talent and sensitivity that would forever be beyond his reach.

But the hunger remains. And he is so lost in his thoughts that he almost misses its solution, almost loses out on a prime opportunity.

Terence stops the bike, looks back.

And there it is, the answer to his needs.

Smoke rises from a black metal trash can, its sides rusted. Back from it, in the entryway of a warehouse, silent this late at night, sleeps a man. Black. Nappy hair poking out of a coat wrapped around him like a cocoon. Terence feels the heat of his blood and the thudding of his heart. Music. He considers the coat wrapped around him so tightly for only a second: why so cold on this hot night?

Quietly, with stealth perfected through years of practice, Terence dismounts and moves the bike to a wall, hiding it in the shadows. He walks with purpose toward the sleeping man, a silent force, a whisper of black against black. Invisible.

He stands above the man, looking down. There's no beauty here. No sexual rush. Yet, the throbbing of his life force is hypnotic and Terence wants to savor the moment, letting the desire and hunger build. It's so much better that way: slow, steady, delayed gratification. Like the most perfect sex.

Terence knows he can bring a chill this slumbering man has never dreamed of. He descends, gliding, so quiet the man does not murmur or awaken. Gently, like a mother unwrapping her baby from its blankets,

Terence opens the coat. The smell is putrid, body odor rising up, sweat and defecation. But underneath it, the sweet note of blood, warm, with a tang of copper, awaits. Terence squats down as the man's eyelids flutter and for just a second, their gazes lock. He lifts the man like a lover, like the mother in a pieta, and lowers his head to his throat. The man cannot even struggle or scream as razor-sharp fangs pierce the dark flesh.

And then the blood is spurting in steady jets into Terence's mouth. It is delirious. It is delicious.

And the man is emptied as quickly of his life force as he earlier had emptied a bottle of cheap fortified wine.

When he roars off on his Harley, there is nothing left of the homeless black man but a pile of ragged clothing, bones, hair, and pieces of flesh too tough for Terence to digest.

Chapter
Four

1954

WHEN EDWARD AWAKENED, milky gray light was streaming in through the open airshaft window. Borne on a cold breeze was the smell of the apartment below, something greasy and fried. Edward stirred and even the simple movement of turning away from the window set his head to pounding.

God, how much did I drink last night? Edward put a hand to his forehead, where pain bloomed behind his eyes, expanding and insinuating itself into his entire face, making it feel like a throbbing messenger of hurt. He fell back against his pillow and closed his eyes; nausea began to roil in his stomach.

This was no ordinary hangover. He would get no painting done today. This was why, in states of despair and after nights like the previous one (*what had happened?*), he often promised himself he would stay away from The Tiger's Eye and drink no more, or no more than, say, a glass of wine with dinner, when he could afford it. The cost was just too high; not only did it empty what little cash he had in his pockets (dollars that could be invested more wisely in luxuries like food and rent), but also it exacted a larger, and more painful, toll in time. And time was a resource he could never renew, like money. Poor as he was, there was always the chance to make more money. Somehow. But time, once spent, was gone for good.

He would pay for whatever happened the night before with this entire day. It bothered him that he couldn't remember anything from last night. *How did I get home? What happened once I got here?* Edward wondered and tried to retrieve the memories, but it was as if they were never there, as if most of last night, after leaving The Tiger's Eye, was a void. Blacking out was a line he had yet to cross and the thought of it made him even queasier. He didn't want to become one of those drunken has-been painters, regaling others in a bar about what could have been to cadge a free drink before he even had his first gallery show.

Even though it felt like the almost palpable pain behind his eyes would push them out, Edward managed to get up on his hands and knees and crawl to the little sink in the corner of the room. He was glad, for once, that there wasn't much in his stomach.

He turned the spigot on and lapped at the cold water like a dog, not bothering with glass or even cupped hands. The water helped calm the queasiness, and its chill was a balm to his aching head. Did he have what people in polite circles referred to as a "drinking problem"? Had he crossed a line from social drinker to alcoholic? Would he begin to lose weekends?

After drinking what seemed like gallons, Edward squatted and splashed water on his face, letting it dribble down his naked body. He closed his eyes and breathed deeply, keeping his mind blank by concentrating on the cool water. He opened his eyes.

Looking down as the cold rivulets ran through matted chest hair, making their way south to a pitiful looking penis, shriveled and tiny, bereft of almost any blood (that was mostly in his brain, causing him the most delirious pain as a reminder to keep away from the booze), he noticed something wrong.

There were several small, vertical scabs on his inner thighs. Three or four on each. Precise lines, their slightly irregular appearance due only to the crustings of blood. They looked deliberate.

What had he done to himself?

Edward grabbed a bath towel from the floor and dried the cold water from his face and body. He didn't need anything to make him feel more chilled than he already did. He trembled slightly.

These were cuts. Thin and almost elegant, they probably had to have been made with a razor.

What had he done? What had been done to him?

He looked around his apartment. The dull, midday light revealed a few spots of blood on the floor, a smear of it near the door: crimson fingerprints on the wall, turning black. His own blood.

He felt bile rising up and scampered on his ass backwards, collapsing on his damp mattress, rolling himself into the loose sheets and shivering. Did he really not remember what had happened?

Or did he just not want to?

He lay back, trying to breathe slowly, deeply, to quell the quaking that seemed to be veering close to seizure. There was a wall in his mind, one he had erected, and he was afraid to peer over it. Yet flashes assailed him.

Terence looking up at him from beneath Edward's spread thighs, his face smeared with blood.

He is smiling.

Edward turned and, as he did when he was a child and afraid of the monsters hiding in his bedroom closet, pulled the sheets over his head. But the sheets were not thick enough to keep out the memories, flooding in, quicker now that he had opened the gates.

"It's sharp enough that it won't even hurt. You have nothing to be afraid

of." The glint of stainless steel, a straight razor. Glimmering, even in the dull light.

Edward turned over, face down in the pillow, and whimpered. "No, I don't need to remember."

And his super-ego responded: "Yes, you do, so that history won't repeat itself."

And his id chimed in: "Yes, you do, so that you can do it again. It was good. So good, remember?"

Edward swallowed; his tongue felt dry and rough, like a cat's. But he didn't think he had the energy just now for a cross-room trek to the sink for more water. He tried to summon saliva from somewhere deep inside, like someone in a desert digging deep for ground water.

He saw Terence again.

He was naked, and his body was perfect, which made Edward wonder once more if he was heading down the right path with the expressionism of his art; if he shouldn't be perfecting realistic strokes so he could capture the beauty of what was before him. To capture beauty like what was in front of him, Edward had thought, would be real achievement. He could record and memorialize something outstanding.

"God, you're gorgeous. How did you get so pretty?" He had reached out a hand to touch Terence's flat stomach, to feel the cobblestones beneath. He imagined putting tongue to the white, silky flesh stretched taut over pectoral muscles.

But Terence had held up a warning hand. "You can't touch."

"Why not? Isn't that what we came here for?" He was so hungry for this man, he felt near tears.

"We came here to get to know one another better. I like you. I like your work. But you must know: I'm not a queer." The dark irises flashed. "At least not in the sense of the word you're probably thinking of." He snickered.

Edward had felt a momentary flash of shame. "But I don't understand."

"Can't I want to be close to you without wanting to stick my cock inside you? Can't I be your friend? Can't we be intimate in other ways?" Terence brought his face close to Edward's.

Edward was drunk, emboldened by spirits. "But I want to be close to you in all ways. And right now, I want to be close in the physical sense." He remembered a voice that became pleading. "Listen, you don't even have to do anything. Just lie back and let me suck you. You can close your eyes and pretend it's a woman down there." A nervous giggle had escaped him. "A mouth knows no gender." He had hated himself for begging, for putting himself in the position of being the one who wanted and not at all being the one who was wanted.

"That's not true."

Had he spoken aloud? He didn't think so.

"I want you very much." Terence had turned, exposing the turgid flesh between his thighs; at the same time, exposing Edward's thoughts. How had he known? "I just think there's a better way for the two of us to commune other than the pedestrian fumbling most people pass off as real intercourse."

Edward felt coarse, crude; he wanted to chastise himself. But he couldn't draw his gaze away from the rigid column of flesh rising up from the thatch of silky blond hair. He wanted to touch it; everything else was blotted out by this desire. It was almost all-consuming.

And then he recoiled, scrambling back just slightly, away from Terence, desire beginning to ebb as it combined with repulsion. It was such a tiny thing, yet seemed so out of place.

A drop of blood stood poised at the tip of Terence's penis. It dribbled down the shaft, to be replaced quickly by another. "You, you, you're bleeding," Edward whimpered, gesturing with an unsteady hand.

Terence looked down at himself, then up at Edward. He was grinning. He put his finger to the blood, then put it in his mouth. Scooped some blood from the shaft of his penis and held it out for Edward to lick. "Take this all of you and drink it, for this is my blood. The blood of the new and everlasting covenant." He snickered. "Go on." He edged his finger close enough to Edward's face that Edward could smell the metallic aroma. "Taste."

Edward moved back a little more. "I don't want any." He longed to feel the queasy delirium of being drunk, but suddenly, his mind was clear, and he was afraid. He didn't understand what was going on. This was turning into a nightmare.

"What? Do you want to lick it from the tap, so to speak? Sorry, fella, I don't do that." He leaned in close. "But I will do something, something physical that will make me very happy. And I can tell you're more the type that likes to make his partner happy. From giving pleasure, you derive it yourself. Tell me, Edward, am I wrong about that?"

In spite of the fear that had cleared his head, Edward was intrigued. Part of him wanted Terence to leave. What scared him even more was the thought of trying to get rid of him, of the inevitable conflict, and who would win. Another part of him wanted this man to stay with him, that part was willing to take whatever Terence was willing to give him, which is why he asked, "What do you mean?"

Terence slid close. Close enough so if Edward reached down, he could touch his sex, just encircle it with his hand, hold it. But he had a quick vision of a hand swinging out so fast the arm was a blur, a vision of himself flying across the room to land, hard, against the wall, his spine snapping and seeing himself collapse, like a marionette, to the floor, barely breathing. So, he simply stayed still, like an animal in the clutches of something much more powerful, frozen and submissive because there was no other option.

"What is it?" Edward whispered. He could barely speak, terror and lust warring within him.

Terence breathed in, then met Edward's gaze full on. "There is something, a little ritual if you will, that can bring us closer together. I would only want you to do it if you really wanted to... I'd like to drink your blood."

Edward stared back, lips parted. *Get up and run, you idiot!* he thought, but stayed rooted to the floor. He suddenly realized he could barely move, and that all of his movements, since he had taken a few tokes from Terence's pipe, were cloaked in a kind of nightmare slowness, as if he were moving in something heavy and viscous. Like clotting blood, perhaps. "You're not serious."

"Oh yes. Very serious." He cocked his head. "Are you worried that I'll hurt you? Worried maybe that I'll kill you?"

"I don't know what I'm worried about."

"I won't do either." Terence's eyelids were getting heavier, the hooded look that came with lust. And seeing the lust in his face gave Edward a feeling of power, making him forget completely the possibility he was being seduced, being manipulated.

It was then Terence brought out the straight razor. "Just a taste. All right?"

Edward said nothing. He didn't move.

Terence must have interpreted Edward's silence as acquiescence. He brought the blade close, paused with it just above his thigh. "It's sharp enough that it won't even hurt. You have nothing to be afraid of."

And Edward, trembling, had lain back, spreading his legs a little further. Terence was right: it didn't hurt. There was a slight chill as the metal made contact with his flesh, replaced by a warm, crawling sensation as the skin broke and the blood, freed, began to trickle down his thigh.

But not for long. Terence's mouth was on him, sucking and moaning.

Edward turned and felt sick. The memories scattered as he struggled to bring something up. But there was only a little yellow bile he swallowed back down, bitter and acid.

I won't do it again, he thought. And even as he thought it, he was wondering how he would find Terence again. Wondering if he would appear once more in the Eye of the Tiger.

Chapter
Five

SHE HAS BEEN alone so long the sound of a knock at her door startles her. Elise turns, head cocked, questioning. She puts down the charcoal pencil and goes to quiet the pounding.

The pounding grows louder as she skirts easels, a drawing board, her meager furniture. "All right, all right." *Who can it be?* Her life has become cut off from everyone she has ever known: family and what few friends she once had. When you become a cut-rate streetwalker, somehow the desire to keep in touch with Mom or Cathy from high school just isn't there anymore. "Yeah, Mom, today it was the same old, same old: blew a dozen guys, let six fuck me, and took one up the ass. But, hey! I'll make the rent this month." It wasn't the kind of news, either, one posted on the alumni website.

"Jesus! Give me a second." She struggles with the locks, wondering: *Do policemen ever make house calls to prostitutes? At least in any kind of official capacity?*

She swings the door open and memories rush in, images forming and dispersing with the rapidity of montage. Terence. Gone are the chains and leather. Tonight, nothing more than jeans and a crisp white button down cotton shirt. Asics running shoes. He looks devastating. But not devastating in the way most people would interpret that word; his appearance begs a more literal interpretation. The pedestrian, everyday clothes don't make him appear more normal, but emphasize his ashen pallor and dark-eyed intensity. The street clothes can't mask a hunger that's frightening. She really hadn't expected to see him again. That's the great thing about the business: one is always meeting new people.

"What do you want?"

"What? I get not even a hello?"

Elise leans against the door frame, crosses her arms across her chest. "Why? When I didn't even get a goodbye?" She starts to close the door. "Now, if you can't tell me something as simple as what you want, I really don't have time to be standing here."

He smiles. His teeth are tiny, baby-like, pearls between thin pink lips. "Isn't the answer obvious? I wanted to see you."

"Didn't you see everything you wanted when you were here last time?" Elise recalls how, against her wishes and her will, he had devoured all the art she had created over the past months, drinking in her vision, raping her creativity. She wasn't ready for a showing. She doesn't know if she ever will be.

Terence laughs, his deep voice dead, an echo. "Yes, as a matter of fact I did. I saw probably more than you realize."

Empty words. Does he mean to praise her? "Okay. You've seen me. I'm busy, so, please, could you go now?" Elise begins to close the door again.

Terence puts up a hand Elise cannot fight. The door stays open. She stares, waiting.

"I want you to come with me, meet my friends."

His friends? Elise cannot imagine the ghouls that would number Terence among their friends. Would they be like him, locked in some sort of pseudo-goth glamour? Besides, it's been so long since she's met anyone (other than in her role as professional caregiver), she wouldn't even know how to act. What would she say? What topics could she talk about? "That's impossible. I don't have time."

"It might help your art." Terence gives a small smile.

This statement intrigues Elise. "In what way?"

"Experience. Isn't that what you feed from? Isn't that what inspires all artists?"

"Oh, please." Elise tries again, without success, to close the door. "Save the art school platitudes for the kids at the Art Institute downtown." She sends a pointed stare his way. "Really. I'm very busy. The best way I can 'help my art,' as you put it, is to keep working at it."

Terence sighs. "Look, I won't take up much of your time."

Elise shakes her head. "Really. I think you should be going. This foot in the door routine is just irritating right now. In about five minutes, though, it will be illegal."

"What if I make it worth your while?" Terence takes out a wad of green and presses it into Elise's palm. For a moment, she is tempted to slam the door in his face. Instead, she looks down and counts five hundred dollars. She realizes she has become more of a whore than she realized.

"All right, I'll come with you, but for just a little while."

They roar down Sheridan Road, weaving between cars, making their own lanes as they speed between two rows of moving traffic, surging forward. They squeeze between parked and moving cars and buses. Elise prays no one will fling open a door as they whiz by. She imagines how quickly it would happen, her body flying through the air to crumble in a heap on the pavement, the slow stream of red darkening the asphalt. The sirens. The upended motorcycle wheel, spinning forlornly. Perhaps cinema would be more her forte. Or perhaps she can store the image for later retrieval. Already, she is wondering how the broken body on the road would look in a painting of black and white, the only color the trickle of blood from the victim's head.

But there are no accidents. The wind whips through their hair. She clings to Terence's back, wondering why pressing against him offers no respite from the chill of the wind off the lake, just a block or two to the east. She lays her cheek against his back. After all, nothing separates her flesh from his but white cotton. But even this divider seems to throw up a wall against warmth.

Have I done the right thing? Elise asks herself. *Going off with a stranger, someone who, just last night, betrayed me?* But Elise knows Terence is right when he says she needs experience to create. And if the experience turns out to be bad, or even fatal, well then, who will know the difference?

Terence rounds a corner near Loyola University and continues south. Now, the broad expanse of darkness that is Lake Michigan is to their left. Elise looks over at the water, how the moon glows silver and distorted on its surface. She has a quick image of playing in the icy surf one early summer day, the air fresh and filled with promise. Idyllic. She wonders if this "vision" is merely a figment of her imagination.

"Almost there now," Terence yells back, the wind stealing his words almost before they reach her ears. "I hope you're ready."

"I hope I am, too," Elise whispers.

The bike sputters as Terence comes to a stop. He pulls between two parked cars on Thorndale. The absence of the Harley's engine roar seems strange, making the more commonplace night sounds of traffic and insects underscored by the pound of the surf seem surreal, as if they exist in a void.

"Where are we going?" Elise runs fingers through her windblown hair, trying to smooth it.

"Home." Terence begins walking away from her. *It must be wonderful*, she thinks, *to have such confidence, to know that when you start to walk away, someone will follow.*

He is walking toward an old mansion, one of the only ones left in this mile or so long strip of high rises fronting the lake and having the feel of southern Florida, if not the warmth. Elise has passed the old house many times, and had noticed it because it was an anomaly, here on this strip of high-rise apartment buildings. "I thought this place was abandoned." It had always looked so, and looks so still. Its windows are black and empty (eye sockets whose vision was stolen in a gruesome maneuver); the yard sports patches of bare earth and weeds, and the entire façade radiates emptiness. The house seems solid and has the earmarks of architectural confidence and even style, but the overall effect is fearsome, as if the house disguises something alive and waiting, breath held, attempting to look innocuous to lure the unwary.

"No, not abandoned, my dear." Terence stops and turns. "Although

I suppose it's not unfair to describe it as lacking a certain *lived-in* quality." He snickers and begins moving toward the broad and crumbling concrete front steps.

I suppose he's expecting me to ask what he means by that. Elise will not give him the satisfaction. She follows him up the stairs and notices he does not remove any keys. He simply stops, hand poised on the doorknob.

"You're going to really like my friends. And I'm sure they'll love you."

In spite of the mockery that is a nearly constant key he sings in, there is none of that in the simple statement. On other lips, 'they'll love you' would probably be welcome, calming to a new visitor.

But on Terence's, the phrase sounds like she is being described as an entrée, words to be followed with, "I'm sure you'll be delicious."

A quick chill. "I don't think this is going to work." Elise turns, heading back out toward Sheridan, where there are plenty of cabs.

"What are you talking about? You mean we came all this way for nothing?" He lays his hand gently on her arm. "Now, don't be silly. You'll come inside. You don't have to stay long."

It all sounds so reasonable, Elise thinks, stealing one last glance at the lakefront before following him inside. Part of her wonders if it will truly be her last.

Inside, Elise paces, heels clicking on the dusty wooden floor. Outside of a gallery, she has never seen such a collection. But no, not even a gallery would contain such an eclectic mix of art: representational mixed with wild flights of fancy, abstract sculptures welded from metal, looking violent and harmful, sitting next to a figure carved from marble in a classical manner (the careful chips and missing digits on the one hand made for a convincing replica, Elise thinks; such attention to detail). Perhaps a museum might yield such a mix, but in a museum, there are separate rooms for separate periods and styles. There is logic and organization. In a museum, there could not be this anarchy of form and vision; this chaos that somehow makes a statement on the hunger human beings have for expression and creation.

There must be a defining element, Elise is certain, *that ties all of this together. Something I haven't yet been able to decipher.*

She has already decided, even if she has yet to meet any of Terence's "friends," that she must come back. She will need to study what's here. Some of it looks alarmingly authentic. But art worth millions stashed in an unlocked house that appears abandoned?

It can't be.

Terence left her alone only moments ago. "Wait here. I'll be right back." His exit was so quick, she almost didn't realize he had gone. But Elise doesn't care how long he keeps her. For the first time in months, she feels alive as she drinks in the genius of the work. She hadn't realized she was starving.

And then Terence is back. Too soon. Elise pulls herself away from the figure of a woman, welded from burnished steel, her mouth open in torment or orgasm. The work reminds her of her own; it has the same clinical detachment toward something elemental, be it ecstatic or horrific. She fingers the metal, its smooth finish, wondering about technique and process. *Just a few more minutes alone here*, she thinks.

"These are my friends, the ones I told you about." Two people emerge out of the shadows. First comes a man, much shorter than Terence, but muscular, strength bound into a compact frame. "This is Edward." He gives a lopsided grin to Elise, not showing teeth. He takes her hand and kisses it; the chill and damp of his lips make her think of slugs. He looks into her eyes and she feels something right away: an odd connection. There is such intensity in his pale eyes; she senses how hard he is trying to engage her. It chills her, yet she instinctively is not as afraid of this one as she is of Terence. She thinks she sees sadness in his face, a melancholy so deep she is afraid to even attempt fathoming it.

"Edward," she whispers. "I'm very glad to meet you."

"And I'm really happy that you're here. Terence told us a little about you last night. You're an artist. I used to dabble myself..." Edward's smile is tortured and Elise feels that his story is one of loss and pain. Instinctively, she pulls back, wanting to know more about him and wishing, at the same time, he would just go away. "But that's all in the past." There isn't an ounce of mirth, though, in the smile that follows this statement. "Terence tells us you have something really special, he says you're really gifted."

"Well, I try."

Terence pulls her away. Elise glances back at Edward, seeing one of the clone boys she has seen on the part of Halsted Street that's "Boystown" central. Yet, there is a longing in his eyes that pains her.

Terence takes her hand and says, "Modesty doesn't become you, love." He pauses. "And this is Maria."

A woman emerges out of the shadows in a moment charged with electricity. It hangs in the air like the ozone after a lightning strike. Her movement is so liquid, so gliding, Elise believes she must have planned her entrance. She wonders if there are casters hidden beneath her long, deep red dress.

Their gazes lock. The art in the room fades into a graying pastiche of color, the blurred background of a photo. The floor vanishes, leaving the two women suspended in midair, legs dangling above a black abyss. The huge fireplace loses its charred brick back and becomes a shadowed portal. Even Terence and Edward fade. And Maria glimmers and shimmers, perfection in close-up. Elise drinks her in, her exquisite bone-white skin. Dark curls frame a face of Botticelli beauty. Elise is swallowed up by dark eyes that bore into hers with knowledge and certainty. Elise can't recall a time when she has felt such raw, animal connection. Especially not for another woman...

Elise bows her head, suddenly feeling a loss of words, a loss of self. What to say to this creature so stunning she is almost monstrous?

"I've been waiting to meet you." Maria's voice is broken glass in honey, rough and deep, scarred, as bass as a man's, but decidedly feminine. She moves forward and embraces Elise.

Elise's heart beats so hard the blood rushes in her ears, pounding. Maria's embrace is ice, but Elise doesn't recoil. She pulls the woman closer, wrapping her arms tight, wanting to warm her, to share her heat. Something stirs inside; her heart gallops. She wonders if the organ will explode, leaving behind a shower of red sparks. It would be a good way to die. She breathes deep and buries her face in Maria's black hair, to take in whatever essence these dark strands give off. The closeness and the feel of the silken hair against her cheek ratchets up her desire, leaving Elise helpless, lost, and elated. She tries to pull away, imagining the flood of dopamine in her system as a cascade of silver liquid, trying without much success to convince herself this sudden lust for another woman is nothing more than the release of chemicals within her brain. But if any trickery is to work, any black magic to be successful, Elise knows it will not be self-generated.

Maria finally breaks the embrace. For a long time, she does nothing more than stare into Elise's eyes. She bites her lip as she regards her and Elise again has the peculiar feeling of being suspended in mid-air. Elise wonders if what Maria feels is at least somewhat akin to the rush of emotions she's experiencing. Maria tears her gaze away, runs a hand through her hair. "Terence tells us you are able to create the most astonishing work, that he's never seen anything quite like it. He's very excited. He wants us all to see it as soon as possible." She cocks her head. "With your permission, of course."

Elise isn't sure what to say. What has Terence told them? Is her work good enough for them? But if seeing it will allow her some more time in the presence of this amazing creature, then Elise thinks she might dare risk it.

"I'd love for you to see my work," Elise hears herself saying, surprised the words are tumbling forth, almost beyond her bidding. "I would love for you to come by."

"I think I would love that, too...Elise. Elise, right?"

"Yes."

"From the French? I believe it means something like 'consecrated to God.'"

Elise shakes her head. She flashes on herself on her knees in an alley the night before, wiping semen off her face with a paper napkin. "I don't know. God and I aren't on speaking terms these days."

Terence laughs. "And He's completely turned his back on us. So we can commiserate together."

Maria touches Elise's face and the chill of her hand doesn't feel odd, but electrifying, the cold invigorating. "Perhaps you'd like to share something to eat with us."

"Oh, I don't know. Well, yes, yes, that would be nice." Suddenly, Elise feels tongue-tied. She looks to Edward, who stares away, into the shadows.

Terence is grinning.

Elise follows the trio into a kitchen that looks like something from another century. Here are the same water-stained walls and crumbling plaster she found in the other room. There is another large fireplace, this one less formal, more utilitarian, rough bricks and careless mortar, crumbling together. Inside the hearth is something Elise has seen only in period paintings, or a movie theater: a big black pot (could it be properly referred to as a cauldron?) hangs on a peg above a crackling fire. Steam rises from it. Elise sniffs and can smell roasting meat and the sharpness of a good red wine. She cocks her head. "Beef Bourguignon?"

Terence snickers. "Something like that."

The flame under the stew provides the only light in the room, save for what filters in, gray and flat, through the windows that afford a view of a moonlit garden, riotous with weeds and brambles. The darkness is probably a good thing: electric light would reveal the filth and disuse of the room. Elise is certain she can see heavy cobwebs in the corners. The cabinet doors are hanging off their hinges, some fallen to a rough tile floor.

There is nothing inside the cabinets but shadows. Elise thinks she can detect movement and the twinkling of rodent eyes in one of them.

"I don't usually eat meat," Elise mumbles, cursing herself for putting the "usually" qualifier in. Without it, there wouldn't have been any room for maneuvering when they politely offered her something.

Maria moves quickly to the big bubbling pot, a bowl and ladle in her hand. "Tonight, for us, you will make an exception?" She glances over her shoulder. "Please?"

Terence says, "Oh, restraint. I was hoping you were a hedonist, like us."

Elise scratches at her face, plays for a moment with a strand of hair. "Sure. But not too much."

"Speak for yourself." This from Edward, who leans against a countertop, his face unreadable in the flickering light.

"I get all the pleasure I can handle." Elise takes the earthenware bowl from Maria. "Thank you." Steam rises up from the bowl, bearing up a bouquet of aroma: rosemary and tarragon and a bass note that has a rich, meaty smell. Elise wonders if she is being offered some sort of wild game.

"You need a spoon." Maria pulls open drawers and finally locates a tablespoon. She wipes it on her dress and holds it out to Elise.

"Aren't you eating?"

Edward stands up straighter. "We'll wait for you to start; then we'll serve ourselves."

"Old European tradition," Maria says.

"Oh, well then, all right." Cautiously, she takes some of the stew onto her spoon. It appears to be only meat, herbs, and broth. She brings it to her mouth and the smell is an odd paradox of a delicious aroma and something off-putting, something causing her stomach to roil. She forces herself to take a bite.

The taste of the meat is a surprise, more like pork than beef, with a strange gamy aftertaste Elise finds unpalatable. The broth has a viscous, almost metallic tang. She struggles to control her gag reflex, setting the bowl on the counter. "What is this?"

"Just a little meat, some wine, a few snips of special herbs." Maria is dishing up big bowls for herself and her companions. "Why? Do you not, uh, care for it?"

"No, it's fine. I'm afraid I'm just not very hungry." Her stomach continues to churn. She doesn't really want to look too closely at the reason for her queasiness. "What kind of meat?"

Terence lifts his bowl, bringing it up to his mouth, and slurps up the broth. He lets out a satisfied sigh. "It's just a little pork. What do you think? We're cannibals?"

"No. No, of course not. That would be silly, wouldn't it?"

Edward stares at her, mute. The other two get busy with their food.

"I need to be going." Elise takes her bowl to the sink. Its surface is stained and chipped porcelain. A cockroach skitters across the bone-dry surface. The sudden movement causes Elise to drop the bowl, which shatters. She gasps. "I'm sorry." She reaches for the porcelain knob to start the water's flow and nothing happens, except for a creaking protest. She turns and smiles, stupidly, at them. "Your water seems to be shut off." Elise feels a rising panic. "I need to go."

Maria takes her hand, making Elise wonder where she had come from; it seems Maria took only a fraction of a second to cross the room and appear at her side. "I understand. Let me see you out. My cooking isn't always to everyone's taste." She smiles, and Elise notices that her teeth, like Terence's, are tiny and pearlescent, the canines sharper than the average person's. Elise trembles. If she had more of a supernatural bent, she might think these three were something other than human beings. But she gave up on horror movies and all that crap when she began turning crime scenes into art. The real world is horrific enough.

Isn't it?

"Come." Maria leads her forward. "We need to talk about when I can see you again. We need to talk about when I can see your work."

Chapter
Six

1954

WHY HAD HE done it?

Edward lay back, trembling. He had spent the day trying to feel normal again, to regain a feeling that now seemed alien, fleeing from his grasp. How would he quell the queasiness in his gut, the pounding in his head? It had taken hours just to get to the point where the only thing he felt was fatigue and not the kind of nausea that made him think death wasn't such a bad alternative. He had eaten canned chicken soup and pieces of dry toast, forcing them down with weak Red Rose tea (there was some orange juice in the refrigerator, but the acid in that would have been adequate to start the whole cycle all over again). He had stared out the window, at the parade of delivery trucks, cars, and foot traffic that never seemed to ebb, wondering where everyone had to go. Wondering why there was never a moment when everyone just stopped, when they all simply got to where they were going and stayed. It was thoughts like these that occupied him, that kept him from dwelling on feeling sick and remembering.

So why, as soon as he felt good enough to walk around, had he allowed the fantasy to run rampant, like some caged animal for which he had unwisely unlocked and opened a door?

Edward felt almost like a marionette as he lay on his mattress and closed his eyes. What hands were pulling the strings, bringing to life thoughts Edward would swear hadn't originated in his own brain? Projected upon his inner eyelids were images of Terence, naked. Images of Terence's blond hair, buried between his thighs, ignoring the turgid sex and sucking the blood from slim razor-drawn cuts.

Why did these images excite him? Why did seeing something in his mind's eye like Terence rubbing Edward's blood on his own sex force him to take hold of himself roughly and tug and pull until he spurted all over himself? Why did he pick at one of the cuts on his legs until it bled, then mix the blood and semen and bring some of it to his mouth, where its odd bleachy, metallic smell almost made him vomit once more?

Yet at the same time, the aroma and the taste excited him again, as though the mixture was a potent aphrodisiac.

And now, he lay upon his sweat-soaked mattress, after coming three times in quick succession, feeling drained and out of breath, his own blood and semen a mess across his stomach and running in crawly streams down his thighs. His head buzzed. He closed his eyes, trying to blot it all out, but the simple act of trying to obliterate one sense activated his imagination. The blank, black canvas of the inside of his eyelids caused brilliant crimson visions to bloom.

He stood, inspired, and rubbing his hands over his chest and stomach, painted broad swathes of red and viscous gluey fluids across a bare canvas, then stepped back, panting, to look at the shiny swirls of bodily fluids.

And saw nothing worthwhile.

Later, Edward dressed to go out. He had no money to spend, but would make a circuit of Greenwich Village and somehow find Terence. He felt a curious mixture of dread and desire. Dread because he knew Terence had awakened in him a hunger he didn't understand, and seeing him again could up the hunger, making it worse, making it unbearable. He wondered if his need for this strange man had the potential to drive him insane. Desire because he knew he wouldn't be able to think, or create, or even tend to life's small responsibilities unless he saw Terence again. He was like an addict in that sense.

Was this what love was like? Edward had never known that particular emotion; he had always stood on the outside, observing. If this was love, he couldn't imagine why anyone would court its irresistible, all-consuming siren call.

Could another human being have so much power over him as to render him helpless?

He needed to find Terence to see if he could somehow release the hold this strange and beautiful man had on him, whether that release would come through complete immersion in Terence, or through some means of breaking the bond Terence had forged when he had drunk his blood.

Outside, the night was close. The temperature had gone up as darkness fell, cloaking the city in a moist, heated embrace. Everywhere Edward looked, it appeared as though the people on the street were more than tired; they were dead, zombies walking the street, their pace slow and languid, their gazes dull. They simply existed, driven by legs that would not stop walking, hearts that would not stop beating, lungs that would not stop working, like bewitched bellows. Edward knew he was projecting his own feelings upon the men and women he passed, but that didn't make the feeling he was walking among scores of living dead any less real.

He had no idea where he would find Terence. He had no idea even how he could go about locating a single person, admittedly a unique single person, among the millions inhabiting this small island crawling with humanity. But he knew he had no other choice. Otherwise, he might as well just walk out onto the wooden sidewalks that spanned the Brooklyn Bridge and fling himself into the Hudson River's dark and dirty waters. The prospect had an odd appeal, seeming as encompassing and final as the fever of obsession gripping him. At least the river's waters would be cool, offering a different kind of oblivion.

For all this drama, Edward thought, locating Terence should have been much more difficult than it was. But, as he turned the corner of Horatio onto Greenwich Avenue, he spotted him.

It seemed as if Terence was waiting. He stood, dressed in a white linen suit, near a street vendor selling flowers. The white suit, crisp and clean on this hot and humid night, the flower vendor with his rusting, chipped green painted cart, and the blur of humanity surrounding them looked like a scene created purely to engage his senses. Again, he had the thought he should turn to realism in his work, when such scenes kept springing up before his eyes, perfectly composed, waiting only for the touch of his craft to freeze them. Terence's blond hair was slicked back; Edward could see the dark, lacquered blond underneath a white straw boater. He wore white bucks and his white shirt was buttoned at the throat; no tie.

They had made no plans to see each other, not tonight, nor ever again, for that matter. Yet, there he stood, looking like an oasis of cool on a busy street of people who dripped sweat, whose clothes were stained with dank, odiferous moisture. There he stood, waiting. The single white rose in his hand, Edward knew, was for him.

So how did he know to be here right now, when I came into view, posing, with the light from a street lamp spotlighting him, giving him a glow that other passersby did not possess? How did he know I would come searching for him?

Or does he have the power to compel me to search?

Edward stopped, and the sounds of the night, the groaning exhausts, the honking of horns, the endless chatter of people on the street, seemed to recede as he locked gazes with Terence. The neon and the bustle went slightly indistinct and out of focus, serving only to sharpen the image of Terence before him.

A part of Edward wanted to turn and run. There was still a little of him that held out for what was sane, what was logical. But, as is often the case with love and obsession, rational behavior was no match for the powerful force of desire. Even as Edward was picturing himself turning and running up Greenwich Avenue to 14th, where he could continue running east until he got to the East River, he knew the decision to do anything other than walk toward Terence was out of his hands.

Feeling a queasy mixture of lust and fear, he began walking toward Terence. And Terence smiled. It was like he knew before Edward made a move exactly what he would do. Edward witnessed the satisfaction in his eyes, even at fifty, even at one hundred paces. Terence was controlling him like a puppet, yet even this knowledge did not release him. As Edward neared him, Terence raised the hand with the rose in it, holding it out like one would hold out a treat to a dog.

Edward closed in, reaching for the rose. He clasped it tightly in his palm, so that the thorns would dig into his palm. He tried not to wince as he felt the tiny daggers pierce his skin. He looked down for only a moment at the small network of red holes in his hands before offering it to Terence.

Terence took the proffered hand gently, bringing it to his mouth, like a man about to kiss a woman's hand. He sucked away the blood, causing two teenage girls to stop and stare, then run away, giggling and casting looks back.

"I knew you were coming."

"You didn't just know. You made me."

"Don't be ridiculous. If I had that kind of power, why would I be wasting it on the likes of you?" Terence threw back his head and laughed. Edward could see a dab of his own blood at the corner of Terence's lips. He pulled Edward close. "Maybe I just wished hard enough to make my dream come true."

"Or maybe I did."

Terence spoke slowly. "Whatever brought us together doesn't matter because we are now."

Edward nodded, wanting to lick the blood away from Terence's mouth. Too late: Terence's tongue emerged, a hungry snake, and restored his marble-like face to its original, unsullied white.

"So, what should we do?"

"I'm so glad you asked. I have somewhere I want to take you. Somewhere we can be alone." Terence moved to the curb and raised his hand to hail a taxi.

What awaited Edward was not what he expected.

Chapter
Seven

Present Day

ELISE HAS ONLY two mirrors in her apartment and hung neither of them herself. The first is built into her medicine cabinet (a metal thing circa 1930). The second is a full-length one sunk into her front closet door. She doesn't like mirrors, but accepts their necessity. How else will she know if she has applied eye shadow or lipstick correctly, or if the seams on her stockings are straight?

Otherwise, Elise has grown to hate them. Their silvered surfaces often throw back a person she used to be, someone with ruddy cheeks, lustrous hair, and an irrepressible smile. Now, there are times when she stands for long periods in front of the medicine cabinet mirror, scissors in hand, ready to hack away at the mane of reddish-brown hair that has always inspired envy and desire. It is only fatigue and depression that prevent her from following through on her resolve to make herself ugly. There is also the matter of fear: if she could cut off her hair, why not slash at her face with the scissors? Scars would make the men turn away in droves.

Gradually, she learned to stop looking at herself. Gradually, she became accustomed to the fact that, although her beauty probably remained somewhere in her features, most people saw her now as a nasty streetwalker, a used-up whore who would feel gritty to the touch.

She doesn't want that persona tonight. She leans over the sink, bringing her reflection in close. It is almost like looking at another person. Elise asks this person, "What have you gotten yourself into?" Her reflection stares back, dumbfounded, unable to provide an answer.

Elise has pulled her auburn hair away from her face, pulling it into a French twist. The style gives her the look of a Hitchcock heroine, elegant and cool. It also makes her eyes stand out: wide-set, rimmed in black lashes so long she has been accused more than once of wearing false ones. Without her hair obscuring her face, her cheekbones and the fine line of her jaw also stand out, defining and framing a face that Elise has so often felt betrayed by: why not give this beauty to someone else? Someone with a kind heart, who deserves it more than she?

She has spent the last several months perfecting her face as a canvas for a work called "The Whore By Night," using lurid colors around her eyes — one night a neon lime green with Cleopatra slashes of eyeliner and brilliant crimson lipstick on her lips, another night, the pairing for eyes and mouth is blue eye shadow and bubblegum pink lip gloss of a white-trash Lolita. But tonight she yearns for a subtler effect. The makeup brings out the definition of her cheekbones, the fullness of her lips, the oval shape of her face...just a touch of mascara to showcase the green of her eyes. She wears a long green silk dress, with oak leaves embroidered into the fabric. She steps back and is surprised by the transformation; surprised and grateful that she isn't so far gone that she can't recapture a healthy, youthful look. "Looking your best tonight," she whispers to her reflection.

It has been a long, long time since Elise has wanted to look good for someone, as opposed to wanting to look good as a tool of her trade.

All day she has cleaned; scrubbed Linoleum, dusted what little furniture she has, changed sheets and moved her works in progress to a corner, secreted behind a bookcase. Her best she has put on display, the few pieces she has bothered to frame positioned along the baseboard around the circumference of the studio apartment. Maria will have to squat down to look at her work: the graying strokes of gunshot victims, stabbings, stranglings, and car accidents. Looking around, Elise finds it hard to believe there was ever a time when she used color (pastels, acrylics, watercolors, and oils) or employed cheerier subjects for her art. The person who created a watery, bursting-with-color vision of a Mexican street vendor holding aloft a mango cut just so and garnished with lime and red pepper seems another artist entirely. A dead one.

Elise takes one final tour around the little room she calls home. Electricity throbs within her and the feeling is alien. She hasn't experienced this in so long it almost feels like something drug-induced. There's a dizziness, a rush of emotion. What is it people call this?

Oh yes. Anticipation. Elise shrugs; she'd thought that the emotion had flown the coop, having more to do with ketchup than with her.

The bass of a motorcycle engine trumpets Maria's arrival. Elise turns off the overhead light and hurries to the window to watch. Outside, Maria straddles the Harley. The bike's chrome glints yellow in the sodium vapor light. Maria dismounts, shakes her black, windblown hair. Elise cannot see what she is wearing; darkness shrouds her. With careful movements, she locks up the bike.

Elise feels an unfamiliar sensation break across her features, an odd tightening of muscles. She is smiling.

She hurries around the apartment, using a disposable lighter to light candles she has positioned on every surface. The question comes to her: *Am I a lesbian? Is this the real reason I found, ultimately, no comfort with a man? But why hasn't there been anyone before? Why has this woman in particular captivated me so much?*

And then she sees Maria in her mind's eye. The vision is startling:

black hair contrasted with skin so pale it's almost translucent. Her hair has a blue sheen. Her eyes are so black, Elise could tumble into them, happily lost forever.

The bark of the door buzzer startles her.

Elise hurries to press the button that will admit Maria. "Why did I do this?" She thinks she should be on the street, working. She thinks, for a moment, almost as if the thought came from someone else, that the streets would be a safer place than the territory she is about to travel into.

It is the first time in a long time Elise has actually decided to let someone peer into the world she has created with her art. Fear is part of the reason she wants to keep the light in the room dim. Like a disfigured or merely unattractive person, Elise figures the candlelight will accentuate what's good about her work while hiding its flaws.

It bothers her, as she moves to the door, that she cares so much about what this woman whom she barely knows will think of her work. *Why should it matter? Even if she hates your work, she could still like you.*

No. Love me, love my work. There can be no distinction between the two.

Elise opens the door.

Maria is cloaked in leather. Tight leather pants, a zippered shirt of thin, pliable hide, dark leather boots. The black offers a striking contrast to her skin. Elise swears her heart stops beating.

Maria brushes her lips, cool, across Elise's. "I brought you some wine." Maria sets a bottle of cabernet on the kitchen counter. "And this." She holds up a carved wooden pipe. The pipe is similar to the one Terence had, but the carving on this one is different: a cat's face. Not a domestic cat, something more like a lion or cougar. The choice of beast suits Maria.

Elise breathes in sharply, regarding the pipe, already stuffed with redolent sinsemilla. She can smell its acrid tang rising up from the bowl, like incense. Maria sets the pipe next to the bottle of wine.

"Is that the same stuff Terence had?"

"Yes."

"I don't know if I can handle it. Especially with wine." Elise giggles. "I'll be comatose."

Maria has still not looked at any of her art. "We wouldn't want that. I find that, if we use it correctly, it can make us more attuned." Maria regards her. "Drugs can be used to enlighten and inform the senses, you know."

Elise nods. To give herself something to do, she picks up the bottle of wine, reads the label. Out of the corner of her eye, she regards the bowl. "Where do you get it?"

"We grow it ourselves." Maria grins. "Ancient Chinese secret." She fires up the bowl and inhales, then passes Elise the pipe. Not wanting to disappoint, Elise draws in a lungful of smoke, though she knows it will numb her almost beyond reason. She wonders if the pot is cut with something more powerful.

The women pass the pipe back and forth. Three hits for Maria. One for Elise.

Maria, whose gaze has been on Elise since she entered, turns finally. "Your art. Terence tells me you're a genius. I want to see." Maria's voice comes to Elise through a tunnel, and in response, she gestures to the work positioned along the wall. Elise feels as though her movements are traveling through glue. Her heartbeat has slowed to the point where it's an eternity between beats.

It seems as if hours pass. Maria stops before each piece, black eyes intent, drinking it in. It's as if she's devouring the art, much the same way Terence did. There is a difference though: this time it is not a violation, not a rape. Elise wants to give, to open herself and her creations up to Maria. She wants to explain what she's doing, her process, but her tongue is thick in her mouth, and words are beyond the capacity of her languid breath. She then has the revelation that, if her art is doing its job, as her incapacitated mind puts it, she doesn't need to explain process or intent. All the answers should be there, on the paper, written in charcoal.

She knows Maria will see.

After a while, the walls melt, and Elise sees only Maria, standing in a dark void, her work suspended before her, work that has slouched toward life: three-dimensional, breaking chains of paper and canvas. Finally, Maria turns to her, and Elise tumbles into the blackness of her gaze. Maria nods. She understands.

Time, having stretched, now rushes forward, and Elise is in Maria's arms. Those dark eyes that have swallowed all her art now reach for the artist, claiming, capturing. Compelling. Elise fears the power of those eyes, the lure—fears being swept away, fears getting carried away. Fears losing herself to temptation.

I am already lost.

Lips merge: soft flesh, cold and hot. Tongues intertwine, dueling. Blood races through Elise's veins, heating her core; her vision dims. Maria's flesh is icy fire, glowing in the dim light, the only real thing in the room. Whiter than the sheets they lie upon.

Maria nuzzles Elise's thighs, cold caress calling hot fluid forth. Her tongue darts and circles Elise's clitoris, teasing, toying, probing. Traces a torturous path down. Elise grabs a handful of night-dark hair and pulls. Hard enough to hurt.

Maria only laughs, chill breath a different sort of kiss. And then she rises, writhing upward, to hold herself above Elise—hair swinging down, tickling brush against cheeks and shoulders—and slides down again, slowly, to Elise's breast.

Kissing, suckling, licking. Biting.

A gasp as the tender skin of Elise's areola is broken by tiny, razor teeth. Spots of bright red blood rise against salmon skin. Elise's command of language is gone and she whimpers as Maria's tongue, rough and cold, a cat's, laps away the blood.

"Just a taste," Maria's voice floats above her. "I must have a taste. But that is all. That is all. I would never harm you...my love."

Elise surrenders to the darkness of her pleasure.

Chapter
Eight

1954

THE CLUNK OF the taxi door closing isolated them. Edward sat stiffly against the cloth seat; the noise and bustle of the city shut out. The cab was silent and, oddly, cool. Edward leaned to peer at the traffic going by and didn't see a single cab that did not have its windows rolled down in an attempt to circulate the hot, heavy air, but this cab was sealed shut against the night, almost as if it existed in a different realm. There was no rearview mirror mounted on the windshield, so Edward couldn't make out the face, or even the eyes, of the cab driver. He could only stare at the almost silhouetted shape of the back of a head, broad shoulders. "Where are we going?" He had an urge to grab Terence's hand, an urge born of fear, born of a desire to possess. Terence hadn't said a word as the cab pulled away from the curb, yet the driver seemed to know exactly where to take them.

They cruised through Manhattan, toward Brooklyn. Terence was silent, and if Edward hadn't turned to look at him, he wouldn't have even known he was there. No warmth emanated from his still form. The chill should have frightened Edward, should have had him groping for the door handle, so he could fling it open at the next light and flee into the night.

So why was Edward staying? Why wasn't he screaming and beating on the windows to be set free? Why did he feel that what was ahead of him should be met with anticipation rather than dread?

If he knew the answers to such questions, he would have a better hold on why he was sitting quietly in this silent, cool car with what seemed like an animated corpse. Where was he being taken? And for what purpose?

Edward swallowed and let himself lean back against the upholstery. "Got a cig?" he mumbled to Terence.

Terence offered a Lucky and Edward took it. The silver lighter appeared, flashed, and Edward closed his eyes, sucking in a huge lungful of smoke.

When the cigarette had burned down to the point where it would burn Edward's fingertips, Terence plucked the butt from him, lowered the window just enough to fling it out, and turned to Edward. He held the small pipe he had offered in Edward's apartment the other night in his hand. Edward didn't see him reach in a pocket; the pipe was just...*there.*

"Why smoke cigarettes when you can have this?" Terence lifted the pipe so Edward could catch a whiff of the sticky bud pressed inside its bowl. The smell was bitter, pungent, and strangely attractive. "Cigarettes are so pedestrian. Will you join me in a real smoke?"

Terence fired up the bowl and drew in, making the bud glow a brighter orange in the cab's dim interior. He held the smoke in, released it through his nostrils, then handed the bowl and sterling silver lighter to Edward. "Here."

"I remember the last time. I'm not so sure I should." Edward was already reaching.

"Moderation is the key. A little goes a long way. It will make the evening so much more pleasant. You'll see."

One hit was all it took. The brownstones and shuttered storefronts dissolved from Edward's view. The cab came to a halt outside a subway station. Edward looked up and through dry and blurred vision saw a sign for Church Street. "Where the fuck..."

"We're in Brooklyn, sweetheart. Now get out of the cab. The meter's running."

The two men exited the cab and it sped off. Edward saw no attempt to pay the driver.

"Come." Terence grabbed Edward's hand and his cold touch was electric.

Edward could barely keep up; it seemed Terence was gliding on casters. They went down a flight of stairs into a subway station. Edward thought he saw the name "Bergen" formed from tile on the walls of the station, yet there was no one below. There was no rumble of trains either. The station appeared deserted.

Edward drew on his rudimentary knowledge of the New York City network of subway stations and asked, "Where are we going? Coney Island?" The absurdity of the question tickled him and he giggled. Or maybe he was just trying to avoid the vague terror at the back of his mind. *Why is he leading me into what looks like an abandoned subway station? Bigger question: why am I following?*

"Come." Terence pulled him further into shadows.

Edward pulled himself away, trembling. This was going too far. "No! Wait a minute! What are we doing here? No trains come through here. It's silent. There are no passengers. We didn't pay to get in here." In the shadows, Edward sought to make a connection with Terence's dark eyes. Once he felt he had his attention: "I want to know. I'm not going any further."

Visions of murder danced in his head. A body that wouldn't be found for weeks until its rotting corpse was discovered by a wine-swilling bum who wandered into this empty station seeking shelter from a storm...

"Trust me, Edward. There's someone you should meet."

The drug he had smoked clouded his brain. He had already forgotten what he had asked. His mind pondered another question: if this was truly an abandoned station, how could they have gotten in? Wouldn't such a place be locked and barricaded against the public?

But that question, too, vanished into a hemp haze.

Mutely, he followed Terence to the end of the platform. It was even darker there, but the darkness was fragmented by a sharp line of yellow light, shining out from under two huge metal doors.

"What's behind the doors?" Edward felt a sharp stab of fear. It caused his heart to beat faster and made his face grow slick with sweat. He noticed for the first time the musty air that smelled mildewed, as if hadn't been disturbed by anything living in years. To defy him, a rat the size of a small dog scampered across the platform before him and disappeared into a tunnel. "I don't like this," he said, reverting to a child's protests. "I want to go home."

Terence presented him with his most seductive smile, the tiny, pearlescent teeth almost glowing. "But, darling, we've come this far. And Maria is expecting us."

"Maria?"

Terence stooped and his hands moved near the bottom of the door. There was a click. Terence stood and rubbed his hands together, then wedged a fingertip into the slim line separating the doors, which swung open, releasing the very essence of dankness and a pale lemony light from a wall-mounted lamp, nearly blinding after the gloom Edward had grown accustomed to.

The two men stood at the top of a wide flight of stairs. They descended into blackness. Edward shivered. He could not see where the stairs ended.

A strain of music floated up the stairs. Edward cocked his head. Was it Vivaldi?

Terence put his arm around him, urging him to the first step. "There's another station below this one."

"And what's down there?" Edward reluctantly let his feet descend two steps.

"Maria. And our home. I've visited your home. It's only gracious that I have you to mine."

Edward swallowed hard and let Terence guide him into the pitch.

Chapter
Nine

Present Day

HARSH LIGHT ARRIVES as an unexpected visitor. Elise stirs, turning over, pulling the sheet over her head. How can it be morning already? Yet she hears the birds outside, the traffic, the cries in the street...just another day. The pedestrian sounds are unreal, the soundtrack to a movie. Elise struggles to return to the oblivion of her sleep. Was the night before a dream? She can't remember. She just wants to remove the bright reality of consciousness.

But sleep betrays her, scampering away, casting mocking looks over its shoulder. Besides, it's already hot. Elise whips the sheet away from her moist, overheated skin. Squinting at the sunlight, she wonders where the darkness and the cool cover of night have gone. The air hangs palpable and dead. Elise sits up, looks around her small room.

Night, Elise thinks, isn't the only thing that left her while she slept. Where has Maria gone? The pillow where her head had lain still bears an indentation from Maria's head. She had not expected, for the first time in how many years, to wake up alone again. Her head buzzes, with anger, with hurt, with the fog left over from the pot Maria fed her. Her body aches: sore nipples, sex that feels bruised and chafed. These are pleasant pains, but would have been almost celebratory had Maria still been here with her.

Why should she expect more? Hasn't she learned that life is nothing more than a series of disappointments? Isn't that what she has steeled herself against?

How could it be so easy for someone to come in (a woman, no less!) and just knock over her defenses like tiny green toy soldiers?

Elise dangles her feet over the edge of the bed, squinting at the light filtering in through the vinyl mini-blinds in the window across from her. She will make coffee. She will soak in a tub of cool water. She will buy herself a cat. No, wait—forget the last part.

She will forget Maria. She will forget Terence. She will not permit them entry into her body, her life, her soul. It will be healthier that way. Art or no art, she is striving to be a realist. Romantics only absorb pain like sponges.

Where has Maria gone?

Elise wishes she didn't care. She gets up and ambles slowly across the cracked vinyl flooring to the kitchenette, runs cold tap water into her Mr. Coffee glass carafe, sets it in position, pours some ground beans into a filter, and sets it to brewing. She wishes she smoked, like every other whore she has seen on the street. Somehow, the effect would be right, after a hard night of debauchery and God knows what else.

She leans against the counter, closing her eyes, the breathing sound of the coffee maker as it drips and steams through its cycle a background soundtrack to her thoughts. Memories, like dream images, rush back, knowing no chronology or order. She recalls sensations and has trouble putting them in context. Now, the feel of Maria's hand on her lower back, the cool skin against the fevered, sensitive flesh. The whisper of dark hair across her thighs. The moistness of a tongue and a cool mouth at her nipples, nipping and sucking. Elise hears the whispers, the sighs, the laughter. She sees Maria's eyes above her in the darkness, gazing down at her, rapt and hungry.

Why did she leave me asleep and alone?

The coffee maker is quiet and Elise opens her eyes.

A horn blares outside. "Hey, asshole! You gonna move that?" someone shouts. The horn blares again, louder, longer, angrier.

Elise turns and pours herself a cup of black coffee, gazes down through the steam, and sees Maria's face in the dark liquid. She blows away the steam and the image clarifies: her pale white skin floating on a sea of chocolate. Her hands move up toward Elise, summoning.

Elise looks away, to her drawing board, and remembers her promise to accomplish something with her art every day. But the tools, the charcoal and the heavy-weight paper, do not tempt her. There is something cold and lifeless about them right now.

She is not inspired. The muse has left the house, trailing after Maria like a groupie.

She sips her coffee, the burn numbing her tongue and scorching her throat. She doesn't care. At least she feels something.

But today, she will not take up a pencil or a stick of charcoal and create. Her mind is too crowded with thoughts of Maria. Once upon a time, she might have called this feeling love. Now she wonders if she even knows the meaning of that weighted word.

But she has learned better.

Elise sets down the coffee and walks naked toward the bathroom. A scrub in the shower; quicker than a bath, even though it won't be as soothing. She doesn't have time for soothing. Elise finger-combs her damp hair, pulling it away from her face. She wiggles into a denim skirt, a white blouse she knots at her waist. Black ballerina shoes on her feet. Simple.

Outside, the air is cloying and heavy. She smells cigarette smoke, car exhaust, frying food, all underscored by the bracing, slightly fishy odor of Lake Michigan, just a few blocks to the east. Elise soothes the pounding behind her eyes, concealing them behind a pair of dark sunglasses. She walks the short distance to Sheridan Road, where she can pick up the 151 bus, the only transport she will need to get to the house she remembers.

The ride is a short one. Ten thirty in the morning, rush hour is past, and the green lights on Sheridan Road have been timed so drivers can traverse maximum distance in minimal time. By ten forty-five, Elise is stepping off the bus. The bus driver calls, "Be careful," and Elise wonders if he is referring to stepping down from the bus or if he knows what lies ahead of her.

The house is still the same: a large, white brick box, with dusty leaded glass windows, a black wrought iron fence, a wide expanse of stairs up to the massive oak front door. She notices the empty stone planters, the only things growing in them a few dandelions, some nettles. The yard is a riot of grass gone to seed, Queen Anne's lace, more dandelions, and here and there, a Black-eyed Susan. It would be more fitting for a prairie than a Midwest turn of the century urban mansion.

It occurs to Elise, as she stands outside the imposing structure, that Maria, Terence, and Edward are probably squatting here. She starts up the steps. The really frightening thing about the thought is not the illegality of it (she does, after all, earn her living though commerce that is against the law), but the question that looms: if they are squatting in this splendid old house, how are they keeping others at bay? How are they managing to keep what seems like a practically priceless collection of art here without alarms or other forms of security? Elise looks to the south, where a rag-dressed man is accosting passersby to purchase a copy of *Streetwise*, and adds another question to her list: How are they keeping out the homeless — of whom there are plenty–who would embrace this place as a free palace?

How, indeed?

Elise pauses in front of the house, listening to the almost aquatic flow of the traffic behind her and beyond that, the actual aquatic flow of Lake Michigan as it hurls itself against the boulders at Thorndale Beach.

Elise reaches the front portico and pauses in its shadows. Is Maria inside? Is she still asleep? She imagines finding her new love on a bed of red satin, imagines leaning in to plant a furtive kiss on her brow.

The house appears to be abandoned, darkened, empty. She wonders if these people who came so mysteriously into her life, will leave just as mysteriously. Fear grips her.

She imagines slipping inside, finding the place empty — all the art gone. Perhaps it was never there in the first place. Perhaps Maria and her friends are nothing more than phantoms, dream images made flesh. Elise could be living out her own weird real life version of *The Twilight Zone*. The possibility, she realizes, is not so far-fetched, living the kind of existence she has for the past several years. It would almost be saner to imagine herself going insane.

Insanity would explain a lot.

She'll ponder such mysteries later. Right now, she is making a social call. Let the phantoms answer her knock...

Her signal sounds hollow, reverberating inside. It could be true; in the gray, milky light of day, it seems more likely this abandoned looking house is truly empty and her imagination has conjured up its inhabitants. She pictures scurrying mice and cockroaches, expanses of dusty wooden flooring, unmarred by human footprints, cobweb-choked chandeliers. Yet she continues to knock.

And no one answers.

After her knuckles have become reddened and sore, Elise gives up and turns away. She scans Sheridan Road to the south, looking for another 151 bus to take her home. Disappointment catches in her throat. She hadn't realized until now just how desperate she is to see Maria again.

No bus is in sight. And hailing a cab is out of the question—too luxurious, unless the driver happens to be horny enough to want to trade commodities. Elise doesn't feel like gambling, although she has played such games before, and won more than she has lost.

A chill breeze comes to her from off the lake. Since there is no way to return home in sight, what harm can there be in just seeing if the door is unlocked? The possibility is remote, but why not just give that tarnished doorknob a turn? Where's the harm?

She doesn't really expect it to open. But, in a way, she thinks there can be no other outcome. She is being propelled forward in a story whose narrative is slightly out of control.

The door opens easily. There is no dramatic creaking. No talon-like hands reach out to grab her and snatch her inside. Elise steps into the cool shadows and closes the door behind her. The *thunk* of the door closing shuts out entirely the sound of traffic on Sheridan Road, the rhythmic pull of the waves of Lake Michigan across the street.

"Maria? Terence? Edward?" Her voice echoes. Dust motes play in sunlight streaming in through leaded glass. Elise steps further into the room and notices the art: the paintings, drawings, sculptures are still here. There is something disconcerting about their presence. This time, she notices that all of the art has humanity as its prime subject; even the abstract art retains some semblance to human bodies, eyes, faces. There are no still lifes or landscapes, no sculptures representing a what rather than a who. The thing that's scary, and Elise thinks this notion is so Walt-Disney-haunted-mansionish it makes her smile, is that it seems as though the art is watching her. It chills her even more, this legion of inanimate people eyeing her as she makes her way further into the room. She can imagine hands on sculptures coming to life and reaching out for her. She shakes her head to clear it and calls out, "Maria? Maria, it's Elise."

No one responds, and Elise continues through the gallery that makes up most of the first floor. She steps into the kitchen and finds it empty. By daylight, the room looks even more unused and barren than it did in the darkness the other evening. Don't the three of them ever eat? In one corner is a refrigerator, a relic, the kind with the motor on top. Elise opens the door and a strong odor of rot and mildew emerge. Inside, there is only a bouquet of withered roses, the petals blackened and ready to crumble at a touch, perhaps even a breath.

She moves toward a window near the back of the kitchen, over a grime-filled and rust-stained porcelain sink. Outside, sunlight glares down on weeds, some of them as tall as she. She turns and notices, for the first time, a staircase in the room. Servants probably used it at one time. There's nothing grand about it, just a door frame and a simple flight upward.

She has come this far. Why not see where these stairs lead? Something tells Elise now would be a good time to turn back. For one, she is trespassing (whether her new "friends" are squatting here or not is beside the point). For another, and more importantly, she doesn't know what might await her upstairs. She could flee this strange house a lot more easily from the first floor than from the second, where the only quick exits might end in broken limbs or death.

But she puts her foot on the first step anyway. Unlike the front door, it does creak. Elise's heart begins to thud. *Listen to yourself. Listen. Go home.* But she puts her foot on another step. A vision of Maria briefly stays her ascent up the creaking, narrow staircase, but she forces it away. She grips the wall for support as she makes her way up.

An image from the night before assails her: Maria biting her breast hard enough to draw blood. She can see, in sickening close-up, the droplets of blood which rise from the puncture wounds on her soft, white flesh. She can see Maria's upward gaze and the flicker of a smile as she lowers her head to lick away the blood, to pause, watching the droplets appear again, and then repeating the action, moaning softly at the taste.

Why don't you turn and hurry back down these stairs before it's too late?

It's already too late. Part of her recognizes her desire to flee as a lie and another part, the part that's stronger and winning, tells her that nothing associated with Maria could be harmful to her. She ignores the queasiness and the sweat popping up on her brow and mounts the last step.

Upstairs, it's quiet. A long hallway is before her: three doors on the right, two on the left. She can see the handrail for the front staircase, its rich, burnished wood hidden under a thick layer of dust. The walls are covered with peeling wallpaper, cabbage roses Elise can discern only when she gets close. Parts of the wall are losing their plaster, exposing rotting holes and wooden studs.

Is Maria sleeping behind one of these doors? Elise wonders. She's rooted to the floor, unable to move for the moment, paralyzed by the very sensible desire to flee and the very provocative desire to begin opening doors.

Elise starts down the hallway, comes to the first door. She pauses outside, biting her lip until she tastes blood, then takes a deep breath and swings the door open. It complains loudly, the creaking of metal against metal akin to a scream.

The room is empty. There are two large leaded glass windows that may be facing Lake Michigan, but the glass is so clouded and dirty it's impossible to see anything outside except the silhouette of a nearby tree branch. Still, the windows do their duty of admitting light, grayish and watery as it is. Elise steps into the room, turns. It's a large room, with brass wall-mounted light fixtures topped with stained glass. The walls are crumbling plaster; in places, Elise can even see the naked brick and mortar. She walks to the closet, opens it, and flings a hand to her mouth to stifle a scream.

Now, will you please have the good sense to turn and get the hell out of here? Run! Run as fast as you can.

But Elise does not run. She stands, panting, and stares down. Her face is cold, white, and slick with sweat. Her stomach churns.

Lying on the closet floor before her are two intertwined skeletons. Both appear to be women; there is still dry, straw-like hair attached to each skull: one reddish, the other blonde. Clothes lie in a heap nearby. They seem like the kind of things she'd pick for herself, to wear in her work as a streetwalker. Leather mini-skirts, spike heels, cheap costume jewelry litter the floor.

Elise leans against the door frame, struggling to regain some composure, to stop the churning in her belly, to bring to a close the shrieking in her brain that makes her face feel like it's quivering, trying to send some strength to her legs to prevent her from falling.

She doesn't know how long she stays that way, frozen in the doorway of a closet where two women, perhaps two women like herself, were dumped after being killed, or worse, trapped inside to die. Elise doesn't want to, but looks down at the interior of the door and sees what she expected: claw marks.

There is no spit left in her mouth.

After a while, who knows how long, Elise begins to breathe normally again. The horror of the skeletons remains terrifying (*thank God for that, thank God I'm still human enough to have normal feelings*), but, at the same time, the scene takes on a numbing aspect allowing Elise to turn away from the desiccated bodies and close the door.

The option to leave is still with her. There are still no signs of life in this house.

She closes her eyes and stands in the muted sunlight for at least a quarter of an hour, not allowing herself to think. Then she rationalizes her still-present desire to see Maria by saying to herself she has to see her, to discover what's going on here. It's the only right-minded thing to do. Surely, there is some explanation for what she's seen. Perhaps the bodies are an art installation, not even real, crafted from plaster, silk strands for the hair...

What, are you crazy? Get the fuck out of here! Now!

She ignores the voice and exits the room. This time, if Maria is behind one of the other doors, she will find her. Find her and confront her. Find her and love her.

Oh God, what's wrong with me?

Elise stands frozen in the hallway. She notices she's trembling, and wonders how long her hands have been quivering. The stairs down are just a few steps away.

There is a sound: a slither of cloth hitting the floor, almost imperceptible. Elise turns and believes she knows, now, behind which door at least one of them slumbers. Taking in a lungful of air and letting it out slowly, she screws up her courage and walks toward the door at the end of the hallway, from behind which she assumes the sound has come.

She pauses outside. A large, dark-stained mahogany door is before her. She leans in close to the wood, listening. But it's still. Is this the wrong door?

That question has only one answer. Elise places her hand on the doorknob, but doesn't turn. She waits. Her heart is thudding against her chest, painful. Blood is rushing in her ears. Opening this door, she thinks, could have far more significance than the simple act of swinging a panel of wood inward.

"If I told you your art is some of the most meaningful I've ever seen, would you believe me?"

Elise recalls Maria posing just such a question to her, only last night, but already their time together is taking on the sepia tinge of a memory far older than just a few hours. The question had confused her, then. Was Maria being genuine or merely flattering her for her own selfish purposes?

"No, really. There is something that comes alive in these drawings you do. You draw death, but by making it so real, you emphasize life. There's a contrast there and I understand it. I understand *you*."

And Elise sees Maria then, standing before her, holding her face in her hands with all the care of a patron, someone who has a deep appreciation for beauty, who knows beauty that goes far beyond merely being pleasing to look at. Elise recalls the dark, dark eyes of Maria boring into her own, seeing her pain, her vulnerability, but also her talent, the essence that gave her no choice but to create.

That frozen moment before Maria leaned in to kiss her.

Again, Elise tells herself such a woman would never do anything to harm her. There has to be an explanation for everything, and the only way to get that explanation, to resolve things, is to confront her. Elise turns the knob and swings the door open slowly, trying to make sure it doesn't creak, trying to take her time because of the very rational fear of what might be lying in wait for her on the other side of the door.

She pauses at the threshold. It takes a few moments for her eyes to adjust to the darkness.

All three of them are there, lying next to one another on a huge canopy bed. A red velvet coverlet conceals much of their sleeping forms. Heavy red velvet curtains are drawn at the window. Elise experiences a flash of jealousy that almost burns. She hates the thought that Maria left her bed to return to this one, is sleeping with these two men, with *these* men, one of whom is pompous and arrogant—a user.

But she realizes she doesn't know what their relationship is, what history they share.

Elise waits a little longer, hand on doorknob, until the light in the room becomes gray and she can see well enough to approach the bed. Her resolve withering, she thinks maybe it might not be a bad idea to postpone her confrontation, no, make that *talk*, with Maria for a little while. What is she going to do? Shake her from sleep and make demands:

"Why are you living in this abandoned house?"

"How do the three of you support yourselves? How do you pay the bills? How do you eat?"

"Do you eat?"

"What are those skeletons in your closet?"

Elise lets loose a mournful laugh at this last question. She's never thought of it before in such a literal sense.

No, she will wait. Slowly, she moves closer to the bed. She wants just one more look at Maria; just to see her again will be enough. She approaches, a small smile creasing her features. *Just a chance to lay my hand on her cheek while she sleeps will make this trip worthwhile.* As she nears, she sees Maria's tousled black hair sticking out from under the top of the coverlet.

She freezes.

Something is wrong. It takes her a second to figure out why this tableau is so disturbing, and when she does, she doesn't want to accept what she sees: These people don't appear to sleep. There is no rise and fall of chests, no sounds, no drowsy slow movements.

They lie still as corpses.

Suddenly, the darkened room seems oppressive, the flocked wallpaper closing in. Elise moves nearer, noticing that Maria's face looks different from the one she remembers with such passion from the night before. All of their faces, in fact, look scarred; darkened areas rim their mouths. Elise brings her face close to Maria. Crusty dried blood covers Maria's face in patches. Elise finds she cannot swallow when she sees tiny flecks of skin in the corners of Maria's lips.

She cannot stand. Elise drops to her knees next to the bed. She is panting and her shortness of breath makes her wonder why she felt no breath from Maria when she leaned in close to her face.

Her stomach roils. The room spins. She is certain she will faint, but steels herself against the possibility, though she is not sure she can stop herself. She raises her head enough to look again at Maria's face in repose, just to reassure herself she isn't hallucinating, but it's all still there: the crust of blood, the sickening, still-moist bits of flesh, like rotting meat.

Perhaps she's hurt herself. *Stop it!* Elise admonishes with an internal scream. *Just stop it. Your own eyes are not lying to you. Your eyes have been the one reliable thing in your whole miserable life.* On shaky legs, Elise manages to stand. She is biting the loose area of flesh on her hand between thumb and forefinger.

It's kind of a relief. Common sense is rushing in, replacing her wild desire and near obsession for this strange woman who managed to carve a significant place in her life in such a short time. Was it through trickery? Seduction? Black magic? Hallucination?

Elise stands and stares at the dark shapes in the room: the armoire, the fireplace, the heavy draperies pulled tight against summer's light just on the other side. She realizes she must leave. If—later—she hears a motorcycle pulling up outside her building, she will hide and will not come out until the knocking at her door has ceased and the sound of the motorcycle diminishes as it rumbles away.

She will go back to working on her art, but she will also work on getting someone else to look at it. Someone who at least appears to breathe, who does not sleep with blood on her face.

The thought of the blood causes a fresh wave of horror to hit her. And the horror pumps up a rush of adrenaline, enough to make her walk to the bedroom door quick and sure. *I can do it*, she thinks, *I can really do it*. She begins to walk faster, the doorway yawning open before her, welcoming: a means of escape.

Just as she gets to it, though, Maria's voice from the bed stops her. "Elise? Elise, please don't run away."

Elise turns around slowly, feeling herself pulled in two directions at once.

Maria is sitting up. The red blankets have fallen away; her breasts are ghostly white in the darkness. The sight is so beautiful, it weakens Elise. She swivels her head toward the open doorway to regard it longingly, as if someone has actually placed hands on her shoulders and is preventing her from walking through it.

"Elise, my darling. There's so much I have to tell you. So much you don't understand." Maria holds out her hand. "Come. Lie beside me and let me tell you, tell you everything."

And Elise starts toward her, wanting so much to feel the touch of that cold hand on her skin.

"Don't be afraid, my sweet. As you know, I would never harm you."

And then Maria smiles. Elise raises a knuckle to her mouth, to stifle the scream.

Maria displays not teeth but rows of tiny fangs.

The room blurs, then darkens completely as Elise collapses.

Chapter
Ten

1954

WITH EACH DESCENDING step, two warring factions in Edward's psyche revved up, arms drawn for battle to the death. The common sense camp, which, even before he ran into Terence, was a rag-tag team, weak and disorganized, was attempting to band together to convince Edward that taking even one step further down into the gloom and shadows, the cold, mildew-scented air, and the ghostly strains of Vivaldi's *L'inverno* was one step closer to insanity, pain, or even death. This camp, fear heightening its readiness for battle, was urging Edward to flee, knowing him well enough to realize that his fight abilities were, at best, very limited.

The other camp, the one that Freud would call the id, and the one others might refer to as the hedonistic faction, was a stronger bunch: wild, hearty, and unaware of their own strength, or perhaps heedless of it. Ruled by pleasure, a disregard for danger, and a love for the unknown, this group urged Edward forward, arguing that, first, he might miss out on great pleasure and love if he were to turn back now, and second, his art might prosper from what promised to be a unique experience.

It didn't really matter which side Edward paid more heed to, because while his mind was reeling Terence was leading him further and further down the long flight of wide stone stairs.

They reached the bottom, and Edward tapped around with the toe of his boot, searching for a path free of obstacles. Terence had no problem moving through the darkness.

"Give me a second," Edward whispered, although he wasn't certain why he suddenly felt the need to use a softer voice. "I need a second for my eyes to adjust."

Terence moved behind him and encircled Edward's waist with his arm. He laid his chin on Edward's shoulder. "Not much farther."

The closeness, Edward thought, should have made him feel more at ease, but it served only to ratchet up the tension. Terence's chill body against his own was at once deliriously exciting and oddly repellant.

Edward didn't know if his eyes would ever adjust, but gradually they did. He could see enough in the almost pitch darkness to know they were in a second subway station, this one below the first. This one was deep beneath the streets of New York City. Above, people traversed crowded sidewalks ignorant of the bizarre little journey taking place below their hurried paces. To his left, a deeper shade of darkness indicated where the platform dropped off to the tracks. Ahead of him was the even darker entrance to the tunnel, so black it appeared almost palpable, a solid wedge of black; Edward imagined it felt like icy velvet. He could just make out the slightly curving tile work above the opening. He wondered how long ago a train had last snaked through here. He wondered how long ago anyone had stood on this platform, entering or exiting a train. Had anyone *ever* stood here?

A cold whisper of breath touched his ear. "Ready?" Terence's breath was fetid; it had a note underneath of something rotting. Edward shivered, imagining what was going on inside Terence, beneath the pallid exterior; were worms writhing inside, the stink of their movements escaping out of his open mouth?

There was no turning back now. "I guess so." Edward didn't know if he was heading toward his death, and the thought, curiously, did not terrify him. He imagined death in this scenario as a welcoming embrace, a soft landing, removing him from worldly cares.

"You need to let me lead you. I know my way around better than you do."

"How did you find this place?"

Terence took both of Edward's hands in his own and, walking backward with an almost feline grace, began leading him toward what Edward was sure was the tunnel entrance. "I've often found that life is much livelier if one allows a little mystery. Some questions remain unanswered. Some questions have more satisfying conclusions if their responses are delayed."

Edward wished he had the faculty of standing up for himself, the strength to not accept Terence's silly, couched-in-elegance response. But all he did was slog along behind Terence, relying on him for safe passage.

At the entrance to the tunnel, Terence released his grip on Edward's hands. The sudden lack of contact almost induced in Edward a feeling of falling. He reached out to Terence, his hands those of a blind man fearing a pitch into an abyss. The metaphor wasn't far removed from the truth.

"Now, I'm going to drop down from the platform onto the tracks so we can proceed into the tunnel. Once I'm there, I'll help you get down."

"This is crazy." Edward felt like he was whimpering, adopting a childish tone he had assumed he had left behind a long, long time ago. But then, how would he have known he would have ever faced a situation akin to the one he was confronting now? "What if we step on the third rail? We'll be electrocuted."

"Do you really think I would let you be harmed?"

Edward wanted to respond: "How should I know what you would or wouldn't do? I don't even know you, beyond the fact that you like to drink blood and are leading me into the tunnel of an unused subway station!" But all he said was, "No." He could see the ghostly glow of Terence's white suit as he squatted, then leaped into the darkness of the subway rails. It was like watching a glowing skeleton. Edward's common sense told him that now would be an excellent time to turn and run. But common sense was being drowned out by a hedonistic chorus, who were singing to Edward the praises of the undiscovered, telling him his life lacked excitement and that to turn away from something as unusual as this would be the folly of the pedestrian. No real artist would ever deny himself such a bizarre experience.

"Coming?" Two white forms, oblong, reached up: Terence's arms, poised to lower him. "My Edward, so untrusting. Do you really think I'd let anything happen to you?"

Edward took a step closer to the edge. "Are you sure I'm not too heavy? How much do you weigh, anyway?"

Terence sighed. "I'm stronger than I look." He snapped his fingers. "Come on. I won't let you fall."

Whatever would happen, would happen. Edward closed his eyes and stepped off the platform's edge.

Terence's embrace was amazingly strong. Edward felt like a child in his arms. He had expected to be helped down, but Terence was able to easily lift him and swing him through the air, gently setting him down on one of the large wooden beams that ran horizontally beneath the metal tracks. Again grasping his hands, he began to lead him into the tunnel. "It's not far."

Edward followed him down a short length of track, making sure his feet never came into contact with metal. The music grew louder as they approached. After about thirty or so paces, Terence stopped. "This way."

The two turned to the right and suddenly, they were in a smaller, lower tunnel. Gone were the train tracks. Edward's feet crunched in gravel and dirt. Cobwebs brushed across his face. He heard the twittering and rustling of rats. Something scurried down his collar, making him gasp.

But he noticed that the light at the end of *this* tunnel was growing brighter as they approached. He could now smell something warmer above the damp mold: roasting pork. The music grew louder and he could differentiate the strings: the violins in *continuo*. The music and the warmth were doing little to allay his fears, but Terence's cool firm grip and his movement through the tunnel, effortless and graceful, helped make him feel a bit more confident this adventure would not be his last.

The tunnel ended. The two men stood poised at the entrance to a high-ceilinged room, a cavern.

Edward had never seen anything like this. The ceiling of the space disappeared into complete darkness, so he had no idea how high up the ceiling was, or if it even existed. Perhaps the room continued upward into infinity. Likewise, the shadows claimed the corners of the room, so it was hard to tell how truly large it was.

What he could see took his breath away. Save for a couple of flocked wine-colored upholstered benches, what might have been called, in an earlier era, swooning couches, there was no furniture in the room. There were candles, hundreds and hundreds of them: pillars, tapers, and votives in a variety of holders. There were tall stands of metal, twisted into gothic crosses and spikes. There were lanterns, with flames encased in glass. Chandeliers had somehow been suspended, and these were all lit with candlelight, casting out sparkles and reflections from crystal and gold. A blazing fire occupied the center of the room and a bubbling pot, steaming, sat atop the flames. The music sounded almost as if an orchestra was playing, but he could see no musicians, or even a radio anywhere. He was too dumbfounded to ask about the source.

The candles illuminated a vast and varied collection of art. Paintings and drawings had been mounted around the space on easels. Some hung from wires suspended from that eerie, undefined ceiling. The paintings were all of people, in various ages, sizes, colors, and races. Some were impressionistic; some representative with an almost photographic attention to detail, still others seemed informed of a more romantic sensibility, *a la* Rembrandt. There was nothing expressionist and Edward thought for a moment how good one of his body-slammed paintings would look here. Unique selling point: *you need to fill this niche; it's missing from your collection.*

In addition to the paintings, there were sculptures, all people in various poses, done in various styles and media: marble, plaster, *papier-mâché*, wood, and metal.

And in the middle of all this stood a woman.

She stood beneath the flickering light of a chandelier, which held what seemed like dozens of candles. Beneath this illumination, her appearance wavered, so it seemed cast from shadows and light. Like Terence, she was deathly pale, but unlike Terence, there was a kind of warmth to her beauty. There was none of the ferocity that made Terence at once so off-putting and so attractive. She had a mane of black hair that flowed over her bare shoulders and a fine-boned face, porcelain, the dark eyes glowing. Her lips were full and red and her smile, directed only at him, was composed of tiny, pearly teeth. Edward was transfixed, pulled into her gaze. For moments, everything vanished around him, including Terence. There was an odd connection in their eyes, one he had never before experienced. The woman wore a clinging, wine-colored velvet dress that exposed her shoulders, but hung and puddled on the floor. The dress was liquid in the way it clung to her; it could not have been more revealing if she had stood naked before him. Again, the urge to capture this woman on canvas was fierce, right here, in this unnatural light. He wondered if he had the ability to make a painting glow the way she did.

Terence was nudging him. "Edward? Edward, my dear. I thought you didn't swing that way."

"What?" As if he had been awakened from a dream, Edward turned to Terence, who was grinning at him.

"I'd like to make proper introductions, if you don't mind. This, my friend, is Maria."

The woman moved forward. She had been as placid and immobile as the sculptures surrounding her and if it had not been for her eyes, he might have doubted she was even alive. She extended her hand and Terence reached out to grab it. Surprisingly, the flesh was supple and warm and her touch felt like a current of electricity going through him. Edward snatched his hand away, stunned. He gaped at her.

"Don't be afraid." Her voice was surprisingly deep and resonant; their cavernous surroundings made it even more so. She reached it and encircled his hand with her own once more.

Edward lost himself in the warmth and the satin texture of her skin. "I'm not afraid." He wanted to say more, like tell her he was awed more than fearful, but words like that might only be taken as pretense. "I'm very happy to meet you, Maria."

She squeezed his hand, released it. "Are you hungry, Edward? I've just eaten, but there's plenty more." She laughed. "All of it quite delicious."

Edward looked to the steaming cauldron and sniffed the air. The roasting meat smell made him sick. Whatever was roiling inside the pot, he was certain, would not be something he'd want to force down his gullet. "I'm not hungry right now. But thank you." He smiled. "Maybe later."

"Perhaps a different form of sustenance, then?" Terence stepped forward. In his hand was the little carved wooden pipe.

"Oh Lord," Edward said. "Not that again."

Maria laughed again and her laughter lent an aura of normalcy to this strange meeting. "Your reaction is common. Just take it easy. A little bit of this goes a long, long way...at least for those not used to it."

Terence fired up the bowl, took a hit, and held it out to Maria. She snatched it away from him and offered it to Edward. The bud inside was glowing orange, giving off the essence of incense. "How rude you are, Terence! Our guest! Our guest!"

Edward swallowed. The smell alone was intoxicating and Maria's effort to be hospitable, he felt, could not be refused. He took the pipe from her hands and drew in tentatively, letting the smoke enter his lungs slowly, where he imagined it rolling inside him like a fog.

"That's my boy," Terence said softly.

Mutely, Edward watched as Maria took the pipe and drew in a huge lungful of smoke, only to emit it moments later. The smoke spiraled upward, to be lost among the shadows claiming the cavern's ceiling.

In seconds, Edward felt his mind go numb; his face felt as if it were vibrating. His body filled with warmth. All of this was very pleasant and he giggled.

"It doesn't take long, does it?" Maria took his hand once more. "Why don't you come over here and sit down?"

Edward thought that sounded like a very good idea, indeed. He let Maria lead him across the space and, like a child, allowed himself to be folded into a sitting position on the settee. Across the room, Terence was ladling a bowl of something from the pot. As it slid from the ladle to the earthenware bowl in his hand, Edward could make out pieces of meat almost raw in a deep, viscous red broth. It made him want to gag.

Terence brought the liquid to his lips and slurped some up. He took a few more bites and then held the bowl up to Edward. "Are you sure you don't want some? It's delicious. Maria is a wonderful cook. She's Italian. They know how to put food together."

Maria was smiling at him, and Edward noticed the large, strong nose, the raven hair again, and how those and her other features conspired to create something from southern Italy. Perhaps, he thought, the broth was red merely from tomatoes. He thought not, but it was easier to entertain himself with such pedestrian fancies.

Edward closed his eyes for a moment, feeling an odd floating sensation. Beneath that, there was a sudden, and acute, hunger. "What's in the soup?" he asked, tongue thick.

Maria answered, "A bit of this, a bit of that."

Terence snorted. "A little of her, a little of him."

Edward shuddered.

"He's joking, of course. It's simply pork, with a few vegetables, a little basil, some Roma tomatoes, lots of Chianti."

His repulsion faded. Edward reached out for the bowl. "Maybe just a little."

Terence handed it to him and Edward's fear was overcome by a hunger that grew more relentless with each passing second. He dug into the soup. The meat was surprisingly tender, as if it had been cooked for a long time. And, yes, he could taste tomatoes, and wine, and herbs. Never mind the coppery tang beneath all this. Perhaps that metallic note had been transferred from the pot in which the stew had been cooked.

He finished quickly and set the bowl down on the floor.

"A little capper, then?"

Edward took the proffered pipe from Terence and drew in more deeply this time. The smoke hit him quickly and he lolled back, supine, on the settee.

"Let's make you more comfortable," Maria said, kneeling at his feet and beginning to unlace his boots. Edward made a vague purring noise, lifting his foot slightly to make it easier for Maria to remove his boots.

Terence moved in close and began to unbutton his shirt. His hands felt smooth and, at last, warm against his bare skin. Edward could do nothing but lie there, barely lifting his limbs as he was relieved of his clothing. Whatever happened, Edward was certain, would be wonderful.

He lay naked before them, watching as each shed their clothes. Their bodies were so beautiful, crafted from marble. He couldn't wait to taste them: to kiss, to suck, to feel the tenderness of their embraces.

He closed his eyes and surrendered.

Chapter
Eleven

ELISE IS ALONE. There is only a wan light, barely dispelling the shadows, not even enough to really see anything. Elise curls into herself, almost fetal. She isn't so sure she wants to see anything. There is a vague, sick dread filling her up. The terror isn't rational, but knowing this doesn't make it any less real.

Elise scrunches her eyes together and puts her hands over her ears. She can hear squeaking and the restless fluttering of leathery wings. Bats. They hang from the ceiling above her and their tiny, skin-crawl inducing movements tell her they are readying themselves for flight. But before they fly away, they will be hungry, and the heat of her, she's certain, will rise up like an aura around her, attracting them. In fact, the smell of her flesh, the warmth of her body, and the pulse of her blood beneath it all is probably like light to a moth and their tiny twitterings are like gossip, word spreading fast that there is a small feast here.

She cringes as she feels a small bony claw on her shin. She draws her leg in toward herself, shaking the tiny, almost weightless creature off. But it's gone for only a second. Like a fly, it hovers then lands on her again. This time, it's brought a friend.

It's only seconds before she feels the puncture of their tiny teeth. And then, almost as one the whole group arises and covers her, all fluttering wings, ember-glowing eyes, and razor sharp teeth. Piercing.

And Elise screams and screams. Screams until one of them ventures near her open mouth to nip at her lips and then her tongue, where the blood is sweeter. It squirms further inside, so she can't close her mouth, so she can't scream, so her eyes are stuck open in dumbstruck horror.

Elise awakens. Her face is slick with sweat and she's trembling. She doesn't know where she is. Her arms are still pinwheeling, trying to bat away the dark, furry shadows that covered her moments ago.

Gradually, her racing heart slows its frantic beating. Her breathing slows to normal respiration. The sweat on her body begins to cool.

Slowly, she focuses, and Maria is above her, looking down, dark eyes alive with concern. She's holding a cool cloth to Elise's forehead. Elise gets up on one elbow, and the room spins. She returns her head to the pillow and lets Maria continue her ministrations. The cool touch of the cloth and Maria's gentle demeanor are comforting, yet they seem like a lie. A part of her wants to return to her nightmare. In a dream, at least for Elise, there's always a sense of unreality, that with enough will, she could awaken and escape. Being bathed in cool water by a beautiful, but oddly cold and hard woman is surreal, but Elise knows it's happening. She's lying on a red velvet settee near the fireplace. She turns her head and can see the huddled forms of Terence and Edward, still asleep in the huge canopy bed, bodies intertwined. Terence's arm lies protectively over Edward's shoulder. But they don't move. They are as still as corpses. Elise doesn't want to think about the dark stains here and there on their faces. She doesn't want to think about Maria's teeth.

"Better?" Maria whispers. "You fainted, but were only out for a few minutes." Maria moves the cool cloth around Elise's fevered face. She smiles. Gone are the rows of tiny fangs. Elise wonders if she ever really saw them. Her face is clean, smooth and white as a marble tombstone. Only the fire in her dark eyes breathes life into her countenance. "Do you feel all right now?"

"Yes." Elise's tongue is thick in her mouth, a speech impediment. "Could I have some water?"

Maria doesn't move, yet suddenly she holds a cut crystal tumbler of water. Elise gulps it. She is parched; she feels almost dry from within. While she drinks, she casts around for something to say. She feels numb, her mind buzzing and empty. Finally, she settles for the truest, simplest course.

"What's going on, Maria?" She isn't certain she wants an answer, at least not a truthful one. She is as thirsty for lies as she was for the water. Even if she knows it's not the truth, any sort of somewhat rational explanation will calm her. At least she can tell herself that whatever Maria spoon-feeds her must be the truth. Why would she lie? All sorts of absurd notions run through her mind, involving suggestions of the supernatural or insanity (hers or theirs, she's not sure). None of these notions seem plausible, yet how does one explain?

Maria smoothes Elise's hair back away from her face and presses her gently back on the couch. Elise allows herself to recline, accepts the kiss, cold, from Maria's lips. "I'm going to tell you the truth now. But you won't believe it. Not at first, anyway.

"I know this idea has come to you and that you have probably rejected it. I can't blame you. Most of you with your modern ideas and technology have no concept of things lying beneath the surface of palpable reality. Gone are the notions of romance...of the inexplicable. But you, my love, are an artist. And artists are the only ones that understand things not explained by science or numbers. You, or at least most of you, rely more on intuition. That's why we like to traffic with creative humans. I hope you understand us, because it's rare I find a mortal who does."

Oh now, this is getting too weird. I don't know if I want to hear any more. Hearing words like 'mortal' and 'human' used in the context of conversation, as if referring to something foreign, makes her head pound and induces her desire to flee. She takes another sip of water, gets to a half-sitting position again, testing her strength. The best thing to do, she knows, is to put her feet to the floor and walk right out of here before Maria can continue. But the semi-erect position brings her a new wave of dizziness and perhaps in a moment, Maria will laugh, tell her she's joking. Elise lies back down, staring up at Maria, like a child waiting for the rest of a bedtime story.

"A mortal? What are you talking about?" The room is closing in on Elise, almost as if the walls are alive and able to move closer to one another. Her breath quickens again, close to panting. The panic is rising. She thinks of horror stories about vampires and blood being leeched from helpless, terrified people. Her synapses fire with red-cloaked imagery, making her tremble, run hot and cold all at once.

The answer, it turns out, is simple. Maria smiles. "We are vampires." Maria leans close to Elise. "I know it sounds absurd. And the stuff of legend, of your modern-day horror movies, is mostly untrue, stories made up to frighten, to entertain. But vampires do exist, few in number, and we are three of those few. I don't know if we're really the 'living dead' as some have called us, or if we're just different—a new kind of animal, an organism born out of the carcass of a dead human being. Maybe we're just another form of evolution, something as much a part of nature as you are. Maybe supernatural is a word that shouldn't be applied to us. Perhaps 'supernatural' should be reserved for ghost stories."

She pauses. The words hang in the air like dust motes dancing in sunlight. Elise wants to laugh, but there is no humor in her desire. It is the giddy laugh of hysteria, just before a shriek. She shakes her head, trying to keep the despair at bay. "Please don't do this, Maria. It's been so long since I've had anyone in my life. Please don't turn out to be insane; don't turn yourself into some Anne Rice heroine."

Maria laughs. "Oh, that's a rich one. When one of us is feeling blue, we pick up one of those Anne Rice books and we laugh and laugh." Maria runs the back of her hand across Elise's cheek. "I do love you. I knew that underneath all the angst and the existential torment, there was someone who could make me laugh. I'm good at sensing these things." She grows serious once more. "But it's true, Elise. We are what I've said. We need human blood to exist. I know you saw the blood on our faces. I apologize for that; we are such messy eaters. But sometimes we just get so hungry and we forget our manners."

Elise wonders if this is for real. She wants to laugh, too, to let Maria know she's in on the joke. She wishes it were a joke. "You're joking with me, right?" Elise already knows the answer, but a part of her still holds out hope for the finger in the ribs, the confession of morbid punchlines and misguided mirth.

Elise nods. Hot, sour bile rises at the back of her throat. This cannot be. She has been alone too long. The streets have warped her. This too is a dream. But the hand in her own feels real enough, solid. In fact, its icy hardness reminds Elise of stone. She yanks her hand back, recoiling at the dryness, the chill. "But sometimes," she sputters, "sometimes, you feel warm." *Please,* Elise thinks, *give me something, anything, to cling to. Half-truths, lies...*

"For your sake, I wish I could say what I'm telling you is all a joke. But we both know it isn't. How would I explain away what you saw earlier? My fangs are efficient tools, nothing more." She takes Elise's hand in hers, squeezes. "Feel that? Feel the cold? No warmth runs through my veins. Surely you've noticed."

Patiently, Maria takes her hand gently again and presses it to her breast, inside the robe. The skin gives only slightly. "Feel that?"

Elise doesn't want to acknowledge what Maria is trying to tell her. "What? I don't feel anything."

"Exactly."

Elise pulls her hand away and turns to hide her face in the crushed velvet of the settee. There's no heartbeat, no matter how hard she presses her hand; there is no thump of a beating heart beneath her flesh

Muffled, Maria's voice comes to her. "Elise, in spite of the fangs, in spite of what we have to do to survive, there's nothing to fear. All of us, me especially, admire you. We care about you, your art. You're brilliant. Brilliance we don't often see. Especially as time passes. We would never harm you."

Elise turns back. The beauty of Maria's face, her body, the shine in her eyes...she's the most beautiful woman she's ever seen. And even though her body is cold, she radiates warmth, and intelligence, and understanding, understanding Elise has not yet encountered in anyone else.

"Terence, Edward, and I have been together for a long, long time. Ages. I know this will sound fantastic, but I have been with Terence for about two hundred years. Edward has only been with us for around sixty or so. He is still new to all of this. He can tell you, though, that when we find someone rare, someone special, like you, we don't hurt them." Maria lies down beside Elise, fitting her body against Elise's back, following the contours of Elise's body with her own. "I want you to know about us. Let me share with you a little of what's important. Little by little, our whole story will emerge, especially if you stay with me." There is something plaintive in Maria's voice as she speaks these words.

Elise tries to relax, closing her eyes as Maria spins her tale.

"First, it's rare we forge any actual connection with human beings. It usually doesn't work out. And, don't hate me for this, but in order to truly survive, to *live*, we have to look at humans as food." Maria rolls her eyes and grins wickedly. "It's funny: the more they 'progress' the easier it is to look at them as entrées rather than people. It's like the whole race gets dumber and dumber with each advance in technology. I wish I could tell you how many victims Terence alone has taken when he comes upon one on a cell phone. They hardly notice him until he's biting into their neck. I can't imagine what the person on the other end of the call thinks. No signal! Searching!"

Elise curls further into herself. This is just too weird. She wants to laugh. She wants to cry. "You refer to human beings like they're something different. Aren't you..." Elise's voice trails off as she wonders how to pose the question. "I mean, weren't you..."

Maria nods. "Yes. Yes. I suppose I was once a human being. It's been so long that I've forgotten. I don't look at things that way anymore. We're not human. We're not superhuman; we're different. That's one thing that sets us apart from the human race: perception. We acknowledge there are things going on that might not be part of our immediate perception. We, for example, have moved and merged with masses of people for hundreds of years, and no one ever notices we're anything out of the ordinary. Because humans believe only what their eyes can see. And sometimes that's wrong. And sometimes there are things you sense in a different way. The brush of something soft on your neck, the people who appear in dreams you've never seen before, things like that are testimony to other worlds that exist all around you.

"So, yes, I was once a human being, like you. But, aside from needing blood to continue to survive, I've also honed different ways of seeing. And a lot of what I've learned about such sight, I've learned from people like you. People who can remove the covers from their eyes, open them and truly see things in a way that's different from the conventional, from how most people see things. These are the kind of people I feed on in a different way." Maria sighs. "I've been around a long time, so I can sense it when I meet one. Someone like you. Someone like Edward. Believe me, there aren't many.

"But you want to hear our story." Maria looks dreamy-eyed. "There's so much to tell. You just have to come to know us and let the story leak out gradually. We don't have time to sit here and go through everything. What would interest you? That I grew up as a child in Venice when the city was still new? That Terence knew Oscar Wilde and Dante Rossetti, but that he knew Wilde much better, if you know what I mean?"

Maria shakes her head and summarizes her story, mainly with Terence, a story spanning continents and centuries. She tells of their nocturnal existence, their pursuit of blood, flesh and art. How, at various times, their desire for each of these things has caused conflict and pain. How, at various times, all three things combined, bring them the most delirious physical, intellectual, and emotional pleasure. Maria tells her how easily they accrued their wealth through the centuries (mostly through black-market buying and selling of paintings and sculptures) and finally, their kin.

"I don't know if you can immediately understand what we are." Maria takes Elise's hand in her own, almost as if to warm it. "That will take time, and it has to be time you're willing to freely give. If you were like us, you'd discover the luxury of not living as if you're racing to beat the clock. Immortality, or the enhanced possibility of it, gives us tremendous freedom."

Elise shivers. "I don't know what you mean. I'm not sure exactly what you mean by that." She swallows, mouth dry, confusion reigning. When will Maria's face break into laughter? When will she tell her this is all a joke? It must be.

"Oscar Wilde?" Elise giggles, in spite of the fact that dread grows inside her, heavy and warning.

"Ask Terence. The two were quite close."

Elise shakes her head. "I'll have to do that. But I don't want to wake him just now." She closes her eyes for a second, perhaps hoping when she again opens them, something different will appear. She is disappointed. "So, are there others like you here in Chicago? Nearby?"

"I don't know. We don't really mix with others like us, although there is a loosely-knit society the world over, with its own rules and logic, pertaining only to us. I believe we are rare, so perhaps not. There have been times, when we lived in other places, where we saw more of our kind. Anne Rice would have you believe New Orleans is crawling with us; not so." Maria laughs. "Here, in America, the places I've found most populated with others like us are Pittsburgh and Kansas City. Not very romantic, but what can I say?" Maria shakes back her hair. "Terence, Edward, and I are pretty much alone. What need we have for togetherness, we get from one another."

Elise doesn't know anymore what she'd call togetherness. She tries to get up on one arm, so she is no longer touching Maria.

"Sometimes, we want someone to join us."

Elise turns to search Maria's eyes. Maria cuts off the connection by closing her own eyes. She whispers, "It's too soon to talk about that."

Lovingly, Maria strokes the whitening skin of Elise's face, her long, blood-red nails gently passing over milky warmth.

"Really, there are very few of us. Forget the lore you read in pulp novels. We do not form a new vampire each time we kill. The process is complicated, involving ritual and faith, two concepts you moderns seem to have lost stock in. Those of us who have survived are spread throughout the world, feeding quietly on society's outcasts, of which there are many. I would guess there are no more than a few hundred of us, and we've had hundreds of years to perfect our techniques of hiding, our techniques of hunting.

"I don't know all the history, or even why we exist. Our biggest influence on the world, the one most noticeable anyway, is in something you might find bizarre, or even silly." Maria stops and brings out a bowl filled with dried marijuana; leaves, buds, stems and seeds mingle, all redolent of resin, glistening in the dim light. "This is part of our ritual, developed over thousands of years. We used it at first to stun and pacify our victims, while on our systems it had the opposite effect. It awakens our senses, attuning them to your thoughts, your auras, your health, everything about you, before we kill."

Elise stares down at the marijuana, afraid she will be sick. Who would have thought that fun and games with bongs and power hitters when she was in art school would someday have ties with the living dead? She wants to giggle, but she's afraid that, once she starts, she will never be able to stop. Never.

"It's pure, this. Mortals have taken it upon themselves to trade and grow their own, but what they grow is polluted, impure. Hardly the same thing. But I suppose if you're looking for some stamp of our existence it would be this, and that we introduced it to the world." With one hand, Maria rolls the marijuana into a slim cigarette, expert; the joint is perfect. "Let's smoke this now."

"No!" Elise gets up from the settee and runs from the room, from the house. All of this is too strange. What can she do to forget?

Chapter
Twelve

1954

EDWARD AWAKENED. HE was back in his apartment, but had no memory of how he arrived there, or when. He looked down at his clothes and saw he was still dressed in the same jeans and shirt he had worn the night before, when he had met Terence and the two of them had taken a trip to the depths (it seemed as if one of them, either Maria or Terence, had referred to their place as "the depths"; the name fit in many ways).

But had last night happened? Had he really spent an evening in a cavernous room in an abandoned and hidden area of the New York City subway system? There was a nauseating sense of the surreal as Edward recalled the night before. How Terence had been waiting for him, not outside his apartment, which would have been normal, if not a little creepy, but several blocks away, as if they had arranged to meet. He remembered the trip with the silent cab driver and the descent into the bizarre underground space: its cold, its dim lighting, the stench of mildew in the air. How could it have seemed so romantic to him? How could he have done what he had done?

But he didn't want to think about that now. Whether he would have a choice in shutting out his memories was still in question. Concentrate on the present, he told himself, concentrate on getting up, moving. Those things, once so simple, now seemed alien. He felt profoundly weak as he lay upon his mattress, a chill air blowing in from his window. Too weak to even get himself up on his elbows. His entire body felt infused with a lethargy that made him feel as if he had suddenly gained 500 pounds. He couldn't move. He didn't know how long he had slept, and wondered if it was only for a very short time. He felt so *tired*, beyond exhaustion. All of his strength had been sapped. If they weren't automatic, Edward didn't know if he would have had the strength to keep his heart beating and his lungs drawing in air.

So he stared at the ceiling, tracing a hairline crack from one side of the room to the other. He mustered up enough energy to turn his head and regarded his paintings, arranged along the baseboard of the opposite wall.

Everything was ugly. Childish. Amateur stuff. Crap. What had he been thinking? Slamming his paint-smeared body into canvas, as if that were something original, as if it were communicating something other than the creator's desperation for getting noticed. It was children's figure painting, except with a larger "brush." It was a ploy for getting attention, no more sophisticated than a four-year-old flinging himself on his back in a screaming and kicking tantrum.

When he got enough energy back, he should gather his work up and take it downstairs. There was a place in the back where the janitor burned trash. He could have a bonfire—and then maybe his paintings would actually have some beauty, if only for a fleeting time. He imagined the flames crackling: the orange, the black ash, the way the air shimmered and distorted just above the flames.

Turning his head away from his work, Edward felt nauseated by the smell of turpentine and paint. Those smells once had a resonance. They were exciting, arousing even, like the smell of a man's armpit, or the aroma of semen. They fired up a desire within his soul, not unlike lust, to create.

But now the thought of painting, and sex, for that matter, offered no appeal. All he wanted was his life back, his energy. If he had believed in God, he would have prayed and offered up all sorts of things, his creativity, his left testicle, for a shot at being normal. Getting out of this apartment and finding a job somewhere, maybe as a teacher, or something more humble. Didn't garbage men make enough to get by?

He saw the three of them in memory, the music silenced and their bodies intertwined. The sex was nothing new for him, even if it was rare. But the sex had led to something darker, something more soul stealing. They had bit him; their razor sharp teeth piercing his skin and sucking out his blood. The pleasure was delirious, making the most sensational orgasm seemed pedestrian by comparison. He saw their mouths, ringed with blood. He remembered their eyes, bright, almost feral, with desire. He felt, again, their warmth. It was the warmth of his own blood running through their veins.

The thought sickened him. And he knew that the previous night had marked a turning point, had been a true loss of innocence. He wondered if innocence was a quality one could ever regain.

He didn't know if he could ever return his life to what it once was. There truly were, Edward thought with despair, points of no return.

He turned away from the memory of the previous night, not wanting to confront what he had done, whom he had become in the small hours of the morning, when the city darkened and slowed above him. It was no wonder he suddenly craved a normal, pedestrian life. Craved even turning away from his "inversion," as Freud called it, and getting married and having two children, a boy and a girl. A place in New Jersey. Hoboken, maybe? And if he couldn't turn away from his love and desire for his own sex, maybe he could become a more conventional homosexual and find himself a "roommate" or "friend" as they were coyly referred to here in the Village, to hide what could not be hidden, but what discretion and decorum dictated remain concealed. He would spend weekends on Fire Island, attend the opera, and cruise the baths when his roommate traveled on business.

A normal life, he wondered, *is that now entirely out of my grasp? Have I reached a point where it's too late to turn back? Have I jumped off a cliff into an abyss of deep red? Have I embraced something that has damned me?*

"Oh shit," Edward whimpered. "Stop it with the fucking melodrama, you queen." He forced himself up on his elbows and found it was possible to manage a somewhat vertical position without expiring. His back and neck felt weighted down, as if gravity had increased during the night and was fighting to pull him back down. But as the minutes ticked by on the old Westclox on the wall opposite, his strength was returning, not in waves, but in dribbles, and that had to be good enough.

There was a small, cane-bottomed chair positioned near the window. Edward would sit in this chair from time to time, to catch the breeze, to smoke, and to ponder. Edward made this chair his goal. He needed to get to the chair so he could sit and think, put last night's events in some sort of order, some sort of perspective.

He wasn't sure why, but he felt his life depended on it.

And remembering it while sitting near a window seemed to really matter, because it proved he was still human, that he could sit and think like anyone else. Lying on his back was too much like them. He remembered leaving them, remembered their deep slumber and the look of contentment on their faces. It was all coming back.

He rolled over and crawled across the dirty wood plank floor, thinking of nothing else save getting to that chair. The trip across his soiled wooden floor was a long one, one in which the rip in the knees of his jeans grew larger, enough to expose the flesh beneath, enough to rip the skin and cause a trickle of blood to emerge, leaving a crimson smear. Edward paused to regard the swatch of color on the hardwood and thought how his new companions probably would have already lapped it up, leaving the floor as clean as if it were brand new.

Edward pulled himself up on the chair, his face near the window, where a cool breeze, a gusty wind actually, was whistling through. He swore he could almost smell the Hudson, beneath the exhaust fumes.

He stared outside for a long time, not thinking. He smoked three cigarettes down, until his throat felt scorched. But at least he felt something, something human.

After he had tried to eat some of the food they offered, Edward had partaken once more of the powerful weed only they seemed able to procure. The marijuana numbed him and made the actions that followed those of someone else; he was merely an observer.

What he saw was himself, stretched across a red velvet settee, naked limbs white against the plush fabric. The contrast was stunning, almost unreal. The velvet outlined and softened his naked body, which looked better than Edward would have thought, given his diet of coffee, cigarettes, and alcohol. He was slim and sinewy. On his face was a look of rapturous intensity, his eyes bright with desire, his mouth hanging open, lips moist, as if he were panting or already in the throes of some delicious ecstasy.

They were kneeling next to the settee. At first, they didn't touch; they only observed, building his anticipation. It was as though they knew exactly what they were doing to him by waiting, by not giving in to the delirium of touch. Here was a young man desperate to feel flesh against flesh and withholding it made that desire all the more intense. Yet, there were rules. He didn't know where they were written down or who had the authority to enforce them, but instinctively he knew the rules of this game. There was to be no talking, no pleading, no wheedling, no seductive tones. He was not allowed to touch them. Supplicant, he had to wait.

They heightened the waiting by at last bringing their hands up, but not touching...not yet. They moved their hands over his body, just above the field of his flesh. He wanted to arch his back to bring his skin into contact with their hands, but knew that would be insubordination, so he remained still while their hands slowly circled, moving in arcs inches from his flesh, flesh becoming more and more fevered with each rotation. He didn't know if the heat was in response to their almost-touches, as if they could raise heat from his body like magnets with their upraised hands; or if the heat came from within, his lust and need stoking up his internal temperature.

He watched as his body grew slick, and beads of sweat popped up and rolled off his chest, his stomach, his thighs; watched as his pale hair became darkened by perspiration.

And then Terence's hand landed on his thigh, gentle, the touchdown of a butterfly. He whimpered. Maria kissed his neck, barely a whisper.

This time there would be no razors, no slim, almost elegant lines carved into his thighs. Maria bent over him, and as naturally as a doe lowering her head to graze, lit on his neck and nipped him gently, teeth so sharp he barely felt pain. He watched as she moved back to admire her work, the small puncture wounds in his neck, and saw her bring her hand to her mouth in delight as the first blood began to trickle and flow.

All of this he observed from a kind of distance, through a tunnel. There was no horror in his second self as Maria and Terence both got up from their knees to more dominant positions and opened their mouths in strange smiles, which revealed teeth changed from normal to rows of tiny, razor-sharp fangs. He thought for a moment, *This is the part where I scream; this is the part where I struggle against them and bolt away*, but there was no energy for such thoughts, let alone actions.

"You should have it," she whispered to Terence. "He's your acquisition."

And when Terence knelt once more, Edward swung back into himself to feel, as one, the touch of Terence's lips against his flesh, sucking, licking. He needed to know what it was to provide the sustenance that Terence needed.

Maria's hand on his shoulder. "Not too much, now. This one, we're thinking of keeping."

And Maria went down to his thigh, where his erect and quivering sex brushed against her hair. Again, she opened his flesh and this time took the blood that issued forth.

Edward squirmed and let them continue to bite and suckle, until his entire body was a mass of small drained wounds.

It was then he became light-headed, drifting in and out of consciousness. These memories came in flashes: he remembered reeling as Maria mounted him (his first woman!), her face smeared with gore, flushed with high color; recalled crawling across the room to Terence, who taunted and laughed at him, calling him a faggot. The ridicule somehow made everything even more intense. He recalled Maria's touch on his hair, feather-light, as she held his face close to the concrete floor while Terence took him from behind. Terence screeched with glee as something in Edward broke and caused more blood to come forth, to run (but not for long) in trickles down his thigh.

Edward shook his head, scattering the memories like dream images. He sucked in the cold air and wondered if last night had been a dream, but a quick look down at his exposed arm told him it had not: there were small, round scabs all over him.

He stood and filled glass after glass of cold water from the kitchen tap, gulping it down until he felt his belly would burst. It was then the knock at the door came.

Edward turned, glass held in mid-lift to his mouth, eyebrows together. Could it be Terence? The very thought seemed odd and out of place; the whitish sky and light outside precluded his appearance now. He and Maria were in their element only in the shadows, under cover of night. He didn't know why he thought this, but it was so right it was a form of certainty.

So who, then, had come to call? Edward seldom had visitors (other than the ones who followed him home occasionally from the Tiger's Eye, but they were all doomed to never repeat their crossing of his threshold); his friends, the few he had, had vanished one by one, disappearing into domestic bliss, into drug addiction, one a suicide, another an expatriate, trying to recapture Left Bank glories in Paris. And his family...well, they had never understood him and the silence that grew year after year was more and more comfortable and less of a shame.

The knocking was more insistent. Perhaps it was just the building's janitor, needing to gain entrance to spray his apartment for cockroaches. It had happened before. Edward gulped his water down and set it on the counter next to the sink.

The knocking sounded again.

"I'm coming! I'm coming." Edward struggled into a pair of jeans, pulled on a shirt.

He opened the door. Before him stood a smiling woman. Her screamingly red hair was pulled into a tight French twist, so taut it pulled back the skin of her face. Her skin was pale, her eyes bright green, her lips a lacquered red. She wore black horn-rims and a small black velvet pillbox hat. A green chartreuse coat, of some sort of nappy fabric, hung to her knees. An inch of black dress showed beneath the coat; its emergence seemed calculated. Her feet were squeezed into black stiletto pumps.

Edward and the woman regarded one another. The woman never stopped smiling, as if she had a secret and was bursting to share it; her eyes actually twinkled. Edward cocked his head. This was no one he had ever seen. "Something I can help you with?"

"I'd like to introduce myself." For someone so young, the woman's voice was deep, not raspy, but smooth. There was a slight New England accent that was nearly undetectable. Edward was certain she had been schooled in elocution. The woman extended her hand and Edward stared down at it, noticing the bright red nails, almost claws; they contrasted with the whiteness of her skin. She withdrew her hand, but continued to smile.

"My name is Olive Greene." She gave out a short bark of laughter. "You can laugh; everyone does. But it's my real name. My parents either had no sense of humor or tremendously cruel ones. I still haven't figured out which."

Edward didn't say anything.

"Would you mind if I stepped inside?"

"The place is kind of a mess." Edward pulled the door closer to his back. "What is it you wanted, Miss Greene? If you're here to sell something, including religion, I haven't the resources to make you happy, so you might as well move on to greener pastures."

"Well, I guess we can conduct our little meeting right here in the hallway. It does have a certain *je ne sais quoi*." She sniffed the air. "Or maybe it's just cabbage." Olive Greene laughed again.

Edward stared. "So what is it you want? I need you to get to the point. I'm not feeling very well today."

"Okay. Now, that we've dispensed with the pleasantries, perhaps we can get down to business. Do you know a Mr. Sukie Grace?"

Edward scratched his head. The name *did* sound familiar, and maybe on a better day, it would have conjured up an image to make the familiarity clear. But today was not that day.

"The name sounds kinda familiar, but I'm not registering anything."

"Mr. Grace is a friend of my boss's. My boss is the owner of a gallery in Soho. Anima/Animus?" Olive Greene cocked her head. "Maybe you've heard of it?"

Anima/Animus was a name that rang bells. It was one of the most respected galleries in New York City, perhaps in North America. And its dedication to abstract expressionism had earned it mainstream coverage in places such as the *New York Times*. What did Anima/Animus have to do with him? And who was Sukie Grace?

"Who's your boss?"

"As I mentioned, he's the owner of the Anima/Animus gallery, on Houston. His name is Paul Gadzinski."

Sukie Grace's lover was Paul Gadzinski. It all came together now. A few months ago, a young man, scarcely more than a boy, with wispy blond hair and a willowy frame, had followed him home. Not from the bar, but just from having seen him on the street. The two had exchanged glances, each turning to look back at the other several times, in the mating dance homosexuals everywhere were familiar with. On the third head-swivel, Sukie Grace had changed direction and followed Edward back to his walk-up. He waited around outside until Edward came back downstairs and let him in. For the next hour, they didn't exchange a word, concentrating on each other's flesh. It wasn't until afterward, panting and sweating that talk turned to art...and Grace's understanding lover. He hadn't mentioned the gallery's name, perhaps from a fear of being seen as a name-dropper, or, worse, a liar.

And Edward, in a very rare moment of openness, perhaps buoyed by two orgasms, gave his new friend a show of his work.

His new friend was very impressed.

But it never crossed Edward's mind something more would ever come of their meeting. He seldom saw his paramours more than once, so why should this one lead to something that could change his life?

Edward rubbed his forehead. "It's all coming back to me. I know who Paul is. I know Sukie. We've met before. But what brings you here?"

"Sukie's recommendation. He was quite impressed with your work." She grinned. "On canvas, I mean. I have no idea about any other aspects of your creativity."

Edward felt himself redden.

"You're blushing. Quaint." Olive rummaged in her purse for a card. She held it out. It was embossed with the name Anima/Animus in large block letters and the gallery's address and phone number. "We're doing a show next month, called 'the New Wave.' We're looking for five new artists, talented souls no one will be familiar with, for the show. You're one of the ones we're considering. That is, if you're interested."

Edward simply stood still, breathing through his mouth. After a long moment, he nodded.

"Anyhoo, drop by the gallery tomorrow morning at ten, if you'd be so good. Mr. Gadzinski would like to talk with you. If you can bring a sample of your work, that would be terrific, too." Olive Greene cocked her head. "Does that work for you?"

Edward nodded.

"Good. We'll see you then." Olive turned and began her descent down the treacherous staircase, framed by peeling wallpaper. Somewhere a baby was screaming. Edward watched her, thinking she looked like a flower in a Dumpster.

Edward closed the door and leaned against it. There was something he didn't immediately identify fluttering around within him. Was it elation? Was it possible to move so suddenly to the opposite end of the spectrum with just one small bit of news? But Anima/Animus was big news. The biggest! It was the kind of place that made artists and maybe this prospect was enough to restore his faith in himself, his work, if only for a little while.

He wondered what Terence would have to say.

Chapter
Thirteen

Present Day

ELISE STARES AS a cockroach skitters across the floor and scurries under the baseboard. She wishes she were somewhere else, floating down a river maybe, anywhere but here. She imagines the slow, gurgling flow of emerald water, the gentle rocking of a raft beneath her, and the heat of a summer sun on her back. This is how she vanishes. At the end of the river, she notices the black cobwebs clinging to the ceiling and the fantasy winks out, like a neon light at closing.

She wants to pull back when the calloused hand touches her calf and gives it a squeeze. It's like she's woken from a dream.

"Hey, babe, thanks. That was great." His voice comes to her from a distance, although he sits next to her, dressing, on the bed. She turns her head from the pillow, where she had closed her eyes, and looks at him. He is a middle-aged man, in his fifties, maybe, with a hairy pot belly, a hairy back, and a bald pate ringed with too-dark black hair. His face lacks a chin, the fact of which he tries to hide with the help of a goatee, also too-dark black. Had he said what his name was? Does it matter? He had wanted her to call him "Daddy."

Elise doesn't reply to his insincere thanks. She hoists herself up on one elbow and puffs her lower lip out, blowing air upward to clear the sweaty strands of hair from her face. She reaches out toward the wall and traces the crack's progress.

"That was some hot time." He laughs, unaware of her inattention. "You around on Howard Street a lot?"

She forces herself to meet his gaze. He's grinning like a schoolboy after his first time, a mixture of pride, cruelty, and remorse all projected through the thin lips, and too-white Chiclet teeth. Elise tries to think of what makes this one different from the others she has taken on today. They all blur into one, and what does it matter, anyway?

"Hey." The man touches her shoulder, and Elise recoils. Getting fucked is so much easier to bear than the gentle touch of a hand. She hates it when they touch her, or worse, try to kiss her. "I asked you a question."

Elise sits up straighter, wishing for a cigarette, even though she doesn't smoke. But it would add so much to the scene: the flame of the Zippo, the dismissive expelling of the smoke, the blue fog obscuring the trick's face. Perhaps she should pick herself up a box of Marlboros for later. "Yeah, you can find me there just about any evening, looking for friends." She gives her most winning, and fakest smile, and forces herself to jab him in the ribs. "Friends like you."

The best kind of friend... She thinks of the three wadded-up twenties he has already left on the nightstand. She has lain with four other friends today.

She watches silently as he checks his pockets, making sure he has everything. He slides a pair of black framed glasses on his doughy, featureless face. Elise thinks he looks like Mister Magoo. She'd laugh if the image weren't so depressing.

"See you around, babe." And he's gone.

Elise curls her legs up close to her chest. She tries to shrink into herself. She tries not to exist.

It takes Elise a while to muster the energy to move from her bed. When she does force herself to cross the floor and go into the bathroom, she does so only because of an urgent pressing against her bladder. She sits on the toilet and pees; it burns a little, and she thinks it's probably time to visit the city STD clinic. Occupational hazard.

She wipes herself and moves to the shower. Should she turn a light on? An orange glow filters in through frosted glass; light from a streetlamp outside. She strikes a match and puts it to the wick of a candle that sits in a jar on the back of the toilet. She reaches out and turns the knobs for the shower, getting the water steaming, just shy of being so hot it will scald her. Stepping in, under the hot flow, she closes her eyes. After a while, she picks up soap and scrubs herself hard. It's the only way to get rid of her customers' smells, their essences. The water, combined with her frantic scrubbing, leaves her skin red and tingling. She emerges feeling marginally better.

Later, she throws on a pair of men's boxer shorts and a T-shirt and sits at her drawing table. It's late, after 3:00 a.m., and the street outside has grown relatively quiet. Elise's eyes are open wide and even though her body is weighed down by fatigue, her limbs heavy, she knows it will be hours before she receives the blessing, and the oblivion, of sleep.

She tapes a piece of drawing paper to the board, takes up a black crayon, and begins scribbling, darkening the paper's surface until it's nothing but a surface of black wax. Then she takes out her X-Acto knife. She carves, and carves, not even pausing to notice the gradual lightening of her room, how it fills with gray light, bringing form and definition to her meager possessions. Finally, she sits back, breathless, face slick with sweat.

The psychology of what she has drawn is not lost on her: the blackness, the picture carved out of the absence of color. She has drawn Maria. Not the Maria she has fallen in love with, but a grotesque monster. Present are the black eyes, the waving hair, the long, delicate neck. Gone is the beauty. Elise has drawn in a gaping mouth filled with tiny, pointed teeth, each perfect in their detail, each a blade of horrific destruction. She has managed to capture an expression of both hunger and ferocity, distorted almost beyond recognition: desire out of control. Part of her wants to crumple up the work, thrust it deep inside some Dumpster in the alley behind her building, or even further away; the etching could have the power to taint her. But the other part knows this is more than just art: it is expression of her fear, fear that, deep down, she knows is real, knows that it's doing its work in trying to protect her. Keeping this piece of artwork within view could be the key to her salvation.

But can she appreciate the art? She is too close to it to be objective, her mind clouded by the confusion of not even being sure who she is, or what she wants, anymore.

These last few weeks after meeting Maria have been an exercise in self-numbing, blocking out as much as she can by taking on trick after trick. She has a dresser drawer stuffed with crumpled cash to prove it. She has thrown herself into artwork that, even for her, is bizarre. She approaches her art with abandon these days, but it's not the abandon of creative freedom. She works with the renunciation of thought, blocking her mind of sensation and memory and letting her hands and eyes work together from instinct, almost as if they have no direction from her brain.

These last few weeks, she has needed the respite. She is certain that she must block out how she rushed, with a silent scream, from Maria's home—and her news. It seems to Elise that there is no other course remaining other than obliteration. Oblivion is the only way she can keep her sanity. On the day Maria told her about the vampirism (had it even been real? Or was it a nightmare?), Elise felt as if her skin had been peeled away, left raw to experience everything with painful sensitivity. That sensitivity did not fade; it needed treatment, and Elise found it in the worlds of mindless sex and instinctual creation.

The days lately have all become the same: Elise finding herself on her back, or knees, crouching, opening herself to strange men as much as six or seven times a day. Sleep, her primary means of achieving oblivion, eludes her. And when she does sleep, it's fitful, plagued by images of flowing blood, fangs, bats. Or worse, hot erotic images of her body intertwined with Maria's, always ending with being bitten and drained.

So she fills what hours she is not a "working girl" with a new kind of creativity, which could be brilliant, mediocre, or even horrible. Elise has no objectivity; she cannot begin to make an honest assessment of her own work. She wonders what a psychiatrist might make of the horrific images she has crafted, images full of perverse longing. Fangs, blood, bodies torn apart, cannibalized, she makes Munch's *The Scream* look like something created for Disney.

Yet, none of this has worked. It is as if Maria, with her face of fragile beauty, calls to her. And for all Elise knows, she does. Who knows what telepathic powers this demon woman has fine-tuned, especially if it's true she's lived for centuries. Perhaps Maria sits broadcasting desire, nightmare images, and even a kind of love to Elise, willing her to return to her cold embrace. Even while on her knees in some alley, a dark figure spouting his seed on her face, Elise recalls Maria: the face floating to her dreamlike, smiling, hands outstretched to touch.

The sounds of traffic, men groaning, sirens, and all the other aural detritus of her urban existence vanish with these visual images. She looks up and sees a man, wiping away a drop of semen from the tip of his penis, and all she can hear is her beating heart.

Elise puts the X-Acto knife on the ledge at the bottom of her drawing board, and stares at it, wondering what it would feel like to cut herself, to watch the trickle of red emerge, to taste it. She once had a friend, back when she was a teenager in Cleveland, who used to cut herself in secret, hiding the scabs and slashes under designer clothing. When Elise discovered her friend's covert passion (she had walked into the bathroom, found her crouched in the bathtub, slicing her thighs with a razor blade), she asked, "Why? Why do you want to do this to yourself?"

And her friend had answered, "So I can feel something."

Elise had never understood that response. Until now.

The burning beneath her eyelids signals drowsiness coming on. Often, this signal is a cruel one, taking her to her bed, where, maliciously, it vanishes, leaving her to lie wide-eyed and staring at the ceiling.

But sometimes it delivers, and Elise heeds its call.

She gets up from the drawing board and moves to her bed; the sheets are in disarray and smelling faintly of her sweat. She sits down cross-legged on the bed, back against the wall. One of the last things Maria had said to her comes back:

"The one thing in the lives of you mortals you can never change, no matter how hard you try to deny it, is your desire for love."

Elise wants to be able to laugh at the saccharine sentiment, except she knows it's true and it's more of a curse than anything. Oh, to be free of the bonds of love! When will they develop a pill that will block the brain chemicals that bring on the euphoria and the hunger for someone else? Elise thinks it will be as popular as Viagra.

And Maria's voice sounds again, this time louder, a real presence in the room. "I love you, Elise. Come back." She hears Maria's voice, almost as if she were in the room with her, kneeling by her bed, stroking her calf and peering into her with those bottomless brown eyes. Elise lies on her back and closes her eyes. Feel: the brush of her hair across

Elise's leg. Listen: the whisper of satin as Maria shifts in her gown.

Projected on Elise's eyelids, a montage of images: Maria's breasts, her thighs, the feel of her tongue at Elise's ear. Elise touches herself, settling into the sheets, remembering.

Chapter
Fourteen

1954

EDWARD HAD ONLY three dollars and thirty nine cents. He counted the bills and change once more, just to be sure, but the amount was right.

He swept the money off his kitchen table and scooped it into his pocket. "It will have to be enough." It was a rare morning (or day, for that matter) that Edward could entertain the idea of taking a cab anywhere, but this was one of those mornings. It wasn't far to the Anima/Animus Gallery on Houston, but if he was going to bring a couple of his canvases, large, unwieldy things, he couldn't very well hoof it, or even take public transportation. Besides the impracticality of it (visions of him struggling down the street with his work, getting caught in the wind, spun around), he didn't need the stress such a journey would cause him.

His meeting was still two hours away and yet Edward had already gone through two of his shirts, staining them dark beneath the pits, leaving a dark line down the center of his back. His heart raced; his mouth was dry.

This was the meeting that could make all the difference, that could throw his career into the prominence and recognition he had dreamed of since before he came to New York, since he was a little boy in first grade, when his teacher had taken his drawing of an Indian around to the other teachers, to boast of her precocious six-year-old and how his work looked nearly good enough to pass for an adult's, while his classmates were drawing stick figures and birds in the shape of V's. It meant so much.

He knew he would blow it. Knew he would find his tongue thick in his mouth and be unable to talk, let alone charm or impress. Or else he would babble senselessly, saying whatever popped into his head, eliciting stares from the clever, hip people at the gallery. They would exchange glances as he rambled on, rolling their eyes and giving a mute thumbs-down to the crazy young man in the sweaty shirt and the paint-stained chinos.

The one scenario Edward could not imagine was one in which there was awe at his work and, after viewing it, a meaningful dialogue would occur, one in which Edward was offered a spot in this important show. It was hard for him to imagine leaving the gallery proud and eager, but this time with the desire for public and critical acknowledgment.

But the clock was clicking past nine and he needed to get another shirt on (this would have to be the last, perspiration or not), and bind together with twine the two canvases he planned on bringing.

He took one last look at the paintings, uncertain if they were the best examples to represent him or if they were merely...well, crap. Who knew? Did any artist ever really know? It seemed there was no middle ground between cocky arrogance that made someone think their work was beyond reproach, the key to seeing the world in a whole new light, strong evidence of its creator's brilliance and once-in-a-lifetime talent, and abject self-loathing and lack of self-esteem that told the artist he was nothing more than a poseur and his work wasn't even worth the materials he had used (wasted?) to create it.

No matter. These would have to do. Either they would like them and offer him a position in the show, or they would politely decline them, offering icy assurances and the hope his work would find a home elsewhere (the Dumpster behind Abraham's Deli, down the street from his building, most likely). Later, he could always drown his sorrows at the Tiger's Eye; that is, if they were willing to run a tab for him.

He had chosen *Number Six* and *Number Nine* to take with him. *Number Six* had been done about seven months ago. He had splattered a background of lime green, so much paint the color was almost a solid hue, and then he had painted himself chromium yellow, a screaming brightness that conveyed buoyancy and zest. He had thrown himself on the canvas with his arms upraised, then with his legs kicking out, with his movements at progressively higher levels, moving from left to right across the surface. The effect, Edward hoped, was one of vibrancy and joy, of life.

Number Nine had been done just a few days ago. It was similar to *Number Six*, but its polar opposite. He had first coated the canvas in black, great, sweeping slashes of black, smeared across from top to bottom with his bare hands. For this one, he had painted his body with brilliant crimson, and had recorded himself in various positions of despair and longing: crouched into a fetal "c"; arms and legs splayed like a butterfly pressed to a board; and one turning from his side to his back, where his erection was subtly visible.

The difference between the two was not lost on him; they represented the before and after of meeting Terence. He could only pray the difference was a positive one for his work, even as he knew, personally, he was entering a dangerous territory with *Number Nine*, taking on a much bigger addiction than booze or even heroin.

Muse later. Now, I must go. Edward tied a knot in the twine he had wrapped around the oversized canvases and hoisted them up, heading for the door.

"Wish me luck!" he cried out to his empty studio, hoping there was a taxi close by. He couldn't afford to be late.

Chapter
Fifteen

MARIA'S HEAD POUNDS. It's as though something small with razor teeth has gotten inside her head, digging and biting at her temples and behind her eyes. "Immortality!" she scoffs. "You think the living dead could at least be spared the discomfort of a headache."

She has been calling to Elise all night, ignoring the rumblings in her belly, though they grows more insistent by the moment. This hunger is like a living thing: spoiled and selfish, not willing to stop until it succeeds in reminding her, in making her want to savor the recent past. But she feels she must reach Elise, must make some kind of connection, even if Elise isn't consciously aware Maria is speaking to her through a telepathic wire, thoughts traveling across the expanse of city separating them. This calling, this focused concentration has tired her, has caused this sick headache. She massages her forehead, squeezing her eyelids tight, to send one more image. Perhaps this time, she will get something back. It's all she wants. She concentrates, focusing, now, shutting out the exterior and closing in on just an image, making it real.

There is Elise beneath her, lying on the rumpled sheets of her twin bed. A light sheen of sweat coats her face, making it slick, but also moist. The salt taste of her would stun and delight the tongue. Her auburn hair fans out across gray pillows. She gazes upward.

Maria stares into her eyes, locking with them, drowning in the green irises. Maria holds Elise with her eyes, their minds meeting and merging, desire awakened and aroused — a hungry beast. Maria lowers herself, supported on the warm satin of Elise's body. The connection of their flesh is like the tip of a match touched to dry kindling. The hunger rises up like smoke and flame, all-consuming. Maria dips her mouth to Elise's, biting gently, pulling Elise's tongue into her mouth. Sliding her hands beneath Elise's back, Maria holds her close, tight, attempting to make their bodies one, to blot out anything that separates them. Isn't this what so-called lovemaking is all about? The moment where two bodies merge and anything separating them dissolves. Maria imagines candlelight, the smell of wax, shadows flickering on the wall. She hears music, muted, but rising above the ebb and flow of the urban soundscape just outside: the horns, the hum of engines, the voices raised loud. The music is something minimalist, perhaps just the high notes reaching their ears; Philip Glass, maybe.

Gently, she moves her tongue from Elise's mouth to her ear. Taking the lobe between her teeth and biting, not hard enough to draw blood, but just enough to let her know she's there, to send a shiver down Elise's spine. Moving her tongue up to lick her inner ear, the fine down of pale hair growing there, almost invisible. Breath on wet flesh, then a whisper: "Come back."

Maria opens her eyes. It's almost as if she has been set down in a place she has never seen. She looks around the room, taking it in. The communion and the effort have left her drained. Gradually the room filters in: plank flooring, oak pedestal table and ladder-back chairs, with their straw seats, gathered round it. The remains of a meal, service for one, chills on the table. Chicken bones, a baked potato skin, congealing grease. The room is redolent with the odor of the food; it makes Maria nauseous.

She looks down at the boy who had devoured the meal while she watched, less than two hours ago. She remembers his sparkling blue eyes and the way he seemed to alternate the words, "like" and "fuckin'" to the exclusion, almost, of the rest of the English language. It gave him a certain distinctiveness, a vapid boyish charm that went perfectly with the skateboard (hand-painted in purple and green and now resting in a corner of the kitchen, propped against the wall), the purple Converse shoes, and the uniform of cargo pants and oversized T-shirt emblazoned with the name of a heavy metal band Maria had never heard of.

Reaching down, she tousles blond hair; varying shades of yellow, white and soft brown mingle in the dim light. She remembers his face, freckles and a gap between his front teeth, blue eyes trusting. She remembers the lithe form of his body, white and graceful, legs long and lean, muscles not yet stretched to manhood. She remembers the pale swatch of pubic hair above his sex.

Maria reaches out with her tongue and snares a piece of flesh from the corner of her mouth. The taste of it, the moisture and the sharp tang of blood still clinging to it, bring her back to this world she inhabits, this ebb and flow of hunger that really isn't different from the world the living inhabit. Flecks of blood Maria missed dot the floor around the boy. His stomach is ripped open, exposing entrails. Little is left of the face of boyish innocence: red tissue beneath where his skin was, tissue that speaks of musculature that once made the face frown, smile, cry, and laugh. Pieces of flesh are ripped from his limbs in jagged, reddened lines.

Maria wishes, for just one moment, she could have taken what she needed from the boy and then returned him to the way he was. Assuaging her hunger is never a delightful thing, never really a pleasure. The food rumbles in her stomach, mocking.

What is it the kids call it these days? Addiction?

Maria jumps at the sound of a footfall and a familiar voice. She looks up dully, but does not otherwise move; she brings her knees up to her chest.

"We have to find her. We can't leave her out there." Terence has entered the room, dressed in jeans and a black T-shirt. He has washed the blood from his face and looks cool and smooth.

Maria had almost succeeded in forgetting she shared her home and hearth with others. "Good evening to you, too. You don't waste any time, do you? No need to exchange pleasantries when there's someone out there to be killed. Isn't that right, Terence?"

He stands before her, as if he has materialized there, brushing the blond spikes at his forehead back. They flatten and rise up quickly, a resurrection of sorts. Life, death, and rising up again: it's all around them, in the smallest of ways. His stance and sneer makes her wish she could think him away.

"You know we can't allow her to go on, knowing what she now knows." Terence bends down to lick some loose flesh from the boy's ravaged face. "Delicious," he whispers, and grins at her.

"Why? She won't tell anyone." Maria wants to move over the boy, shielding him with her body to protect him from the violation of further ripping and renting, to give what remains of his corpse some dignity. What they have done has completely lost its allure. It now seems inelegant, base, the product of a hunger that knows no will, a desire completely out of control. They are nothing more than animals, no different from a silent winged owl, swooping down out of the black sky to grab a mouse in its talons. "Of course I know there are rules against mortals knowing about us. Of course I know that." Maria laughs, but there is no mirth in it. "I'm the one that taught you the rules, our traditions..."

Terence's eyes bore into hers. "Then you know you've already broken it. Our first law, Maria, and you've ground it under your heel as if it didn't matter." Terence takes a deep breath. "It's cardinal; it's the one thing our survival hinges on, the one thing that ensures we don't become extinct, the few of us left..."

"Would extinction be such a bad thing?" Maria's laugh is bitter. "What do we bring to the world? What do we contribute? Pain and loss? Heartache? Oh yes, Terence, I don't think the world would mourn our loss."

Terence shakes his head. "I know you don't mean it. And I know you remember what you made sure Edward and I both know, that allowing a mortal to live with the knowledge is the worst thing any of us can do. It renounces everything we are, and have been."

"You don't need to be so pedantic, you insolent bastard. I know. We've had this talk before. Over and over."

"Yes. And it doesn't seem to make any difference."

"I told you, I'm trying to bring her back. She'll come."

"And how many nights now have you sat in darkness, trying to reach her? Don't you think you'd know if she wanted to hear from you again? She's ignoring you." Terence is very good at sneering. Over the centuries, he has perfected the scowl and frown. "We know where she is, Maria. It would be a simple matter to go and pick her up. Edward and I could"

"No! She didn't ask for any of this; I don't want some Nazi strong-arm maneuvers used on her."

"She has to die."

Maria shakes her head. "That solution is out of the question."

"That solution is the only one."

Maria shakes her head, her brow creased, frowning. If she allowed herself, she could perhaps shed a few tears, but she hates the sight of them, crimson instead of clear, a painful reminder of the truth. "Let me try to bring her here. Give me a little longer." She feels ridiculous; he is her progeny and she is wheedling like a spoiled child begging its mother for a treat.

Terence slowly shakes his head. "It's not up to me to tell you what to do. But as I said, I've seen you sitting here night after night, with your little telepathic headset on, broadcasting to no avail."

"Who says it's to no avail?"

"She isn't here, is she?" Terence reaches down and thrusts his index finger into the boy's entrails, brings it up crusted with blood and pinkish matter. It disappears into his mouth and emerges clean. Terence smiles with impossibly white teeth.

"No, but she'll be here. I promise."

"I wish I could trust you." Terence paces, the floorboards making no sound beneath his weight. Feline grace.

"I wish you could, too. Why are you so eager?"

Their eyes meet, flashing: competitors. Yet Maria can treat him with the condescension of victory. Elise could never be his. He discovered her, and in his fashion, she was his infatuation, brought home to share with the family like a proud trophy. With his looks and his devilish charm, women tend to fall for him immediately. The fact Elise didn't, and worse, preferred Maria, makes Elise's existence unbearable. It has nothing to do with tradition, and they both know that. He wants to get rid of her because she is not his. Who would she tell about them? Who would believe her? She would be locked away in a mental institution before she could say "Blood-sucker." No, what Terence is about, what Terence has always been about, is punishment, the infliction of pain and suffering. Even now, as Maria looks up at him, he has the pose down just so: the appearance of deep thought, as if he is considering her question.

Terence says, "You know it's been our life to collect the creativity of the mortal, to preserve it as we have." He frowns. "It's the only thing they can hold over us, so we worship. We always have. I don't want anything more from her other than some of her art." He smiles, a death rictus. "That's all."

"You just said, and I don't think I misheard you, that we need to kill her. That it was the only way..." Maria shoves the blond boy's corpse away and stands, bringing her face close to Terence's. She can smell a mixture of cannabis and blood on him. "Oh Terence, think about who you're talking to here; don't change position in midstream. I know you too well. You want her dead." Maria sighs. "And besides, some of her art is not all I want." Her eyes flash. She stops, uncertain if she should continue, wondering how her desire will be taken by Terence, or even the agreeable Edward. Should she tell them? Should she admit that after eons, she is finally in love? Even to her mind, it sounds preposterous.

"What are you talking about?" A smile plays about Terence's lips; already he is preparing to mock.

Maria realizes she need say no more. Terence knows. The knowledge glints in his eyes. But she can't help herself; words tumble out of her in a rush. "I want her to become one of us." There, it's on the table. Maria searches Terence's face for signs of insubordination, waiting for him to rile against her. "Another tradition," Maria whispers, "We can make others, Terence. Where do you think you emerged from?"

Terence laughs until he is gripping his sides. Laughs until there is no longer any humor, until it becomes painful. Abruptly, he stops. "You can't be serious. And besides, you're not the only one who knows the traditions backward and forward."

Maria casts her eyes down; she knows what's coming. And she knows, too, deep in her silent heart, that what Terence is about to say will be right, will be an irrefutable truth. "And I suppose you'll make certain that Elise and I reap fitting punishment for flouting tradition."

Terence shakes his head. "Of course not. What kind of hypocrite would that make me? If you hadn't gone against the rules, I wouldn't be here. Edward wouldn't be here. But, Maria, you have to understand, we can't keep doing this. It has to end somewhere. And you know what will happen to her. You know. Think of Edward."

"*She* is all I can think about." Love can be such a selfish emotion. One would think, in the hundreds of years Maria has walked the earth, she would have become immune to its siren call. But, in the face of the real thing, she is as helpless and dumb as any teenage girl.

Terence sighs, pretending patience, or perhaps sympathy. "I thought it would always be just the three of us. Remember? When you made Edward—and what a mixed blessing *that* was—we decided our little trio, our *family*, would be the end of it. If we ever let anyone into our circle again, it could only be someone who was already one of us. We agreed, Maria. We agreed because it made sense. We made a pact for a reason."

"But?"

"Take a look in Edward's eyes!" Terence shouts, and his face reddens with the blood of the boy. "Never again. You said it, Maria."

"Never is a very long time." Maria smiles. "We could use a change. We've gotten stale. Life is a bore. All the Harleys and whores in the world can't change that. Elise can bring something new into our dynamic." Even as she's saying the words, she knows she is rationalizing, but that's what lovers do to justify their ends. "And do we really know that Elise will be the same as Edward?"

"You're a fool." Terence turns away. "A selfish fool."

Maria feels the anger growing inside, its flame leaping up, stirring up the calm. "Just because you've never loved anyone! Just because you've used your charms to lure and seduce only to get what you want and then to kill! Don't be self-righteous with me. I love her. What's wrong with that? Why can't I have her? Why can't I have someone who loves only me?"

Terence scoffs. "Love? What a concept."

"Just because you don't understand..."

Terence cuts her off. "I understand love. It's what I feel for you, for Edward. It's not what you feel for Elise. If you truly loved her, you'd want to take nothing more than some examples of her art. Real love isn't selfish. Real love is about doing what's best for the object of your affection."

"That's shit. Don't you, of all people, preach to me about love." Maria casts her eyes downward; she can't help the sinking, defeated feeling inside: he is right. And yet, she wants Elise so much. "It's shit, pure and unadulterated."

"No, it isn't, and you know it. And you know why."

This stops Maria, and she lowers her head in shame. "Isn't it time for you to go somewhere?"

"Don't avoid the issue, Maria. If you bring Elise over to us and make her one of us, you know what it will do to her."

"What it will do is make her happy! At one with the person she loves most!" Maria cries.

Terence hisses. "Happy? That's a good one, coming from you. Shall I call Edward? Ask him about happiness?"

The pain in her head comes back, stabbing. She doesn't want to hear this. In fact, she wants to claw Terence's face, make him hurt. "We don't know that. Just because she'll have a different perspective as one of us doesn't necessarily mean anything. The trade would be worth it, Terence. Eternal life."

"You're pathetic. How can you say you love her?" Terence turns away, heading for the door. Over his shoulder: "There's really nothing more to discuss here, Maria. We have to do something about your little artist friend. We do...or I will."

Maria shivers, a sensation she hasn't had in a very long time. "She's coming back to us. Soon."

"Good!" Terence shouts over his shoulder. "Maybe then we can get what we really should have from her, for our collection, and we can end this nonsense."

"How can we end it? She knows! She knows!"

Terence waves her words away with his hand. "Goodbye, Maria. Poor thoughtless, lovestruck Maria. It's almost quaint."

Chapter
Sixteen

1954

AFTER A SPATE of gray days, energy-sapping humidity, and showers that seemed too lazy to do anything more than produce a half-hearted mist, New York was alive again. A northeasterly wind had blown over the city, clearing away the depressing weather with a few gusts. It was now one of those perfect autumn days, when the sky was a blue of such brilliant intensity it almost hurt to look at, the color so intense it seemed the birds flying through it would be stained. The few clouds above were of the fluffy, cotton-ball variety, cumulus to inspire the imagination, to make one a child again. Here a dragon, there a reclining nude woman, *a la* Rubens. The temperature was in the upper 60s, hot in the sun and with just a nip when one walked beneath the shadow of a building or tree.

It was the kind of day that inspired people to play hooky. It was the kind of day that made even the most mournful, the most misanthropic, yearn to get outside.

It was the kind of day that perfectly suited Edward's mood, as he strode across Washington Square, toward home after his meeting at Anima/Animus gallery. Only yesterday, New York had seemed grim, a prison with the only escape route, suicide. Today, Edward recalled why he had come here in the first place. People on the street yesterday had seemed nothing more than shuffling zombies, all of them plagued with various maladies ranging from acne to obesity to shiftiness and beyond; today, they were now unburdened by their problems. The light made everyone beautiful. If he could, Edward would have whistled.

The city was vibrant. Alive.

He sat on a bench in the square. Pigeons immediately rushed over, expecting something. Yesterday Edward would have shooed them away, alarmed at their filth; now he felt disappointed he had nothing to give them.

He lit a cigarette and recalled the meeting.

The staff at Anima/Animus Gallery had been more than hospitable. In fact, they, like Edward right now, had been jubilant when he stumbled into the gallery, sweaty and awkward, lugging his oversized canvases behind him. He felt nothing like an artist, but more like a sour-smelling deliveryman. He toyed with the idea of playing the part and just leaving, coming back when his face wasn't shiny with sweat, in a shirt that wasn't stained dark in the armpits. But that shiny face would still be the same, dry or sweat-slick. Now was the time.

Olive Greene was sitting at the reception desk (more of a small glass-topped table, really). Her red hair was pulled once more into a tight French twist and today she wore a form-fitting black dress, patent leather stiletto heels, and sterling silver jewelry.

Almost as if she were reading his thoughts, she called out, "You can just put those against the wall, young man. I'll see to them in a minute." She stood up from the desk, dug in the small, square black patent leather clutch on its surface, and crossed the glimmering hardwood, heels clicking. "For your trouble." She held a dollar bill out to him.

"Uh, I don't think you understand. I'm..."

"I know who you are, silly boy."

"Then why the charade?"

Olive Greene put him at ease, somehow made him feel more confident. He snatched the dollar bill from her hand and put it in his pocket before she could close her mouth.

She shook her head, "You artists are all alike. Money-grubbing, even as they deny it with their last, alcohol-perfumed breath." She cocked her head. "I admire that."

Edward, grinning, reached in his pocket.

"No, keep it." Her gaze had moved to the canvases leaning against the wall.

"Is he here?"

"Who? Is that with a capital H? God?"

Edward snorted, ran a hand across his damp forehead. "You know who I mean. Paul Gadzinski."

"Well, some think of him as God. Especially Mr. Gadzinski himself."

Edward didn't need to hear he would be meeting with an egomaniac with an overly inflated view of himself. The fact Mr. Gadzinski thought of himself in divine terms wasn't funny to Edward; it was intimidating. He didn't like talking about himself, let alone selling himself, and his conversational and kiss-up skills had been honed to the sharpness of a dull pencil. He tried to smile at Olive, but it probably came out more a teeth-clenched grimace. "So, um, is he here or not?"

Olive, obviously realizing Edward wasn't going to attempt to join her in mirth, said, "Of course he's here. You have an appointment." She sighed and looked at her fingernails, which were lacquered black, something Edward had never seen before. "I can go fetch him. Why don't you have a seat?" She pointed to a row of chrome seating, with back and seat cushions covered in red suede. He thought of the back of his soaked shirt. "That's okay. I'll just stand."

He watched as Olive walked through the gallery, heels clicking, and disappeared behind a door at the very back, with a frosted glass window that warned, "Private." *Now,* Edward thought, *now is the time to gracelessly bow out. I can slip out the door and be around the corner before either of them return.* He continued to sweat, but now the perspiration wasn't from heat or exertion. His mouth was dry. Would he even be able to speak? *Go ahead,* he allowed himself, *go ahead and run. Let the paintings speak for themselves. If they like what they see, there's no reason for me to even be here.* The paintings would look no better or worse with his commentary. In fact, his stumbling, inarticulate ramblings could harm more than help.

He was just inching toward the door when Olive's mannish voice assailed him. "Halt! Stop right there! Where do you think you're going, mister?"

Edward tried to find some spit to swallow, but came up empty-mouthed. He froze, heat rising to his face. He turned, grinning, and groped for his cigarettes. In a barely audible voice, he said, "Just thought I'd duck out for a smoke while I waited."

There was a small man standing next to her. Paul Gadzinski was not what Edward expected. He expected someone with a goatee, dressed in beatnik clothes, wearing sunglasses, maybe. The ultimate in hipster cool, a complement to Olive Greene's sophistication. Instead the man staring at him was unremarkable: slightly overweight with a bald pate ringed in the palest blond hair Edward had ever seen. His flesh was doughy and soft, and the only things that stood out on him physically were a pair of intense blue eyes, so pale they appeared almost translucent. He wore chinos and an Oxford cloth button-down white shirt. Wing tips. He looked like a Hoboken accountant on his day off.

Edward's tension level receded a bit.

"Go ahead and indulge yourself, Mr. Tanguy. We'll wait." His voice was soft, slightly feminine. Edward wasn't sure if he was being accommodating or acidly sarcastic.

Edward shook his head. "No. It can wait."

He paused for a moment, struggling to slide the cigarette pack back into his pants pocket. He stared at Gadzinski with frightened eyes and tapped his foot. Then he realized what he should do: he crossed the short distance between them and extended his hand. "Edward Tanguy, sir. I'm honored to meet you."

Gadzinski placed an extraordinarily soft hand in Edward's, barely returning the pressure. He removed that same hand and held it up, as if to stop him. "Please, I don't need the flattery. I need good artists. Let's see what you've got."

Edward was relieved the man felt no need for small talk. He crossed back, went over, and hoisted *Number Six* up.

EDWARD FLICKED THE butt of his cigarette away and watched the pigeons scatter elsewhere in Washington Square, alighting at the feet of an old, purple nylon-scarf-wearing woman who even the pigeons could discern had a soft heart for the ornithological. The meeting he had just left, he supposed, could be called an unqualified success.

When he had put the first painting down in front of Gadzinski, his hands were trembling so much the canvas wobbled. He drew in a great, quivering breath and grasped the wooden edges of the canvas framing tight enough to make his knuckles go bloodless. He kept his head low, in a defeated stance, ready to take the punishment and scorn that was surely on its way. He didn't dare look at either Gadzinski or Greene. He couldn't bear to see the distaste in their eyes, or worse, their pity.

He grew even more concerned when no one said anything.

A vein in his forehead began to throb; sweat trickled down his back. Unnerved by their silence, he finally forced himself to look up.

Olive Greene was smirking. But that wasn't so much of a worry; a smirk seemed to be the woman's preferred expression. And besides, her opinion didn't have the importance of Gadzinski's.

Gadzinski, however, looked transfixed, staring at the canvas, lips parted and eyes moving over its surface. Edward didn't have the confidence to interpret this as a good sign. In fact, he read the intense look on the gallery owner's face as shock. He had to be appalled Edward had summoned up the nerve to bring this crap into a gallery with an international reputation. Edward closed his eyes, trying to get some spit past the huge ball that had formed in his throat. He bit his lip until he tasted blood. The coppery trickle energized him and gave him the courage to speak. "You don't like it, do you? I'm sorry..."

He forced himself to make eye contact with Gadzinski; better to just get it over with. Then he could go home and reconsider his artistic ambitions.

Gadzinski shook his head. "I think it's brilliant. I think you have the talent, Mr. Tanguy, enough to wield major influence and take abstract expressionism to a new level."

As the praise started tumbling out of Gadzinski's mouth, blood rushed in Edward's ears, making it hard for him to hear. His face flushed. Surely, Gadzinski was teasing him; could the man be so cruel? Was he supposed to laugh and then gracefully accept the criticism that would follow this little act?

"I'd be honored" Gadzinski stopped. "Mr. Tanguy, look at me please."

Edward lifted his head, blinking and stared into the blue of the man's eyes, waiting.

Sometimes good news could be as stressful as bad.

"I'd be honored to show your work. In fact, I'm revising my original plan, which was to have you show with several other artists, and am thinking of a solo exhibition. I think we need that, with all the requisite hoopla, as soon as possible." He turned to his assistant and cocked his head. "Olive, check and see what we have available in the next couple of weeks. If there's something *less* exciting than Mr. Tanguy's work here," Gadzinski rolled his eyes. "Which would include most of the work we plan on showing soon, bump it back to a later time."

"I'll see what I can come up with." Olive winked at Edward, smiled, and returned to her desk.

Gadzinski said, "I assume you can be ready? Yes? You have more at home like these?"

Edward whispered, "Yes. Are you sure?"

"Oh, how I dread the day when your innocence and modesty dries up, which, I suspect, will be shortly." Gadzinski smiled. "Leave the two paintings here and go home and get together eight more pieces of your best work. Olive can take care of having them transported over here. She'll also be in touch about when...but it will be soon."

"Okay." Edward wished he had something clever to say, or at least something to say. He turned, dazed and dizzy, and wandered toward the front of the space, needing the fresh air of the crisp autumn day outside, needing to foul it with a lungful of cigarette smoke. He was too shocked to be happy, too stunned to even say goodbye to Olive Greene.

EDWARD SAT BACK on the bench and closed his eyes. It had happened more easily than he could have imagined. He was on his way.

Chapter
Seventeen

Present Day

ELISE STANDS AT their front door, wondering why she has come. She casts her eyes down; the wind off the lake at her back is cold. She shivers, thinks about turning around, and walking to the corner to wait for a bus to take her back.

Take her back to what? A life of selling herself on the street? Depressed days in a little box with peeling paint, mouse turds, and cockroaches? To making herself one with the inevitable, never mind that she has an intellect and can draw dark, warped pictures? Who cares about that? No, she'll fall into the trap like all the rest: first it will be the hard drugs to escape (not stuff like marijuana, but crystal meth, cocaine, heroin, all easy to get in her little corner of the world), and then will come the health problems, the Chlamydia unchecked, ruining what's inside and what's female. She will come to the point where HIV will make a nest for itself in her bloodstream. And with little money, little will to live, and contempt for doctors, she will not be one of the ones she's read about, who find a miracle drug cocktail and go on living, only slightly inconvenienced. No, she'll be like one of the gay boys in the 1980s, who wound up gasping for breath, reduced to skeletal wraiths covered in Kaposi's sarcoma lesions. She could see it all before her.

Suddenly, returning to the bus stop didn't have quite the allure or the feel of common sense Elise thought it should. Why did it always seem, in the end, there was really no free will and that choice was just an illusion? *Freedom,* she thought, recalling Janis Joplin, *is just another word for nothin' left to lose.*

Still, she had promised herself she wouldn't come back here, wouldn't answer the siren call of a beautiful woman whose skin reminded her of milk and roses, and her hair of silk. She promised herself that life, in whatever form and no matter how bad, was preferable to the unending sorrow and isolation these creatures seemed to promise. What's happened to her will, so defiant it caused her to cast away everything for the sake of art? How has she come to bend so easily to a pretty face, a graceful form, the promise of love?

She swallows and raises her hand to knock. Drops it back down.

It isn't just the promise of love. It's the reality of it. The pull of Maria has her in its grasp and it isn't letting go.

Surrender, Dorothy.

The door, painted black, is alive — moving imperceptibly, breathing, waiting; the watchful eye of a cat just before it pounces.

Behind her the sky is a mass of darkening purple clouds, as dusk winds down into night.

They're inside now, willing me to come in. Elise can see them, coming down the stairs, dressed for the evening, their eyes locked on the front door, knowing she is out there, knowing she is tormented. Elise doesn't shiver in terror at the thought of them. She knows they won't hurt her, that she is beyond the reach of their flesh-shredding fangs, their hungry, sucking mouths. For some reason, maybe her art, maybe simply because Maria likes the feel of her and the taste of her skin, she has been elevated to a place of safety and protection.

But they will hurt someone tonight. That's the reality. There is someone out there, a stranger, who will get hurt, who will have his or her blood sacrificed to feed them. Perhaps the twelve-year-old black boy she has seen on Greenview, the skinny one in baggy pants and a hooded oversized sweatshirt, who relentlessly rides a kid's bike, far too small for him, up and down the street, stopping only to ask what time it is, or when a stranger calls down from a window. He's making a living, just like Elise. He's all alone, just like she is. He wouldn't be missed, except maybe for a moment, by those who depend on him for their daily fix of whatever potion he sells. It's no wonder he keeps the hood of his sweatshirt up at all times, cauling his face, hiding it in shadow. Or perhaps they will take Betty, the old streetwalker Elise has spoken to on occasion. Overweight, well past forty, with missing teeth and too-dry dyed red hair, she is no longer a hot commodity and has trouble even finding someone to heed her bargain rate of five bucks for a blow job in an alley behind the liquor store. She certainly wouldn't be missed. Nor would the man on the corner, a young guy, too robust and handsome to be begging, but who daily stands there exhorting strangers to give him a quarter, a dollar, so he can get back to the south side on the el. No one, not even anyone on the south side, would be looking for him.

But whether they're missed or not isn't the point. They're alive. They have every right to go on living, and these people inside have no right to take it away.

She turns, looks longingly at the ebb and flow of the traffic rushing by on Sheridan Road. She's frozen. The rational part of her, the part that tells her the people inside this house are insane, homicidal, or worse, what they say they are, prods her to flee. But that part isn't strong enough to inspire her to move more than this half turn that places her back at the door. She has no choice. Logic tells her to stay away; the danger is real. But her emotions, an artist's curse and blessing, cause her to place her hand on the doorknob and turn. Somewhere she has read that the artistic temperament is not a temperament at all, but just another form of insanity, a way to escape the real world and hide behind the imaginary, creating an alternate existence that could never satisfy, and that as they get older, artists just become more and more insane.

Even as she's thinking this, she's wondering about the forbidden fruit for which she longs so irrationally. *Fuck it.* She pushes the door open, hungry for the fruit, all the more tempting because it is forbidden...and starving for something as simple as the feel of a lover's arms. She slips inside, a whisper, shutting the heavy door behind her. The door closes almost of its own accord, the heavy oak swinging back silently, as if the house itself is unbalanced, so that gravity pulls the doors shut (like a trap after the prey has entered). Her heart pounds; her stomach is in knots. These responses are not because she's afraid, but because she now has the prospect of Maria close at hand.

She can't wait to see her.

Inside the foyer, it is quiet. Elise moves silently across the marble tiled floor, heading for the gallery. Her hands tremble and blood rushes in her ears. Funny, how it all comes down to blood rushing.

She stops. She opens her eyes. She pauses outside the tall archway opening into the gallery, standing breathlessly outside the arch, back to the wall. *Go inside*, she tells herself, forcing one foot in front of the other. She closes her eyes, gingerly feeling her way, not sure what she's afraid of seeing.

A hundred, no a thousand, candles glimmer, casting flickering illumination on the sculptures, paintings, and drawings. The shadows and warm yellow light bring the pieces alive. The paintings shimmer, and the sculptures moves: a gesture, a leap, a twirl caught in periphery. Elise is still in the light, her senses for a moment quiet, absorbing.

This quiet doesn't last long. There, in a corner, warmed by the light of the flames, is Maria. She wears a flowing dress of white lace, no shoes. Her hair is brushed away from her face and her dark eyes drink in the light. Elise could fall into their darkness. The connection between their gazes is electric, the culmination of days of psychic connection. Now, Elise understands why she was so helpless to leave, why the thought of turning away from the door just moments ago was something that just couldn't happen.

They don't speak. Who has need for words? The communication between them is so complete that it makes the words look like crude tools, inelegant and in a different league from this silent connection they share. It's pure emotion, pure understanding, with no need for definition.

The walk across the candlelit space seems distorted, longer than it actually is. Desire and anticipation makes their course toward each other something seen through a tunnel, a weird lens, elongating distance.

Finally, they are in front of one another, close enough to touch, and each pauses to drink in the smell of the other. There is caution; Elise supposes neither of them want to spoil the moment's perfection, or make a false move. Almost imperceptibly, they raise their hands, stretching.

Finally, they embrace. Elise fears her heart will explode; the adrenaline has the force of a shot of coke, or crank. Maria's proximity causes her breath to quicken. She no longer cares about the iciness of Maria's touch; she wants to devour her. Her mouth finds the silk of Maria's body, sinking her tongue into yielding flesh.

Their bodies intertwine, nearly become one. They sink to the floor and hold each other, attuned to their breathing which soon takes up the same rhythm and pace.

"I knew you would come," Maria whispers, kissing Elise's ear.

Elise feels hot liquid at her eyes but doesn't want to analyze what's causing the tears. "I knew I would, too." Whether the inevitability was a good or bad thing was something she would save for later analysis.

"Yes." Maria draws a small pipe from between her breasts. "I've been saving this for us, for when we could be together again." She hands it, along with a silver lighter, to Elise.

Elise wants to giggle, but reins it in, afraid of spoiling the moment. Yet she eyes the resinous bud in the bowl of the pipe warily; she can't imagine being in a realm higher than she is now, and wonders if partaking will send her over some edge beyond her imagining.

Maria grabs her hand and guides the pipe to her lips. "Just a little. It will make things perfect. Trust me."

Maria's dark eyes boring into her own make Elise weak and powerless. Shutting out the thought of where such trust has gotten her so far, she puts the stem to her mouth, lights the bud, and draws in deeply. She imagines the thick, blue-gray smoke inside her, expanding, rolling like a fog through her lungs, tainting and thrilling each of the millions of alveoli clustered there. The smoke smells sweet, with a piquant undertone that makes her think of the incense the priests used to perfume the air at mass when she was a girl. The religious association is not lost on her. She closes her eyes, exhaling slowly, handing the pipe back. Maria's fingers brush hers as she takes the pipe and even this tiny touch is electric.

When the marijuana overcomes, Elise feels once more the reality of everything around her melting into the simple presence of Maria. It is as though the herb has freed her to concentrate on only one thing, and Maria is a huge looming presence, giant, all-encompassing. Elise lies back and pulls Maria on top of her; the weight is light, almost as if she is pulling a comforter over herself. She doesn't remember them removing their clothes, yet now their bare skins merge, each part sensitive and hungry for more touch, an addict after the ultimate fix. The slippery touch of Maria's lips moving down her body, lingering at her nipples, biting gently, enough to break the skin, but not draw much blood, and finally kissing downward, filling her navel with moisture and then moving further, slowly, slowly, until Elise can hardly bear the anticipation.

Maria nestles herself between Elise's legs, the dark silk of her hair brushing her thighs, her tongue speaking an ancient and entirely new language, one much more eloquent than words. Elise arches her back and moans and loses track of her own existence. More than bodies come together: their intellects, their souls merge, unite. It is as though this communion of flesh, sensation, and mind is a rite that makes their union permanent.

This is not a sex act; it's a marriage.

After, they are exhausted, panting and sweating in a mass of clothes on the floor, lying in each other's arms. It takes forever for Elise's heartbeat to return to normal, for her face to cool, for her to become aware of her surroundings once more.

Maria runs her fingers lightly across Elise's rib cage, then gets up on one elbow to peer down. "Thank you for coming back. I wasn't sure you would." She shakes her head. "In fact, I was pretty certain you would not. And that made me think of leaving here. I didn't know if I could bear the proximity. But you returned."

"I don't know that I ever had a choice."

"There's always a choice." Maria brushes some of Elise's hair away from her face. She pauses for a while, staring off into the darkness, the dying embers in the fireplace.

"What are you thinking about?" Elise takes Maria's chin and turns her face toward her. "I can tell...something."

Maria smiles.

Elise notices the smile is tentative, and it's the first time Elise has ever seen the woman lose her confidence and poise, even in this small way. She can tell she's actually nervous about what she wants to say. "What is it, Maria? What do you want?"

"I think you know what I want."

Elise's heart thuds. She nods.

Maria sits up straighter, her lips tighten. She forces herself to look Elise in the eye. "I want you to be with me. To be one of us."

Elise turns away. It's too soon. She hardly knows this woman, and yet feels she knows her better than anyone she's ever encountered in her life. And what she knows of Maria is also a paradox: terrifying and tempting at the same time. She wants to be careful what she says in return.

"I don't know, Maria. I don't know if I can." She gives a small, mirthless laugh. "I'm not even sure I believe in you, in what you are. How can I become something that maybe is imagination, fantasy, the byproduct of an unbalanced mind?"

"You know everything you need to know. I know you believe me when I say we have communicated in a way that transcends human language. You know me instinctively. And, because you're open to that knowledge, because you can actually absorb it, you *can* be one of us." Maria touches Elise's face. "You can. The question really is: will you? Can you give me that gift? I promise to give you just as much in return. More."

As Elise's head clears, she has the urge to flee once more. This is insane. "So you want me to be one of you? So, so what? So we'll always be together?"

"Always."

"And it would mean becoming one of you? How would that happen?"

"It's a gift I can give you. And one that we do not bestow very freely. The last person to receive that gift was Edward, and that was almost sixty years ago."

Elise thinks she hears someone move in the darkness, a sudden rush of air, almost like a sigh. She shivers and peers into the shadows, but sees nothing. She turns back to Maria. "What will happen to me?" She thinks of vampire lore, the Saturday evening "Chiller Theater" double features she watched as a child, *Nosferatu*, and rivers of blood, bat wings, fangs. "How could it not hurt?"

"I promise you. I won't let you experience any pain. I'll lead you through it slowly, my love. The change will take some time, but you'll find it painless."

"And I'll have to do what you do to survive?"

Maria nods, stroking Elise's cheek. "Your perception of it is at odds with what you'll feel once you've crossed over. You'll come to see it as a beautiful thing, more satisfying than sex, more fulfilling than anything you've ever experienced, that much I can promise." Maria does not meet Elise's gaze as she says this. Elise wonders why.

"The idea revolts me." Again, Elise's intellect and emotions war. "I don't think I could do it. First, I couldn't kill anyone. I don't think I could, not even for my own survival. Second, I'd have to consume blood? Just thinking about it makes me sick." Elise sighs. She wants to please Maria, but doesn't think she can go as far as Maria wants. Can't they just be as they are now? Why does she have to become one of them? "Really, Maria, it would make me sick. I can feel the bile rising up now."

Maria shakes her head. "It won't be that way. What you feel now won't be what you feel...after. You won't be the same and you'll experience things in a new way, an exciting way." Maria pauses to look at the moonlight shining on the floor, turning her head, apparently lost in thought. "I wish I could show you how it would feel. But there's no other way to experience it besides doing it, besides actually becoming one of us. It's a kind of heaven."

"Why won't you look at me?" Elise takes Maria's face in both her hands, framing it, and turns the other woman toward her, forcing her to meet her gaze.

"Don't you trust me, Elise? I love you. Can't you see I only want what's best for you, to bring you the kind of joy you can't even imagine now? It won't be as you think. Nothing you've experienced in your life can compare to the joy and pleasure feeding brings."

Elise grimaces at the word "feeding," but feels herself slipping away, beginning to be won over. It's not about the pleasure of "feeding" or any of that mortality stuff; it's about Maria and joining with this beautiful, enigmatic woman that she knows, after only a couple of meetings, more intimately and better than she's ever known anyone in her life. But she has to continue this dialogue, has to be sure. She asks what she thought earlier. "Why can't we just continue on as we are now? Isn't this good enough?"

Maria smiles and shakes her head. "It's wonderful, my darling. But we're not on the same plane. I want you with me forever. I want us to be as one. Your years pass by like weeks for me; soon you will be an old, frail woman, and I'll still be like this." She nods. "Don't you want that? Eternal youth? You'll always be as radiant as you are right now."

Elise whispers, "I don't know," but it's obvious from the sheepish smile and the way she looks teasingly at Maria, like she has a hidden gift for her, that her resolve has all but slipped away. What does she have to cling to in her life anyway?

Possibility, a small voice answers her. But she drowns it out and lets Maria embrace her.

"I'm so happy. It will be wonderful. You'll see. And we can always be together."

Elise collapses into her arms, shutting out thought.

IN THE DARKNESS, in the deepest shadows of the cavernous room, Terence crouches, as silent and unmoving as the sculptures surrounding him. His face is hot with rage. He feels sick with betrayal.

How could Maria do this? It is against everything they had ever agreed on, against what others like them, except even older and wiser, have told them is wrong. It is akin to what the humans thought of as murder: an ultimate crime.

But Terence knows he has never been part of the morality police. The fact this is wrong among their kind isn't what really bothers him. It's the betrayal! He feels abandoned, like a child who suddenly realizes he is not his mother's favorite.

He bites down on his lower lip so hard he breaks the skin and tastes blood. Blood that is not his own. A memory from just hours ago comes back to him.

"Hi. Where are you off to?"

"I'm on my way home from school." She eyes him warily and he can see the tiny war going on inside her: the attraction of a young woman tempered by the fear of a little girl. It is up to him to see that the woman takes the upper hand. He knows from experience this is not difficult work.

"What's your hurry? Why don't you stop and talk with me a little." He smiles. "I'm Terence."

She looks up at him from behind a curtain of dark hair, blue eyes peering out from under a black fringe. There is a sprinkling of freckles across the bridge of her nose. Her lips are full. She is not yet beautiful, but she will be. Or would be, Terence thinks.

He licks the blood away from his lips now and remembers how he convinced her to take a ride on his bike, her schoolmates playing ally to him because she wanted to impress them, roaring off with this stunning older man in front of them all.

Her blood, inside him, is still warm. He had savored her, keeping her chained in the basement, feeding slowly from her over the past forty-eight hours, watching her weaken, until finally she was drained and her young life winked out. For two days, he luxuriated in her terror, watching her lose her mind with fear and revulsion as he ate her.

The lives of these monsters weren't always as romantic and glamorous as Maria portrayed it to Elise.

It isn't so much Maria's misrepresentation that angers him; it's the fact she is being so duplicitously selective in what she tells her...her...*beloved*. How dare she! How dare she leave out the most important part of what Elise might lose should she become one of them?

Terence leaves the room like a chill, hardly discernible. He knows one thing, and this is what enrages him most: he wants Elise for himself.

"SO, YOU'LL BE with me?" Maria searches Elise's eyes for verification.

Elise can see, again, how tentative she is, and it charms her. She sees the hope and the fear. It makes her feel that this is a person with feelings, not some horror-movie monster. She nods. "Yes. I think it would make me happy." Elise pauses. "But what about Terence? What about Edward? Will they be okay with this?" She stops to think for a moment. "Will they even be with us, or will we go off on our own?" Elise realizes it's this last option she really wants. She doesn't know until she utters her question, but the idea of being with Maria alone is perfection; being with two men in addition would take a different kind of adjustment. It's such a huge change; anything to make things simpler would make the transition that much easier. She pictures herself with Maria, a romantic notion, imagining the two of them in some crumbling villa in Greece, surrounded by olive trees and water so blue in the sun it is nearly blinding.

Maria reaches out and touches Elise's cheek. "Terence and Edward will be with us. They are like family to me. No, they *are* my family. We've been together for so long, longer than you can imagine. I will make sure they are all right with the change. You won't have anything to fear or worry about. In time, you'll find them the most delightful of companions. Terence can be, well, *Terence* at times, a little vain, a little self-centered. But, deep down, he's fiercely loyal and can be quite funny. Edward will love having you join us, I'm certain. You have so much in common." Maria looks away when she says this last part, and the fire behind her casts flickering light and shadow on her face. It crackles, and sparks shower out of the hearth as wood collapses and dies.

Neither of them says anything for a while. Elise notices the chill in the room and realizes the fire must be the only source of warmth. Maria doesn't look at her for a long time; it's almost as if she's forgotten Elise is there. But Elise watches as something dark and inexplicable crosses over her features; there's an internal dialogue going on. Maria's eyebrows knit together. She frowns.

Elise begins to grow afraid. She senses something awful is coming up. It's strange for Elise to shift from elation to dread so quickly, like a sunny day when a northern wind blows in, causing the temperature to drop twenty degrees. Elise feels like that now; she watches as storm clouds gather on the horizon. She's tempted to ask Maria not to go on, that whatever she wants to say, Elise can live without knowing. But she isn't that strong. Or that weak. She simply leans back on her elbows and waits.

Finally, Maria turns to her. She takes in a deep breath and her gaze is already beseeching.

Elise steels herself.

Maria waits for a moment longer, then says what she must. "There is one more thing I haven't yet told you. And I wish I could say it's a small thing, but it definitely is not." Maria slides closer to Elise, so their bodies are touching. "It wouldn't be fair if I didn't tell you."

Elise can stand the suspense no longer. "What is it?" she hisses, sorry for the note of annoyance and impatience that marks her words. She's afraid of what's coming next. It seems as though nothing can ever work out for her. She almost laughs, thinking, *not even becoming one of the undead.*

Maria breathes in deep. "When you cross over..." She stops, then starts again. "When you become one of us, things within you might change. You will still be yourself, of course, but your perception will be altered. There will be profound emotional differences; you'll see the world in a new way."

Elise blows out a sigh of relief. She is excited about this new development, this prospect. Sharpened perception? Seeing the world in a different way? What could be more exciting for a creative person? She understands Maria's concern, but this could be a very good thing. She smiles. "That might be good, you know. It could help my art." She smiles. "Sharpened senses never did an artist any harm." She expects Maria to smile back at her. When she doesn't, Elise shivers.

Maria stares down at the floor. Her lips flatten into a thin line, then become lush again as she lets out a rush of air. "And, I have to tell you this, I'm so sorry." She shakes her head. "But I'm afraid the truth is: it *could* harm your art. When perception changes, so does everything else. You're right, it could be a boon to what you create. But it could also take away your artistic sensibilities, your creative 'bent' if you will. That's your choice. It's a risk. But what isn't a risk is my love for you."

Elise bites her lip. Panic rises up, a scaly creature scurrying along her spine. "So you're saying this change could make it harder for me to create? That, essentially, there's a risk I could lose my abilities? That I might no longer be able to paint or draw?"

Maria swallows; her hands tremble. "There are few vampire artists. Your perceptions will be more acute, I promise you, especially with our herb, but their expression will more likely be in the form of the hunt, rather than on paper or canvas."

Elise turns away, bile rising. She pulls at her hair, hard enough to detach some of it, and cries out in a strangled wail. A vision comes to her with all the clarity of a movie: Black night, deeper than any black on her palette. Alone, she wanders the streets south of the Art Institute, streets abandoned, punctuated only by the sounds of the wind and the occasional el train, rumbling. Her face is smeared with blood, and she beats on the doors of the Art Institute, begging for admission. But no one hears except the stone lions guarding the place. Miraculously, they turn their leonine heads to mock her.

Elise struggles to her feet and dashes from the house, salt tears stinging.

ELISE CAN'T STOMACH the thought of public transportation. The bright lights and the crowds are a horror. She pauses briefly on the front porch, vision blurred by tears, the house an oppressive presence at her back. The structure feels more like something organic, something lurking behind her, waiting to pounce. Elise eyes it warily out of the corner of her eye, moving only an inch at a time toward the steps, fearful if she moves too fast, she will be caught up in its clutches.

What to do? How do I get myself home so I can crawl in my own little hole? Silly.

The house seems to move closer as she moves further away. She hastens her pace and trips as she comes down the steps, tumbling forward, and skins her elbow. The pain stings but it's welcome; it reminds her she's human, letting her know she can feel. She looks down at the swatch of black on her arm, the smear of blood. It always comes down to blood.

The traffic swarms by on Sheridan Road, a line of busy bright lights, like the eyes of insects. The air has turned even colder; Elise sees her breath emerging in blue-gray plumes as she runs, a madwoman, up Sheridan Road. She turns west, away from the lake, and heads toward Kenmore. The wind pushes her along, a cold hand at her back.

Kenmore is a good route for traveling north. There isn't as much traffic, and at this late hour, not much of anyone is around.

She glances down at her watch and sees that it's just past 2:00 a.m. Where did the time go so quickly? Had she really been inside with Maria for hours? The pot clouding her brain lingers, making Elise wish she could somehow force its soporific and confusing effects out of her bloodstream and nervous system. She needs to be clear.

It's not until she gets past Loyola University, and has been walking for nearly a half hour, that she notices someone is following her. It was on Greenview she first noticed the footsteps.

She hurries along, trying to vary her pace to hear if there is really someone behind her, someone trying to match her pace, so she won't hear him or her. Home is still miles away, but it's there, and it's home. Never before has she thought of her little rat-hole of an apartment as home, but relatively speaking, it's *Little House on the Prairie*. Suddenly, it appears in her mind as a sanctuary, a shelter.

She wonders if the footsteps had been behind her for much longer than when she first noticed them on Greenview. But when she had first left the house, she was so distraught she probably wouldn't have noticed a Pit Bull snapping at her heels. *Could* it have been that long ago? She imagined she only noticed the footsteps that mirrored her own...what? About fifteen minutes ago? Were they blotted out by her sniffling? Her quivering attempts to gain control of her breath?

The footfalls continue behind her, and she picks up her pace, not wanting to look behind her, not wanting to appear fearful. They draw closer, drawing a chill from her bowels up her spine. She can't stand it, finally, and stops.

There is no one there. The street, at this hour, is quiet, with only an occasional *whoosh* as a car whizzes by, its occupants oblivious to her presence.

But someone, she feels, is *not* oblivious. Over the course of the next few blocks, she repeats the pattern: noticing the sound of footsteps behind her, turning to look, and seeing nothing. When the echo of her own footsteps on the pavement stops, so do her pursuer's.

It wouldn't surprise her if she were going insane. It wouldn't surprise her if these footsteps were some aural hallucination, the beginning of a mental disturbance much more profound.

But for now, she doesn't have the time or the luxury of imagining that someone following her is all in her head. She has to worry about the chance that this is very real. She has to safeguard herself against the flesh-and-blood, fully alive monsters that haunt the streets at this early-morning hour.

Wouldn't the irony of this just be too rich? Elise thinks, quickening her pace. The footsteps behind her quicken accordingly. Irony: on the very night she has blown her opportunity for immortality, a streetwise criminal kills her. Perfect.

Her heart races, and in spite of the chill, a clammy sweat breaks out, coating her face, trickling down her back, tickling in a crawly, unpleasant way. She turns again, the panic rising like something hot and alive, and peers into the darkness. She sees the glow of a cigarette a block or two away; someone hurrying across the street. She doesn't think that person is even aware of her existence. Besides, if someone is following her, his or her footsteps are much closer. But where is that person right now? Elise searches the shadows of apartment doorways, the spaces between buildings. The wind, picking up as it blows across the lake, mocks her, making her think she's paranoid. Isn't paranoia a side-effect of marijuana? She wishes she could laugh, but thoughts of pot and paranoia do little to allay her mounting terror.

She takes a few more steps. So does her stealthy friend. She whirls around to face a potato chip bag and some dust whirling around in a mini-tornado the sudden, cold wind has kicked up.

"Look. I know what's going on, asshole." Elise steels herself, refusing to let even the slightest quaver creep into her voice. "You need to find yourself another route. This one's taken." Elise looks around desperately; in a city usually teeming with life, it is, for once, lonely. Perhaps if she runs back out to Sheridan Road? At least the lights are brighter there, and she has more of a chance of being around other people. She can even hail a taxi, even though she has no money. She could let the driver take it out in trade. It's not like she hasn't done it before.

So she turns and runs. Beneath the blood rushing in her ears, the rasp of her breath, and the gallop of her feet on the pavement, she hears someone running behind her, closing the distance. She wants to scream. She wants to stop, drop, and curl into a little ball. Fetal, letting whatever is going to happen, happen.

When a hand grabs her shoulder, the scream is at last freed.

Chapter
Eighteen

1954

EDWARD WAS A different person as he pressed key into lock just outside his tiny walk-up. It had been so long since he felt any kind of joy that his jubilance was akin to the effects of a drug coursing through his system.

The apartment was cold. Edward hurried to the window, closed it, and listened for the hiss and clank of his radiator. He turned to survey the paintings he had leaned against one wall, trying to decide which eight he should show. It was a tough choice. The show at Anima/Animus gallery would be his professional debut, his first steps into a different world from the one he now inhabited. He didn't want to be overly optimistic, but this show could be the key to a whole new life, a life that did not include living in cold-water flats in ghetto neighborhoods. One that did not include working at menial jobs to make barely enough money to cover the rent with hardly enough left over for essentials, let alone luxuries. Most importantly, a new life could also include validation and professional respect for his work — and that was what was really making him jubilant and hopeful. He already felt inspired, wondering if he should whip off his clothes and pull out the paints and create new pieces for his show.

Hold on now, you're getting ahead of yourself. Edward turned in the dimming light (dusk approached earlier and earlier each day) and thought what he needed, and what he deserved, was a celebration. The Tiger's Eye was only a few blocks away.

Who knew what would happen?

Edward arrived early at the Tiger's Eye. Outside, the night sky had faded from lilac, slate blue, and orange to blackness, yet it was still too early for most bars to be doing a brisk business, even ones like the Tiger's Eye that specialized in poor alcoholics whose dreams had been shattered. Even they, it seemed, preferred a later hour to begin their imbibing, at least in public.

No matter. The place would fill up. Edward slid onto a stool and lit a Lucky. There was still the smell of beer and cigarette smoke to inhale, the multi-colored hues of liquor bottles behind the bar, and the sound of

Eubie Blake playing soft in the background (with Charlie Thompson, the "Lily Rag"). When the bartender approached him, looking particularly delicious with his crew cut, T-shirt and tight black pants, Edward smiled, feeling the kind of confidence that had always eluded him. He only had a few dollars in his pocket, but the way he felt right now, he was certain he would not have to pick up the tab for many of his drinks. Not tonight. Not on this special evening, poised on the brink of the *future*.

"I'll have a Canadian Club; put a beer back on that."

"Sure thing." The bartender appraised him and Edward could tell by his smile he liked what he saw. Edward watched the tip of his cigarette glow in the dim light as he waited for his drink. In a minute, the bartender was back with a squat glass half full of amber liquid (a very generous shot) accompanied by a tall, sweating glass of cold beer, its golden hue topped with a head of white foam.

"What do I owe you?" Edward dug in his pockets.

"Nothing. The gentleman at the end of the bar says to put this on his tab."

Edward pulled his hand slowly from his pocket, wondering whether he should feel his lucky streak was continuing, or if he should be worried. He had thought the bar was empty when he entered. Even now, peering down the length of the bar, illuminated mainly by the soft light over the liquor bottles behind it, he found it difficult to see anyone. He stared, letting his eyes adjust to the low light level and finally saw him, dressed completely in black, stool positioned perfectly so his smiling face greeted Edward.

Edward turned back to the drinks on the bar, heart thudding. Terence. Edward picked up the shot glass and downed it. Holding up the empty glass, he shouted, "Another, please! And put it on the gentleman's tab. I'm sure he won't mind."

He slid from the stool, very uncertain as to whether this turn of events was a good thing or a bad one. The bartender followed him down the bar, shot glass in hand, waiting to see where he would light. He sat next to Terence, staring into his dark eyes for what seemed like a long time, but was really only a minute or two. The bartender slid his beer down and placed it in front of him. Edward smiled, the corners of his mouth quivering. He breathed in deeply. "What brings you out tonight? Slumming again?" Edward felt a low simmering anger and wasn't sure from where it was coming. He had wanted a wild evening out, to perhaps meet a boy and take him home. He wanted to laugh and drink. He wanted to be human, and enjoy the company of others of his kind: ruddy-cheeked young men bent on fornication. Terence, and his subterranean world, didn't apply. Terence was more like something out of a dream...or a nightmare.

He wanted to be among his own kind. Part of the anger, he realized, came from the fact he knew he would throw all these semi-wholesome pursuits away in favor of being with Terence. It felt like, when Terence was around, choice slid from his grasp. He didn't understand why.

Terence eyed him, a slight grin raising the corners of his lips. It was as if he could read the thoughts warring in Edward's mind as easily as he could the front page of the *New York Times* at the news kiosk just outside. "I wanted to see you. I heard that you had some very good news today." Terence slid an ice cube into his mouth, crushing it into oblivion. He grinned at Edward. "Someone's luck has changed."

"How would you know about that?"

"Word travels fast in the artsy-shitsy grapevine. You've seen my home. I'm a collector. Don't you think I have contacts? Don't you think Soho is abuzz with your coup with Mr. Gadzinski? How you're the next big thing? The flame and flicker of jealousy is already raising its ugly head. Tell me they're lying when they say you gave access to your ass to Mr. Gadzinski in exchange for access to his gallery walls." Terence placed a hand on Edward's thigh, sending what seemed like a jolt of electricity through him.

"Don't be stupid."

"Oh, I know it's just envy and despair talking. I've seen your work. No need to exchange sexual favors for a break. You deserve it. Besides, that kind of sexual contact cheapens both you and Mr. Gadzinski. He can get a piece of tail easily enough; there's no need to barter. Not with his influence."

Edward was surprised word had already leaked out about his upcoming show, which was barely confirmed, let alone planned or anywhere near execution. He was also annoyed his elation over getting the show was beginning to be eclipsed by a heat in his belly and further south over the nearness of Terence. That alone should have been sign enough for him to rise, thank him for the drinks, and head back to his original seat, or even straight out the door and up the stairs. There were plenty of other places he could drink in Manhattan. Plenty of other places to find a warm and willing companion for a night of celebration that would ultimately present its logical climax. Even the most lurid sex conducted in an alley or gangway seemed almost quaint in comparison to the dark delights Terence promised. He should go. He should really call upon his will power and get up and leave. There was nothing to stop him (even Edward wasn't sure he believed this) and the night was young and full of promise...without Terence.

But even though he thought these things, he remained rooted to the leatherette stool beneath his ass, drawn to the wan face and exaggerated cheekbones of his new companion, a companion from whom he knew instinctively to flee. Edward felt he was in addiction's grip.

Terence leaned in, his mouth close to Edward's. Edward thought he would faint. Terence whispered, "We should make a night out of it, celebrate. Don't you think?"

Edward leaned back. "I had kind of thought of being on my own tonight." Even as he said it, he knew his thoughts "of being on his own" tonight were nothing more than good intentions.

"Nonsense." Terence's eyes sparkled, even in the darkness. "Believe me, young man, I know how to celebrate. If nothing more, you'll take me up on my offer simply as a learning experience. Besides," and here Terence looked deep into Edward's eyes, "there's no refusing me."

The thought should have angered him. But Terence was right, Edward realized with a mixture of dread and desire. He was powerless, and the smart thing to do was to recognize that and go along with whatever happened. How bad could it be, anyway?

"Where should we go next? I'm in your hands." Edward gulped down the second shot and chugged his beer. "Completely."

EDWARD FELT QUEASY. When he closed his eyes, the room spun. He had reached the point in his consumption of alcohol where he wished there was a chance for remorse, to take back all the Scotch and beer he had downed as he and Terence made a tour of all the drinking establishments, both heterosexual and homosexual, in Greenwich Village's narrow streets. It was hard to remember the number of places they had been. Time was marked by the number of cigarette packages now balled up in his jacket pocket (two; he was working on his third). Terence had been an unstoppable guide to nightlife; Edward thought it should be Terence's picture appearing in the dictionary next to the term "libertine." In addition to all the drink consumed, Terence had pressed cocaine on him, showing him, in various, quieter men's rooms, how to snort the fine white powder up off of Terence's long pinkie fingernail.

Throughout the evening's libations and inhalations, Terence had teased Edward with the promise of a more physical connection than he had previously allowed. He exchanged meaningful, soulful glances with the smitten and hungry artist. He allowed the brush of a hand, or the press of a body against another, to linger beyond what anyone could deem accidental. Terence had even let Edward, after snorting a mound of cocaine off of his fingernail, impulsively kiss him, Edward both thrilled and repelled by the cold, dry lips.

And now, Terence allowed Edward to rest his head on his chest. The public display was all right; they were at Luke's. At this late night hour, the only other men in the bar were those who would approve or envy.

Edward had just about summoned enough courage to slur, "Do you think you could come home with me tonight? Couldn't I just touch you?" He had imagined it would be enough just to sleep next to Terence. But Terence had other ideas. Before Edward could sort and collate the thoughts racing around his fevered brain, Terence asked,

"What do you think of that one over there?"

Through bleary eyes, Edward looked in the direction Terence had nodded. In a dim corner, a pale, skinny young man, almost waifish, danced alone. Alberta Hunter crooned and the boy was lost in her smoky voice, singing about "my man." He moved his hips slowly and had his arms wrapped around his lithe torso. It should have been comic, but it was provocative, probably because the boy was so lost in the music and his movements that his immediate surroundings, Edward was sure, had disappeared. The boy had straight black hair falling into his eyes and his short red shirt had risen up to expose a white belly, sharply defined by muscles undulating just beneath his skin.

Edward breathed in deeply, both troubled by Terence's interest and intrigued by it. Even though he considered himself worldly, he had yet to engage in a *ménage à trois*. Would this be his first? Should he look at it as a gift from Terence? Even though Edward was pretty sure Terence wouldn't allow him to make love to him, perhaps he wouldn't mind watching him with the dancer, directing and orchestrating their movements. The idea had its appeal.

"Why do you ask?"

"I'm intrigued by him, by his apartness from everything around him and his lack of self-consciousness. He's quite beautiful, in a coltish sort of way. Don't you think?"

Edward nodded. The boy had opened his eyes and was now staring at both of them with what looked like complete knowledge of what the two men were discussing. His eyes, even from across the room, were both a welcome and a challenge. "Yes," Edward mumbled. "I do think he's beautiful." He nudged his head closer into Terence's chest and lifted his arm to surround his waist. "Are you just asking for my opinion, or did you have something more in mind?"

Terence grinned. "I had a little something more in mind. What do you think? Should we ask him to join us? Do you think he can appreciate the pleasures of alcohol and cocaine with two gorgeous men?"

Edward stared at the boy, wondering if what appeared lithe in the murky light of the bar was really malnourished and what he was seeing beneath his skin were not, in actuality, muscles, but ribs. Would they be offering him an evening of debauchery and twisted fun, or would they be exploiting the weak? He knew it was the latter, yet it didn't stop him from wanting to please Terence and to assuage his own curiosity as to just where this meeting could lead.

"I think he would appreciate shelter! The nose candy would be a luxury thrown on top of it."

"Oh, don't become a social worker on me. Do you want the boy or not?" Terence lifted Edward's head away from his body, fingertips under chin. "Hmmm? I can procure him for you, you know. For us. Come on, Edward, be wicked. This is supposed to be a celebration. Let me go talk to him. I'll set everything up. You won't have to do a thing, except enjoy him. He looks like your type."

Edward felt abandoned, yet somehow his penis was rising, making his pants tight. It was engorged with blood, diverting the flow of it from his brain to regions south. "What if I don't want to?" His breath eluded him and his heart raced. But Edward knew things had already gone beyond choice.

"You do want to. It will be fun. I'll be with you. We'll do this together." Terence leaned in, his face closer, closer, and kissed Edward deeply, his tongue exploring the inside of his mouth. Edward grabbed and held on.

When Terence pulled away, Edward was even dizzier.

"Yes?" Terence eyed him.

"Yes."

Terence was off his stool quickly, almost as if Edward had shouted, "Go!" Edward watched as Terence crossed the room, elegant all in black, his pure white skin a sharp contrast. He approached the boy, hands on his shoulders, and leaned in to whisper.

The two turned toward Edward. Terence smiled. The boy's features betrayed nothing, only a kind of resignation. To seduce? To entrance?

He led the boy across the bar until they were in front of Edward. The boy suddenly seemed larger, heavier, as if viewing him from a distance had made him somehow a vision. Edward could see that his clothes were grimy and his dark hair, which had seemed so shiny, was really slick with grease. Why, he was nothing but a street waif!

"Shall we go?"

Edward closed his eyes and bit the inside of his lips. *Powerless,* he thought as he stood up, and took the boy's other arm to guide him from the bar.

EDWARD SWALLOWED, TOOK a drag off his cigarette, watching its tip glow orange in the darkness. His throat was burning and the little tar, nicotine, and tobacco-wrapped paper parcel tasted horrible: scorching and sour. His nose was clogged with thick mucous from the ingestion of a prodigious amount of cocaine, so clogged, in fact, he couldn't exhale through his nostrils. He sat on the hard wooden floor of his apartment; outside the sky was lightening, its gray fingers grabbing onto his windowsill and hoisting themselves into his squalid room. The orchestra of car horn, exhaust, street vendors, and footsteps was tuning up, building to a crescendo that would not cease until the wee hours.

His head felt like it had been placed into a vise that an outside force was turning slowly, tightening, tightening.

Edward turned his hand and looked down at the smoldering cigarette between his fingertips. Even though he had long ago passed the stage where he got any enjoyment from them, he kept lighting cigarettes one after another. They helped mask the taste that was underneath. He wanted to eradicate that taste, but it seemed no amount of smoke could burn it away.

The taste was an undercurrent, hinted at, yet powerful: a sharp, metallic tang.

Blood.

Edward closed his eyes, and red swam on the inside of his eyelids. He blinked his eyes open, and winced.

The remainder of the night with Terence had gone pretty much as he might have predicted, if he'd had the wits to predict anything, but his head was so fogged by scotch, cocaine, and lust he could barely predict where his foot would go next as the three men climbed the stairs to his apartment. In his dulled mental state, he had become a canvas Terence could stretch at his will, paint on at his whim, making Edward his own personal creation. Whether the result was art or not was difficult to say.

The boy, whose name was Ned, had been eager for the substances Terence offered, snorting lines of cocaine carefully laid out by Terence across Edward's belly, drinking single malt Scotch in gulps straight from the bottle. Ned didn't say much and his giggled responses spoke of someone who didn't have many brain cells left. He was a desperate boy, living off men who exploited him.

Edward might have felt sorry for him and called an end to the escalating debauchery if he had been clear-headed, if he could have seen into the future and known for certain there was no sexual liaison waiting for him with Terence.

But, like the boy, Edward followed obediently as Terence called out instructions for the two. They were like models, creating tableaux for their rich benefactor's pleasure. They became creations ripped from the imagination of the Marquis de Sade. Here was Edward mounting the boy dry, trying to shut out the boy's whimpers beneath him as Terence clapped and laughed. Terence and Edward held each other's gazes while Edward's hips moved rhythmically, thrusting into the boy, never approaching anything remotely like a climax. There was Ned, on his knees before Edward, endlessly tonguing him with a kind of detached boredom. Finally, Edward exploded down the boy's throat, but only after Terence had dropped his black pants, exposing himself.

But all of the sex was a pastoral scene painted by Monet compared to what followed.

"Have you ever tasted blood?" Terence leveled his gaze upon Edward, who was lying across the boy's lap. Ned was leaning against the wall, legs splayed out in front of him, head tipped forward, and snoring.

Edward turned his head and looked at Terence dully, a disbelieving smile slowly making its way across his face. "What do you mean?" Edward closed his eyes in an attempt to stop the room from spinning.

"Yeah. I guess so. When I've cut myself and I suck on my finger or whatever."

Terence reached out and tousled Edward's hair. "No, I mean have you ever actually tasted the blood of someone else? Have you ever felt the hot rush, the pump from vein into your mouth?"

Edward smiled dully. "You're kidding, right? What are you tryin' to say here, Terry?"

Terence said nothing for a moment, letting the nickname emerge and die in the air like a bad smell.

"What I'm trying to say is that I would like to introduce you to a whole new world of pleasure. What I'm *trying* to tell you is that there are realms of delight out there you haven't even imagined, places I can take you that make pleasures like sex and drugs pale in comparison; pleasures that make those things seem pedestrian. And these pleasures can all be found in the hot, scarlet life of blood. Human blood."

Edward blew out a sigh. "You're sick, man."

Terence lifted Edward off the boy's lap and held him close. He whispered in his ear, "You want to be close to me? You want to share the ultimate in intimacy with me? Then you need to follow my lead."

Edward watched as Terence laid the boy gently across the mattress on the floor. His lithe form and pale skin seemed almost neon in the darkness, a separate form rising up out of the mess of sheets and exposed striped mattress ticking. Edward wanted to concentrate on the alabaster form, how the skin, sweat-slicked, looked like stone. He didn't want to think about what was coming. He tried to concentrate on the simple beauty of the prone boy, trying to ignore the pounding of his heart, the quickening of his breath, and the yammering in his brain, the one he had heard so many times when Terence was around, to flee.

"Let's make this interesting." Terence stood and began shedding his clothes, piece by piece, making a circle around Edward's small apartment, dropping a silk shirt here, black twill there, a sock in the sink, another on top of the radiator.

Edward stared at Terence, mouth open, breathing hard. His body was flawless, like Michelangelo's *David*, only better endowed. Terence was simply the most beautiful man (or should that be creature?) Edward had ever seen, and his beauty was like a shock to his system. He could scarcely move. He could scarcely breathe.

Terence squatted down beside Edward and Edward gazed dully into his dark eyes. He felt helpless, knowing every move Terence made was part of his seduction and he wasn't even resisting enough to make the game interesting. Limply, he let Terence undress him, the long fingers moving expertly over his body, unzipping, unbuttoning, tugging, and pulling until Edward lay bare before him. "Kiss me," he mumbled weakly, sounding desperate and hungry (which he was).

And Terence complied, giving him a deep, probing kiss that seemed to go on for hours, pressing his cool, smooth skin against

Edward's fevered flesh, sweaty and sour from all he had ingested during this night of "celebration." Terence spread himself out on top of Edward, pressing him back against the gritty wooden floor. Edward maintained an erection, which was a particularly Herculean feat, considering the vast quantities of Scotch and cocaine he had ingested. He moved his legs apart, scissoring Terence between them and urging him further.

Terence sat up and shook his head, wagging a finger. "Now, now, my sweet. Don't try to push for a greater advantage than I can give you. When I said we could be intimate, I didn't mean in such a base way. I have better ways of penetrating you, my lad. You'll see." Terence stood and crossed the room to fumble in one of his pants pockets. He returned with the familiar-looking pipe and his sterling silver lighter, glinting from the moonbeams coming in through Edward's window.

Edward propped himself up on his elbows and sighed. "I don't know if I can take any more tonight. My head is already spinning." Edward still wasn't sure if that particular effect was due to the drugs or to Terence's proximity and nakedness.

Terence fired up the bowl and drew in deeply. Holding in the smoke, he held the pipe out to Edward and croaked, "Take it. It will calm you and make everything..." Terence's voice trailed off as he blew a plume of blue smoke into the air, perfuming it with the pungent aroma of cannabis. "It will make everything *sacred*, in a way."

Edward rolled his eyes, but didn't call Terence on the hyperbole. Like a pupil, or a slave, he took the bowl from Terence and drew in, imagining the smoke rolling deep into his lungs, drawing in deeper than he ever had before and resisting the urge to sputter, to choke — and waste the smoke. He knew how powerful this was, and he craved the oblivion it would bring.

Edward was numb. Terence stood and moved to the boy. "Now I'm going to show you. Now I'm going to share with you a way to elevate yourself above the world you have known until this night." Terence put his hand beneath the boy's neck. The boy stirred slightly at his touch, murmuring something. But he did not wake.

Terence held the boy's head tenderly, gazing down at him.

And then he turned back to look at Edward.

In spite of the pot, in spite of the dulling of his senses, in spite of this weird love he felt for this creature, Edward felt an electric jolt of terror go through him, singing along his synapses, making it impossible for him to hold in the shriek.

When Terence looked back and opened his mouth to smile, he revealed not the teeth Edward had grown accustomed to seeing, but rows of tiny fangs.

Edward gibbered, giggled with horror as Terence growled and then tore into the soft flesh of the boy's throat, ripping his skin and unleashing a flood of black liquid that, in the darkness, looked like oil, a liquid quickly staunched by Terence's hungry, sucking mouth. Terence made small noises of pleasure and contentment as he took in the blood that pumped in slower and slower ebbs from the boy's dying heart.

Edward grew silent with shock.

Terence rent the flesh from the boy's neck and his face, gobbling it, exposing the sinew beneath, the muscles that had made the boy smile, laugh, and swallow. The attack was so sudden the boy didn't even have a chance to scream. A scream would have made the whole scene a little more real; the silence lent an even more disturbing edge. But quick, Edward supposed, was better.

Merciful, Edward thought.

And then Terence, his face smeared with darkness, moved back to Edward, who lay frozen as Terence came closer. As he lowered his face closer and closer to Edward's, Edward could do nothing but lie still, a stunned animal.

The kiss that followed was savage, deep, and possessed of a depth and intensity of feeling Edward had never known. He felt he had gone somewhere else. He felt he had died. Terence let the boy's blood flow into Edward's open mouth. It was hot, tangy with metal, and mixed with Terence's saliva, a potent drug.

Edward was lost. The taste of the blood awakened something in him, something beyond love, beyond his understanding. So he didn't resist when Terence urged him wordlessly toward the boy, guiding his head to the open wounds.

And Edward supped, hungrily drawing in the blood of a dead boy, hungrily taking the life Terence offered.

It wasn't until after the pair had nearly drained the boy of blood that Terence bit Edward, digging his fangs into the tender flesh of his inner thigh. He filled his mouth with Edward's own blood and then transferred it into Edward's hungry mouth, causing Edward to orgasm so powerfully he shuddered, banging his head on the wooden floor, eyes rolled back.

When he opened his eyes and looked up at Terence, he saw with an eerie clarity. It seemed lighter in the room and everything had a sharpness to it, as if he had only seen the world through a gauze caul before this.

Terence kissed his neck gently. "There. Now you're one of us."

AND THAT WAS all Edward remembered. He did not remember what happened to the boy's corpse or when Terence took his leave. He knew only that when night fell again, Terence would return for him and nothing would ever be the same.

Perhaps, Edward thought, if he had not blacked out, the course of history might have been altered and the boy would be alive and Edward would not be something that needed to crawl beneath a blood-stained mattress to avoid the nauseating rays of the sun.

Edward curled into a fetal ball beneath his mattress and slept. Finally slept.

Chapter
Nineteen

ELISE CAN'T STOP screaming, her shrieks ebbing away by degrees as she stares, wide-eyed, at the person who has followed her.

And realizes she knows him.

It's Edward. He grips her arms in his hands, eyes beseeching. "Please," he whispers. "I'm not going to hurt you. I just want to talk to you."

Elise stares at him, heart still thudding. She notices the way he looks away when he promises not to hurt her, staring down at the sidewalk, over to the parked cars on the street, anywhere but into her eyes. Is he lying? Is that why he cannot meet her gaze? Does that mean, when he says he doesn't want to hurt her, that he means the exact opposite? Elise doesn't know what to do, and the confusion is so intense, it makes her nauseous. She wants to turn and run. She shrugs out of his grasp and turns her back on him, thinking as she does that it's a stupid move. If he does want to hurt her, turning away from him will make her perfectly vulnerable.

She breathes in deep, trying to slow the pounding of her heart, trying to prevent the hyperventilation that feels imminent, that horrible sensation where the air disappears. It takes her several moments to calm down. She is certain she was going to be harmed...or murdered. She has read about such things in the *Tribune*, and heard the same stories, usually repeated in more graphic details, on the streets each night. But slowly, instinctively, she holds on to what she felt the first time she met Edward. He is a lost soul, like her. And her instinct, and her empathy, tell her she is in no danger.

She turns back to him, wary. He is smiling, supplicating. This is the quiet one, the one who stays in the background, never offering much. Elise has exchanged glances with him, little more, but has always felt he had more to say to her. Her mother had always told her, half jokingly, "It's the quiet ones you have to watch out for."

"What do you want to talk to me about? It's almost dawn, and I have to be getting home." Elise feels she will cry, yet, even though there are many reasons for tears, she isn't sure she can pinpoint even one of those reasons. Her vague confusion finds little comfort from Edward's gentle stance, his warm gaze, and his smile, all of which should reassure her that he has only her best interests in mind.

"There are some things you should know."

"Like what?" Even though the fear is beginning to ebb, her heart is still thudding, and the sweat on her skin feels cold in the night air.

"Things about me. Things that could be about you."

Elise doesn't know what to say.

"Listen, could we walk over to the lake? I just need to talk to you for a few minutes."

Elise shivers, in part at the prospect of being on the lakefront, where the air will be even colder, chilled by the wind racing across Lake Michigan, but more by the chance that Edward is lying. A stroll by the lake could be just perfect: quiet and, at this odd time just between night and dawn, empty. Empty enough so her quick startled scream will not be witnessed, will not be heard by someone foolish enough to try and come to her aid. She searches his face for some sign that might inform her, that might reveal whether his intentions are benign or evil, and sees only a little man who appears to be about the same age as she, whose pale eyes are filled with a kind of sadness and caring. She knows these things might all be part of the mask, a trap carefully laid to catch the unwary and the sympathetic (like her, just like her). And yet, at the same time, she wonders what he could possibly have to tell her. Does it have anything to do with the weird proposal she had tonight from Maria?

In an odd way, she trusts all of them. They could have easily killed her several times over already.

"I see you hesitate." Edward smiles. "I can't blame you. But I promise you I won't harm you." Again, Elise doesn't like it that he looks away from her when he mentions harming her. It could be just a coincidence, but maybe not. (She has a quick flash of herself as a little girl and how her mother could always get the truth from her by pointing at her own eyes, and insisting, "Look right here," whenever she thought Elise might not be telling the truth.) Edward is the only one of the trio she senses has a conscience. Even more than Maria, he seems still to have some humanity clinging to the monster he has become. He looks back up, and his gaze seems genuine, a true connection. Elise lets out a breath.

"There are some things I really need to tell you, things that have to do with what Maria asked you to do."

Elise frowns. Is this little inbred family really so close? Is nothing a secret from the other two?

Edward picks up the reason behind Elise's frown and admits, "Yes, I was listening. So was Terence. We never thought there would be a fourth among us." And it's here she sees his lips form a thin line, watches as his eyebrows move just a fraction of an inch closer together, but it's enough, enough to see the idea of her joining them makes him angry. Almost as quickly, the look vanishes, replaced by a slight, cockeyed smile Elise is certain is meant to charm her. This quiet one's thespian skills confuse and chill her.

"But I have no intention..." She stammers. The thought of a life with them doesn't make sense to her. She hasn't considered being part of some weird family, she only wants to be with Maria.

"I know. Neither did I. Maria can be very persuasive. You and I have a lot in common. Did you know that?" Edward cocks his head. "So, what do you say? Hear me out?"

Elise looks to the east; Lake Michigan is visible down the block. She won't ask herself, "Where's the harm?" because there could be many frightening answers to that question. She will go on faith. She needs to hear what Edward has to say. "All right. I'll come with you. But only for a little while."

Edward looks up at the sky; it's still night, but there is a dullness to it that signals morning's imminent arrival. "A little while is all I've got. C'mon, we'll go sit on the rocks."

They sit, the rocks cold and real beneath them. Elise thinks the rocks are about the only real thing about this whole scenario. She turns to look at Edward's pale profile in the darkness and tries to keep an open mind as he begins to talk.

"They found me in much the same way they found you: a creator, but someone who was lost, whose only connection to the world was through the images that I created with my hands and my mind." Edward smiles at her. "Like you, I was swept up in their strange beauty and their passion for art. Like you, I fell deeply in love with one of them." Edward sighs. "Terence cast a spell on me and it's yet to break." He puts a gentle hand on her shoulder; Elise thinks it feels like marble. "Unlike you, my dear, I was on the cusp of success. I was on the verge of getting serious recognition for my work." He smiles. "Not that your work isn't ready for such recognition, but a very influential gallery in Soho wanted to do a show of my work. They were very excited about it." Edward covers his face with his hands, and when he brings them away, Elise sees a tortured mask: a face contorted with grief and loss. "I gave that up. I gave that up not so much for immortal life—whatever that's worth—but for a chance at love." He lets out a bitter chuckle. "Love for someone who doesn't even love me back. Love for someone who probably never loved anyone other than himself his whole long existence."

Edward nodded. "Coming over to them took it away." Edward stares out at the dark water, eyes shining, lips quivering, until, finally, he breathes in deeply and turns to meet her gaze. "After...I could see better. I could see through the darkness and everything was more alive. There was an aura around people. All that would seem like riches for an artist, but after I crossed over, I couldn't paint anymore. The inspiration and that indefinable need to create just...died. As I did."

Elise hides her own face behind her hands. She wants to cry. She wants to be sick. She wants to envelop Edward in her arms and make the pain he has suffered go away. She wants to turn back time so he has the chance to undo his error. "So you lost your art? You lost your ability to create?"

Edward seems lost in thought as he considers the churning dark water before him. He touches Elise's face and his eyes shine in the darkness. "Keep your art. That's what I want to warn you about, Elise. Don't be like me. I was an artist, and I would gladly give up this hideous, perverse youth to have back just one night of feeling filled with the fire, the need to create, to get lost in the art."

Elise knows exactly what he means.

"You need to get away from them, from us, before it's too late. I'd like to tell you that I'm not a monster, but I am. Just because I can feel regret and can still weep doesn't make that any less true. *Keep your art.* Don't become a monster...paint them instead. Get away. It's simpler than it seems. But you have to go far away; you have to hide."

"You mean you, they, might harm me?" Elise breathes more quickly and hugs herself. Now, she sees the position she's put herself in without even trying: to join them, to spend her life hiding from them, fearful of every night born noise, every pale stranger, or to hold her ground and be dead within a few days...or even hours.

"Yes. You must not trust us, not even me." Edward leans forward, his arms outstretched, and Elise whimpers and falls into them. He draws her close and the two stay that way for several moments. Elise feels him shift and feels the cool touch of his lips on her throat.

Sitting up, she pulls away from him, seeks out his eyes, and muffles a scream. His teeth have become a row of tiny, pearlescent fangs. But here's the strange thing: Edward looks more shocked and frightened than she. And here's what's even stranger: when he realizes she sees, the fangs morph into normal teeth, so fast Elise wonders if she has really seen such a thing at all. It would make sense with all the stress of the past few hours she could hallucinate something as terrifying as what she just saw. Or did she? Perhaps that heavy, powerful marijuana they were always forcing on her had something to do with her vision.

Whatever the reason, she no longer wants to be near him. She looks at him, mouth open to say something, but no words emerge.

Edward says nothing more; there is a line of gray light along the horizon, capping the blackish, churning waters. "I have to go, before it's too late." He looks out at the rapidly lightening horizon. "Although maybe that wouldn't be such a bad thing."

Elise turns her head, runs her hand across the rough gray surface of the boulder upon which she sits. When she turns back to Edward to thank him, he's gone, as if he had never been there in the first place.

And maybe he hadn't.

Wearily, Elise stands. The sky is now purple, bruised-looking, and flecked with orange. She must find her way back.

Chapter
Twenty

ELISE'S WALK HOME is quiet. It's still too early for the swarm of rush hour traffic on Sheridan Road, still too early for almost anyone to be out, except people like her, who come alive at night. She passes a Loyola coed, stumbling back to the dorm after a night where she probably did something she will regret, at least until the next time. She doesn't look up at Elise as she passes, keeping her eyes downcast, a curtain of blonde hiding her face. There is a homeless man asleep in the doorway of a bank, still clutching a bottle sheathed in a brown paper sack, the front of his grimy pants stained dark. A young man hurries down a cross street, intent on getting somewhere. He is wearing a black leather motorcycle jacket and tight Levis, his hair close cropped. Elise wonders if his energy and hurry is chemically induced and what awaits him at the end of his journey.

At Morse, she turns off Sheridan, and walks to Greenview, where she will continue north to her apartment. Something has changed. Her breathing and pace seem easier, her step lighter. She has passed a test, one whose true nature will only be revealed after reflection. But she feels relieved that a chapter has come to a close. She is sad for Edward, trapped in a kind of hell, one in which he will never do what made him Edward ever again. But she is also glad he shared his story with her, making her final decision that much easier. She can now go on.

She can begin turning her life around. It may take a while to find a job that doesn't require keeping late night hours and spreading her legs for men who have enough money to employ her for a half hour, five minutes. But she's young and, unlike her sisters of the night, has not been plying her trade that long. They are trapped. Elise knows what it means to be trapped, because she has just avoided being ensnared — close call. Avoiding one trap has allowed her to recognize another: the kind of life she has chosen for herself was never one she planned on making permanent. But she supposes every woman who got into the rent game had the same thought, at first. And many of them never found their way back.

She will find her way back. She had allowed despair to make a home in her psyche; had allowed bad experiences in relationships to sour her outlook on love. She had let these things take away her hope.

No more.

She has only a few more blocks to go (three, maybe four) when she hears the footsteps behind. She grins and shakes her head. "Not again," she whispers to herself, glancing up at the milky white sky, its illumination full on for this day. She knows Edward is sleeping somewhere dark and wonders if he dreams anymore, or if even that bit of inspiration has deserted him.

She doesn't want to appear nervous or paranoid, so she doesn't glance over her shoulder. She tells herself that someone else is just following the same path as she, someone who is headed to Jarvis Avenue, or Fargo, or Howard Street, to start their day in some dead-end job.

Yet she wishes the quickening pace behind her would turn off the avenue, duck into an apartment building or a house, head for the el. She swallows hard, mouth dry, as the footsteps speed up and get closer.

You're being silly, she thinks, *lightning won't strike twice. No one is following you again. Besides, it's daylight now, things are picking up. Who would be stupid enough to try anything with her now?*

The steps have almost reached her and Elise feels a prickling sensation run up her back, like cold fingers.

"Can I ask you a question?" A gruff voice comes from behind.

Elise keeps walking, putting a little more speed in her step, already casting her gaze about for somewhere safe to run, for a stranger or a group of strangers coming her way.

"I said, can I ask you a question. Come on!"

Elise freezes and breathes in deep. She turns.

A young black man wearing a hooded sweatshirt and baggy jeans is standing in the middle of the sidewalk. He's smoking a little plastic-filtered cigar and appears nervous, shifting his weight rapidly from one foot to the other. His hood is pulled up, hiding his face in fleece and shadow.

Elise closes her eyes and thinks she'd be better off just to answer him; he is probably only going to hit her up for money for the train. Once they conclude their business, she can be on her way. And she will sleep for hours and hours. "What is it?"

"I don't got any money. I just need $1.75 for the train, or even a transfer, if you got one."

Just get rid of him, Elise thinks, digging in her pockets for change, for an errant dollar bill. She is both glad and sorry she didn't bring her bag with her.

All she comes up with is a quarter, a nickel, and three pennies. She holds it out to him. "Sorry, this is all I've got."

He slaps her hand and the change goes clattering to the ground.

"Bitch," he whispers. "Fuckin' white bitch."

She turns to run, but before she takes even a step, he is upon her, one arm pulling tightly around her waist and cutting off her air, the other arm up by her face, a hand clasped over her mouth. "We just gonna see if this is how much you got," he whispers. The low, soft voice is more terrifying than if he were shouting.

Elise struggles, pushes against him as he drags her toward an apartment building parking garage. Her screams are muffled under his hand, but this doesn't stop her from trying, searing her throat with her terror and her desire for help. She kicks at him, but this only makes him laugh.

He has her in the garage in a matter of seconds. They both pause, panting. Once safe in the shadows, he flings her hard to the ground, her head slamming down on the concrete. She sees stars. She bites down on her tongue as she makes impact with the concrete and tastes her own blood.

"No," she whimpers, hands fluttering up like birds to slap, to stop him.

He pulls out a gun, a little snub-nosed revolver.

"You just keep still if you know what's good for you. I ain't afraid to use this thing."

Elise knows from her time on the street that it's futile to fight back against a firearm; you always lose. Even though she knows he might kill her no matter what she does, her only hope for escape lies in cooperation.

"Okay, okay," she whimpers. Her tongue is already thickening. "Just don't hurt me. Please."

With one hand, he rummages through her clothes. She's sorry, terribly sorry, she hasn't worn underwear. His hands linger over her nipples, pinching. He slips a finger inside her, dry, and she winces and yelps with the sudden, sharp pain.

"Nice."

"Please, please don't." She pauses for a moment. "I...I have HIV."

"Yeah? Well so do I. Bitch."

"Come on. I'm for real. You can get AIDS. Just let me go and we can both forget this ever happened."

Elise knows no amount of pleading is going to change anything. She tries to go somewhere else in her mind as he rips the clothes from her, tearing them and flinging them off into a dirty corner. She looks desperately for a place that will take her in, that will at least allow a psychic escape. She shuts her eyes tightly as she feels him on top of her, struggling with the zipper of his jeans. Her thoughts race, going anywhere but here. Thinking of her girlhood home in Cleveland; thinking of a beach in Cozumel where she once walked with a college boyfriend; thinking of the house on Sheridan Road where Maria lives, and the art there. Each place slams the door in her face. In the end, there's only the throbbing pain in the back of her head; the cold concrete against her skin; and the taste of blood in her mouth. She is beyond tears. She goes limp.

And then he's ramming himself inside her and Elise shrieks. His hand quickly covers her mouth as he continues to thrust, each movement sending white-hot jolts of pain through her. She whimpers beneath his sour-smelling palm, afraid she will vomit into his flesh, that he will not remove his hand and she will drown.

Mercifully, it's all over in a few seconds. He pulls out of her and she looks down to see his cock covered in blood. "Shit," he whispers, reaching for her shirt to wipe himself off on. He flings the shirt over her face. "Thanks, bitch. Have a nice day."

And then he is gone. And then she really is sick, turning her head to go on and on, into the dry heaves. But no amount of vomiting can ever rid his memory from her.

Weakly, she gets to her knees. The pain throbs within her. She wonders if she has been ripped, if she needs a hospital. Of course, she does. But she knows she won't go. Sobbing, she struggles into her torn and bloody clothing and manages to stand, to hobble home, hoping no one will see her.

Chapter
Twenty-One

Present Day

SHE WONDERS WHEN these hot jets of water will go cold. Elise has been standing under the showerhead now for what seems like hours, unable to ever get clean again. Rubbing her body nearly raw, first using soap, then shampoo, then defoliating scrub, she's made her skin tingle and discovers abraded places, small patches of blood and torn skin exposed. And yet she continues to scrub, almost oblivious to the pain and damage she is causing, whimpering as the water sluices over her, slightly pink from her torn and bleeding skin.

She turns her face up to the spray, opening her mouth and gulping the almost scalding flow down her throat.

Finally she turns the water off and sits on the porcelain bottom of the tub, near the drain, shivering. A trickle of blood seeps from between her legs.

Mercifully, she has no memory of what happened to her, but it must have been something horrible—she'd never been one to shrink away from trauma. Hell, she'd seen her lover—or whatever Maria was to her—with blood on her face... *Blood.* She's bleeding! She looks down at herself, at her torn and battered body, and the sight nearly makes her faint. She knows only that what happened to her was something horrible, painful, and damaging, but when she tries to grasp the particulars, they scatter away like dream images.

"Maybe that's for the best," she whimpers, sliding forward until her face rests against the rapidly cooling tub bottom.

She lies in the tub for more than an hour. She gets up only when the chill and the shock cause her to shake so badly she isn't sure she can get herself to stop. Staggering to her bed with just enough strength to crawl in under the covers, she pulls them over her head.

Every light in her apartment is on, even though the sun has risen.

Her tongue is thick. It feels like she is under a blanket of needles; even the soft, brushed fleece of her blanket feels rough and chafing.

She closes her eyes and in seconds, slides into a deep, dreamless sleep, almost a coma.

When she awakens, sunlight floods the apartment, usurping the power of the electric bulbs, which are almost humming. She pokes her head out from under the blankets, breathing easier, the air cooling her sweat-slicked skin.

With re-awakening, Elise remembers the rape and the horror and pain of it. She realizes that shock had granted her a few hours of oblivion, but that has worn off. Now, reality sits squarely in front of her, and its knowing grin is hideous. She wishes she could turn back and continue to live in the kind of numbed ignorance she experienced before she fell asleep. By degrees, she manages to get up on her elbows, and eventually to a sitting position. Her breath is ragged and she hurts all over, especially her cunt, which is throbbing and cramping; the flow of blood has slowed to a trickle, but still not stopped. She wonders if she will ever heal.

In spite of the pain causing her to wince and cry out, Elise stands and moves like an old woman across the expanse of her studio apartment to the kitchen sink, where she turns the tap on (cold this time), splashing the water over her face and gulping it down, letting it run until it gets colder, colder. She holds her head under the stream until the cold causes her head to hurt, until the water sluices down her front and starts the shivering all over again. She pulls away, dons a T-shirt and shorts that were on a chair. She sits down near the window, hands in her damp hair.

"Why did this happen to me?" she wonders aloud to the empty apartment. But she's already learned this lesson: that there is little reason to the world, a place where the evil are victorious and the good cast aside, where the evil are squelched and the good were rewarded. It is all a random pattern and trying to figure it out is useless.

Outside, children's voices. School must have let out; she always notices how the noise levels rise in her neighborhood around three in the afternoon. They shout to one another. There's lots of laughter. How can they laugh? Elise wonders. How can anyone ever laugh again?

The flow of traffic outside her window grows louder as the late afternoon traffic increases. Cars pull up, double-park, honk their horns, engines idling just below Elise's window.

How does the world go on? It seems surreal.

She moves to the edge of her bed, icy water dripping from her forehead down her face, and has one thought: *Surreal or real, this is a world I want no part of.* She looks to her drawings and paintings, lined up along the floor, leaning against the walls.

If that's the price I have to pay...

She sits, quiet and as composed as she can be in her discomfort, hands folded in her lap and waits for the voices outside to lessen. She sits and waits for the darkness to fall. When twilight erases the bright yellow sun, she will call Maria. She will not use the telephone (which was shut off for non-payment two weeks ago anyway). She will use only her mind, only her heart. How could she have doubted being with someone where communication between minds is so certain, so secure? The fact they can sync this way foretells a relationship of honesty and togetherness. She thinks of a man, his voice scarred. "Can I ask you a question?" Her stomach turns and she gets half up off the bed, afraid she will be sick, but the moment passes.

Take me. Take me away and love me. She can't help sending the message out to Maria, even though the sun is bright. Who knows what messages penetrate her sleep?

She stands, makes a short circuit of her drab room, and shuts off all the lights. What will she really be losing anyway? She understands the love of darkness and feels like its shadow has been in the wings all along, even before she met Maria, waiting to claim her.

I'm ready now. Ready to come to you. Elise feels like she's walked down a road that ends in blackness. Not in shadow or darkness, but simply ends, as if nothing more exists at its edge. The thought is like what people believed before they accepted the reality the earth was round; that it was possible to fall off its edge and be consumed by monsters.

Take all of me. Consume me.

She returns to her bed and lies on her back, eyes focused on the ceiling, patient for it to get lost in shadows. Like her. Soon.

Chapter
Twenty-Two

Present Day

MARIA STIRS BENEATH the deep red blanket, its heavy damask over her head; it's like someone has lain a rug or tapestry overtop her. Heavy. But she's used to it. It blocks out all light, and that's what she was looking for when she bought it many, many years ago, from a vendor in an open-air marketplace in Venice. How things have changed since then.

She has a vague, uncomfortable feeling, as if someone is pounding on the front door downstairs. It makes her twist and turn in her half-sleep, cursing her handicap, cursing being unable to move when she needs freedom. But to move from outside the darkness would mean death.

It's not really knocking anyway that's making her anxious. The metaphor, though, is apt. Someone is trying to get in touch with her and she thinks it's Elise. Her senses will be more attuned once darkness falls, once she can bring a pipe to her lips, inhale, and transfer the fog in her brain to her lungs, leaving her alert and open.

But she feels vague distress. She is unable to pinpoint the particulars, and this inability makes it impossible for her to rest. She senses there has been harm. She senses a need.

She turns over on her back, then her side. Terence is next to her, still and unmoving. She wants to strike him. She needs someone to share in this agony of not knowing.

After what seems like days, the room darkens. The shadows move under the damask coverlet and penetrate it, much as sunlight penetrates the mornings of mortals. Maria gets out of her bed, not waiting for the familiar stirring of Terence and Edward. She hurries to the window, where the traffic is rushing by like a river of neon-eyed monsters.

She doesn't really get messages, not in verbal form anyway. This kind of communication is beyond words. But if she had to do a crude translation, what she would hear are these bald phrases:

I need you. I made a mistake.
I have been hurt badly.
Come to me.

I want to be with you for all time.

Maria hurries to dress, her clothing practical tonight, with no nods to the romantic. A black blouse, Levis, black boots. She pulls her hair back into a chignon and pauses only to take a deep breath of smoke just before she exits. There is a pipe and a bag on a small table near the front door for precisely this purpose.

She walks into the chill, damp night air, sending comfort.

I will be with you soon.

I will take care of everything.

I will give you the love and nurturing you need.

I rejoice that you will be with me.

Chapter
Twenty-Three

Present Day

IDLY, ELISE SITS at her drawing board, a piece of Vellum Bristol taped to its surface. She is trying to stop herself from sketching, but she can't. Every time she tries to pull her hand back, in which she holds a charcoal pencil, it's almost as though an invisible force puts it back.

The drawing is detailed. In it, she is lying on the floor of the parking garage, one hand held up in mute defense. Her attacker stands over her, shadowy save for enormous arms and penis, both drawn with quick, hard, and deep strokes, almost cutting through to the surface of the board below. The drawing ignites the horrible memory, which is playing on endless loop in her mind, despite her best efforts to block it out.

She has listened to music: the entire score of Prokofiev's *Romeo and Juliet* ballet. She has sorted through piles of whore clothes, stuffing the skirts, the bustiers, the short shorts, the leather pants, the fishnet stockings, spike-heeled shoes, crotchless panties, push-up bras into bags, all headed for the Dumpster outside. She has even run in place until she pants for breath and her body is slick with sweat. None of it makes the memory go away.

She has the idea that confronting it might make it vanish, hence the drawing. But the painstakingly rendered drawing at her fingertips only makes the memory more real, so real she trembles, and feels sick. But something will not let her stop.

As her room grows darker, she senses reassuring messages coming from Maria. The messages wrap her in a kind of warmth and make the memory disappear for an instant at a time. Not enough. She wonders how much will be enough.

She senses Maria is on her way, knows that soon, her life (death?) will be changing.

Scratch, scratch, scratch on the paper: his face is clear, the jaundiced eyes with their brown irises so black the pupils are lost in them, the wide nose, bent slightly to the left, the full lips and the front teeth with the gap. The drawing would be an excellent resource for police detectives, if she had the nerve or desire to contact the CPD.

Why can't she stop drawing?

Why can't she simply wait at her window, intent on the comforting vision of Maria pulling up in front of her building, come to claim her, come to rescue her from a life that is suddenly filled with only pain and degradation.

She sketches her mouth in an O, *à la* Munch. She takes care to draw her eyes, wide and almost bulging in terror, in anticipation of the pain she knows is on its way.

Why can't she simply put the pencil down? Is it because she knows she may never be able to draw like this again? Is it because, even though it's painful, this creation is the only thing keeping her alive?

She draws shadows. A gallery of rats in the corner of the garage, their tiny eyes glowing out of the darkness, bearing gleeful witness to her torment. In one corner a bat hangs down, its fangs dripping something dark and clotted. Snakes slither along the floor.

Monsters, all monsters. Except for her, at the center of things, the damsel in distress.

The symbolism tears at her. She tears the drawing up and scatters it on the floor, tearful and panting. Maria will be here any second, to take her away, to bring her down into a darkness that's safe and nurturing.

Is that possible?

Is what she's contemplating just another way to kill herself? A wild, romantic alternative to slitting her wrists and crawling in a warm bathtub, where her blood will seep out, turning the water crimson?

Of course not, she cannot believe that.

I am almost there.

Elise moves to the window and peers out at the night. A homeless woman pushes a shopping cart down the street, its wheels squeaking, almost drowning out her on-key rendition of "Between the Devil and the Deep Blue Sea." Her voice is surprisingly clear, a whispered soprano, not suited for the song at all, but makes the song's message, about obsessive love, all the more poignant. Elise watches her hobble down the street; the music fades, and finally disappears when the woman vanishes into an alley, probably to discover what edible treats the Dumpsters there hold for her.

Her head aches. *Maybe I should give this more time.*

The memory assaults her, twisting her gut.

I have to go.

She sits down suddenly in front of her stereo receiver and tunes it to a news station. Voices. She hasn't yet tried voices to block out the rapid-fire imagery with which her brain seems intent on torturing her.

Is it providence that makes the weather report end and the next news item to come up just as Elise tunes in? Normally, a grisly story like the one that follows the weather (fog, 70% chance of rain through the night) would cause her to snap the radio off. But the report makes her listen closer with a mounting sense of dread.

The story concerns Alicia Majors, a fourteen-year-old Senn High School honor roll student whose parents had reported her missing. Elise cringes when she hears the girl's body had to be identified through dental records, because "the teenage girl's skin had been flayed, leaving only muscle and bone exposed." Elise stuffs a fist to her mouth when she hears "nearly all of the girl's blood had been drained from her body." She stares out the window desolate, as the story winds up with phrases like, "evidence of sexual assault" and "the last to have seen Alicia alive." Elise closes her eyes and stops breathing when the announcer finally says, "authorities are looking for a tall, Caucasian male on a motorcycle. Classmates report seeing Alicia leave with this man. Anyone having further information should —"

Elise snaps the radio off, doing it quickly, then rushes to the bathroom to throw up what little she had in her stomach, mostly yellow bile.

After she rides out the heaves, she stands to look at her face in the mirror above the sink. Her eyes are bloodshot (she wonders if the force of her vomiting has caused blood vessels to rupture) and tearing. Her skin is flushed.

All of this due to being alive. Due to blood.

Blood that not even the dead Alicia Majors possessed any longer.

It is then the knock at her door comes. Soft, almost a tapping. It is then she feels the force of Maria, her monstrously beautiful face rising up in her mind's eye, her delicate, near skeletal limbs outstretched to embrace her.

Elise sinks down onto the cool of the tile floor, her eyes no longer wet from being sick, but wet from tears. She sobs as the knocking grows louder and more insistent. How long does she listen? Is it hours? She feels like a betrayer, but she cannot bring herself to get up and answer her door, not even to stop the knocking that makes her jump and start sobbing harder with each set of poundings.

She knows Maria will not come inside. Elise knows she has to invite her...and she isn't so sure that decision would be so wise, after all.

MARIA KNOCKS ONE final time, even though she knows it's useless. Her knuckles are raw. What has it been? Twenty minutes? It seems longer.

Maria slides down to the floor outside Elise's apartment and sits on the dirty floor, covered in carpeting so filthy no color can describe it. What should she do? She knows Elise is inside. Her warmth and her scent filter out. She smells the soap, the flesh, and even the blood pulsing underneath. She lowers her head between her knees and stares at the floor.

Of course, she's concerned. She knows Elise is alive, but wonders what kind of shape she's in, considering the pained and panicked tenor of the thoughts she sent out earlier. She is afraid Elise can't come to the door. What she fears more, though, is that she *won't*.

What really scares her is that she's lost Elise. What really scares her is that she won't answer twenty minutes of insistent pounding. And what terrifies her is that there is no answer to the thoughts she has sent. Behind the closed door is a deliberate psychic silence. Maria can't bear the thought Elise may have changed her mind and is ignoring her.

Wearily, she stands once more and raises her hand to knock. *No. It's no good.*

She wishes she could go inside, but she needs to be invited. It's one of those traditions the folklore got right. If she can go in, she can at least see if Elise is all right. She shrugs and her head droops. She frowns as she descends the short staircase to the vestibule. Maria can't believe it's possible to sting with this much pain. She thought she left this part of humanity behind centuries ago. She has lived as a hedonist, existing only for herself and her pleasure. She hasn't counted on falling in love, the ups and downs the emotion could cause. She knows why she has not pursued any attachments for so many years: this pain is insufferable; it is one from which even the living dead have no immunity.

In the glaring, fluorescent-lit vestibule, Maria leans heavily on the steel-framed glass door to push her way out into the night. The door swings behind her, but doesn't latch. She wonders how long the lock has gone unrepaired and if the owners of this building have any concern for its occupants. Probably not, but she does.

She walks by the front of the building and turns the corner. She gives a glance up to the window that opens into Elise's apartment and stops. Elise's face, tired, pale, and almost ghostly, gazes down. Their eyes meet for an instant and, with the connection, Maria experiences a jolt. She is just about to reach up and even begins to lift her hands toward the window when Elise moves back quickly from it.

Maria stops, stunned and embarrassed. She looks behind her to see if anyone has seen. She wants to cry out to Elise, but knows what statement her quick movement away from the window made. It is as much a rejection as if she has shouted, as if she has physically pushed her away.

Maria wants to cry. She feels confused. Despair and rejection are emotions she has not experienced in so long they feel odd, strange, almost a physical twinge. She surmises Elise assumed Maria has not seen her; the apartment is pitch dark and her movement away from the glass almost instant. Elise, though, hadn't counted on the abilities Maria has honed over many years to capture quick movement and to see into darkness.

For a moment, she wants to turn around and go back, pound on the door and demand to be let in. But she shakes her head and continues walking east on Howard Street. Yes, she felt nearly human for a few moments, but she never lost her dignity.

As she walks, her pace picks up, and she finds herself running. What is this dampness on her face? She pushes angrily at the tears, bringing her hands away smeared with blood.

Never again will she let anyone get close to her.

She stops when she can go no farther, when the broad, dark expanse of Lake Michigan stretches out before her. She stands alone on a beach and lets herself cry. She should have known this idea of love, this silly idea, was doomed.

Maria wishes she could walk into the silver-capped waves and disappear. She wishes she had never seen Elise...or her art.

Chapter
Twenty-Four

Present Day

THE BOY HADN'T put up much of a fight. It seemed they never did, anymore. Not since Tina had swooped into town and swept up Halsted Street, leaving death, despair, and a trail of broken promises in her wake.

The small pink plastic bag is still in Edward's pocket, the bottom and corner still retaining small shards of a whitish powder that resembles Drano. The bag had contained an eight ball of Tina, or crystal methamphetamine, if one wanted to get technical. Once upon a time, a little of his powerful reefer had been enough to lure the boys and dull their senses, but now crystal meth, affectionately referred to as Tina, was what the boys craved. Edward could buy a bag from a dealer on Cornelia Street, just off Halsted (also known as Boystown because of its preponderance of gay establishments, including several bars, a bathhouse, and a handful of adult bookstores). Proffering it around in the bars, he was suddenly like the Pied Piper; so many would follow him for a quick snort or two. This "poor man's cocaine," fashioned from ephedrine, drain cleaner, and other toxins, had taken a death grip on young and old in the gay community, in Chicago and across the nation. Edward had never seen a drug spike so rapidly in popularity. He was immune to its charms himself, which made it the perfect candy to lure little boys into his car, so to speak.

And he had used it tonight. Not only was his body craving fresh blood, but he needed to get away from Terence and Maria, both feeling their own personal anguish over Elise, and what needed to be done about her. He hadn't told them about their lakeside encounter. His trip out to the rainbow-pylon-lined street where many of Chicago's gay men congregated was to numb himself, to obliterate the thoughts from his mind about what should be done about Elise. He knew well enough what must be done, and didn't want to think about it. He saw the road in front of him as the watershed in his life as one of the undead, a capper that stood for everything vile and ugly regarding what he was.

So when dusk lowered its purple curtain, Edward arose from the big canopy bed the three of them shared and knew where he had to go.

It was a Friday night, and Halsted Street would be crowded with
revelers, celebrating the beginning of another weekend. The weather
had gotten warmer and the humidity had dropped, ensuring there
would be an even bigger crowd than usual tonight. Edward often
thought of going to Halsted as fishing in a barrel, but he didn't care. He
wasn't looking for a challenge.

After fortifying himself with a bowl of prime sinsemilla, that he
had nurtured himself into reddish, sticky, and redolent buds in the
basement of their house, he dressed for his evening out. Lately, it
seemed the leather boys were the ones who were most willing to do
whatever it would take to acquire the company of Miss Tina, so tonight,
Edward pulled on skin-tight, faded Levi 501s (the crotch carefully
abraded with sandpaper to boost its prominence), a studded leather
harness showing off his defined pectorals to scandalous advantage, a
pair of Harley Davidson motorcycle boots, and a leather biker cap
pulled low on his brow, hiding his eyes and making his five o'clock
shadow and full lips look anonymous, menacing, and irresistible. Years
of practice had taught him what worked and what didn't when one was
out hunting. He could never have imagined being dressed as he was
tonight and, even more, going out in public in this costume, back when
he was alive. Back then, in the 1950s, he supposed there were people
with leather fetishes, but you didn't find them parading up and down
brightly lit and traffic-clogged thoroughfares. Back then, Edward
seldom even wore blue jeans when he went out, sticking with chinos,
plaid shirts, or if he wanted to show off how artsy he was, garbed all in
black (at least that much hadn't changed; the goth boys still lingered
here and there, especially around the alley entranceway to a bar called
Neos on Clark Street; Edward had once hunted there, too).

His mind in a fog, Edward had set off into the night. Any thoughts
of the pathetic mortal they had ensnared in their web and who was,
right now, probably twisting and turning to free herself from its
unrelenting bonds, were banished by the cloud of marijuana that had
dulled the workings of his mind, weaving itself around the coiled pink
structure of his brain. And his blood lust also played a major role in
ensuring his thoughts were not bothered by what he saw as a betrayal of
someone much like himself.

But he couldn't think about that now, as he raised his arm to hail a
cab, not when there was a drunken and lonely boy somewhere to
seduce, his blood and semen waiting for their final spurts into Edward's
hungry mouth.

THE BOY, REALLY nothing more than a carcass now, lies at his
feet. It's hard to decipher what anyone might have seen in him. Edward
nudges the body over on its stomach with the steel toe of his boot so he
doesn't have to look at him. He would prefer to remember the boy when

he was vibrant, when the blood pumping hot just beneath his skin gave his cheeks color, when his vibrant life force caused his eyes to shine.

Yes, that's what I've spoiled, Edward thinks. He remembers talking to the boy in a leather bar called The Brig, where the air was dense with smoke (both cigars and cigarettes), the music was trance, and all the video monitors played hardcore pornography: here a crowd of muscular brutes tied a lithe young man to a St. Andrew's cross and took turns fucking him, while the boy stared dull-eyed at the camera; there a man dressed as a member of the Hell's Angels fisted two other men, on either side of him, their legs in chains in leather slings... Film production had come so far since Edward had surreptitiously watched men wrestle one another wearing posing straps on black and white 8MM celluloid. Edward remembers:

The boy stands alone, in a corner. His bright, alert expression tells Edward he is new to this, and shy. He knows his attention will be welcome, and he knows the power his strong, cocky looks have. He's done it so many times in the past, it is like a routine. The boy will be pliant, willing. And once he has Tina racing through his veins, he will be even more eager to be defiled. The boy has no idea how far defilement can go.

Edward establishes no one will be looking for the boy, at least not for a while (he is from Indianapolis and has slipped away for the weekend, telling his parents he was attending a collegiate football game at Northwestern University in Evanston). It doesn't take long for Edward to ply him with drink, smoke, and drug and lead him to the confines of Steam, the strip's bathhouse, where he bribes the clerk behind the glass entry window to give them a double room without the benefit of a membership card or even ID.

The drug, Edward's compact, muscled physique, and his commanding manner all play into the boy's wildest fantasies once they are alone in the room. Previously inexperienced, the boy becomes an insatiable whore under Edward's tutelage, no limit too extreme. Or so the boy thinks.

The sex is rough, even by leather and S&M standards, but still nothing so far out of the ordinary as to cause any true pain. For their first hour or so, the accent truly is on pleasure. But Edward leads the boy on a climb through dizzying heights of perversion and pain, ratcheting up the slaps, the nipple twists, the sudden thrusting of fingers into rectum, until the boy has a chance to grow accustomed to each level. Edward has done this a million times. The boy is interchangeable with so many others.

Finally, the pain and pleasure are so intense, the boy doesn't even have time to scream when Edward's razor-sharp fangs pierce the tender flesh of his throat. Edward has the boy's windpipe and vocal cords ripped out in an instant. No one passing by their room will imagine anything is amiss; there is more noise in any number of other rooms.

Back in the present, Edward pulls on his cap, and decides on a whim to leave his harness atop the boy's back.

He pauses at the door, whispering goodbye, then presses his forehead to the cheap painted wood. "I should have killed her." He nods. The knowledge, and the certainty, makes him feel sick, in spite of the fresh blood coursing through him, something that had once engendered in him a euphoria he had never imagined when he was alive. Now, it's just another bodily function, like eating or taking a shit had once been, mundane and commonplace. Murder, torture, and the drinking of blood have little more allure than eating an apple. "I shouldn't have killed this young man; I should have killed her, as I planned when I followed her from the house." Edward shakes his head. He knows it has to be done. She can't be allowed to live with her knowledge.

Chapter
Twenty-Five

Present Day

MARIA SITS, MUTE, numb, and wanting to look anywhere else but in the eyes of her two companions. She stares at the black rectangle that is the room's only window; once in a while, car headlights shine from below, moving across the sill, ghostly and suggesting movement, honing in on her desire to be alone, away, and not having to deal with the situation before her. She picks lint off her black blouse, crosses and uncrosses her legs, finger-combs her hair, takes a hit off the little one-hitter she clenches in one hand as though it's life support. She attempts to ignore the near-human anxiety she feels, anxiety that causes one of her crossed legs to swing ceaselessly and manically, her scalp to tingle, and that makes her chew on the inside of her cheek. She had assumed reactions and emotions like these had deserted her long ago. "And isn't it pretty to think so," she whispers to herself, now staring down at the floor.

"Are you even listening to us? Maria? Maria!" At the sharp tone of his voice and the sudden spike in volume, Maria raises her head dully to consider Terence. His long blond hair is in disarray, and his usual impeccable dress tonight is absent; he's wearing a pair of old jeans and a Loyola University sweatshirt (a trophy?). Still, he looks impossibly beautiful, something crafted out of marble or a photograph off the pages of *Vogue*, the model airbrushed to elevate beauty into the realm of the unreal.

"I hear you. What do you want me to say?"

Terence exchanges glances with Edward and Maria reads the quick visual cues that speak of exasperation, that say, "What shall we do with her?"

Edward kneels down before her, sliding his cold hand atop hers. "We want you to say you're with us. We want you to say you understand and you realize what has to be done, however painful that might be. We want you..." Edward's voice goes on, a buzzing drone filtering in and out, with certain words rising above the whitish noise, words like "merciful," "duty," "rules," and "danger." She knows they are trying to talk reason to her, but how can she be reasonable when her heart is broken? (Damn Elise for causing her to fall in love! Damn her for inciting these ridiculous romantic notions...broken heart indeed; but thoughts such as these do little to mitigate her despair.) How can she listen to 'what's right,' and 'doing one's duty,' when the thought of such courses of action fill her with revulsion, fear, and shame?

Their voices filter in dimly, as if they are neighbors on another floor, having a conversation in which she is only vaguely interested.

She tries to conjure up images to send to Elise. Benign things at first, speaking of her love, her devotion, her admiration. *See the two of us by the fireplace in the living room, the flames' light flickering across our faces and making our eyes sparkle. See you showing me your work, the shy expression on your face that shows you're uncertain and that you want me to like what you're exhibiting.* These segue into rougher and more seductive erotic imagery; skin merging and disengaging, tongues dueling, sweat popping out to shine and smooth a silken back, teeth gently piercing the aureole surrounding a nipple, the slow trickle of blood.

She closes her eyes and shuts down the imagery. They are pornography. Elise deserves better. Besides, casting these art house skin-shots out is like casting photographs to the wind. Her thoughts meet only a brick wall, as though Elise has shut down her mind and mentally placed a filter disallowing any of Maria's thoughts to penetrate. And this, Maria thinks sadly, is probably exactly what she's done.

Maria closes her eyes and tries to slip away, to go somewhere else in her mind, somewhere where the sound of water hitting against stone will calm her. But nothing works. There is only this vague feeling in her gut; a queasiness that will not abate. Is it possible for her to vomit?

Edward's hand is on her cheek, stroking. She opens her eyes to see his eyebrows knit together and the sympathetic frown; these speak of his concern for her. Her boys do love her so much! Why isn't it enough? He licks his lips and begins, saying the same words, hoping repetition will aid in penetrating her consciousness.

"Maria? Maria, are you listening to us?" Edward's concern highlights the difference between Terence and him. Terence tonight is little more than a powerhouse of hatred and malice. But it's his extreme emotion and his passion that have always attracted her to him; he may be hard to deal with sometimes, but he has never been boring.

She gives Edward a glimmer of a smile and nods. She turns down the roar in her head, touches Edward, running her fingers across his smooth, bald pate. "I'm sorry. It's just hard for me to think." Maria sits up straighter, and realizes these are the people who have stood alongside her for many, many years, going through euphoric heights, depressing lows, and electric danger that threatened their existence in cities all over the world. "What is it you want to say to me? Hmm?" Maria already knows the answer, but delaying it gives her a small, very small, measure of comfort.

"She knows too much." The words hang in the air like shards of glass, waiting to penetrate, to cut, causing irreversible pain and harm. "I know how you feel, Maria. I don't want to see her die, either. Here's a secret: last night I followed her, intending to kill her, intending to make it quick, so we wouldn't even have to go through what we're going through right now. But I couldn't do it. I was so close. My teeth were ready to pierce her flesh. But I couldn't. Later, though, I realized I was weak. She has to die." Edward shakes his head.

Maria nods. Her tongue feels fuzzy and thick. A headache is beginning behind one eye. These sensations are so unused as to be completely new, frightening and confusing.

Edward continues. "She knows too much. We can't allow her go on, with the knowledge she has."

"Edward's right," Terence seethes, hissing. "Letting this Elise person go on living endangers not only us, but all of our kind."

Maria looks up at him as if she doesn't understand. *If only that were true.*

"You know I'm right, Maria. She'll talk."

Maria rolls her eyes.

"Come now." Terence looks at Maria, sneering. "You allowed yourself to become so infatuated with this mortal you were blind to the laws that have governed all of us since the very beginning."

Edward frowns, the sorrow in his face genuine. It's obvious that he hates this. It's also obvious that he sees no other alternative. "Besides, Maria, she's rejected you." Edward breathes in deep: a beat. "She doesn't want you."

Terence shouts. "Doesn't that make you angry? Doesn't that just piss you off that she threw away the greatest gift a human can ever receive? Who the fuck doesn't want immortality?"

"Right now...me."

Terence goes on, his face close to hers. "Well, maybe if you're too blinded by love and too stupid to see that she's tossed you aside like a used condom from a trick, then you have to consider this: she might hate you now. She might very well be full of rage because you, and us, in essence, tried to take away everything that was valuable. And for what? Because we were in love? Love like yours is no present."

Maria sniffs. What's this tightness she feels in her throat?

Edward speaks softly, in counterpoint to Terence's anger and agitation. "You know what has to be."

Maria feels numb, as if she wouldn't even feel a switchblade to her heart. But the arguments and what she has known for hundreds of years sink in. "I know, Edward, I know."

"You know then that she has to be," Edward sucks in some air, waiting for a moment, "killed." He shakes his head. "What Terence says is true. For one, it could lead to a bunch of self-righteous mortals showing up here ready to kill us. What if Elise leads that charge? We're not as invulnerable as we think. All she would have to do is creep inside, throw open the curtains on a sunny day, and whip off our covers. We'd be ash. But not only that, she could help make real our existence, and that could destroy every one of us." Edward moves close to Maria's face, whispering, "There's no other way. We can't let her live, not with what she knows."

"Edward's right." Terence's anger continues to burn bright, a match against flint.

Maria cries out. This is all too much. "Edward's right! Edward's right!" she shrieks, mocking. "What do you know about love, Terence? You've only hated, cutting a path of destruction and death behind you as wide as it is long."

Terence grabs her arms just before she's about to pummel his chest. "Don't take it out on me! All of us must live by the law. Or we could all perish."

"I don't believe it. I won't!" Even as she says it, Maria knows she must believe it. It's the only truth. She lowers her head and the tears come, painful, blood squeezing through her tear ducts, dripping down her face to land on her jeans in great black drops. She lifts her face to them, anguish stamped across her features. Her sorrow and longing storm inside her, butterfly wings beating against the walls of a sealed jar. She lashes out, knowing that what she's about to say is untrue, ludicrous, but she says the words anyway. She has to; maybe it's a kind of absolution. "What would happen if we left her alone? Nothing! What if, just suppose, she did tell someone about us? For one, we could be gone from here in an instant. And maybe it's time for us to move on, anyway. So what if she told? Who would believe her? Vampires! Blood-sucking fiends!" Maria laughs, but the laugh has no mirth. She continues to smile, teeth clenched. "I'm sure the mortals would rush to demonstrate their safety and their alarm and their credulity." She lowers her head, unsure if the convulsions racking through her are sobbing or abject laughter.

Edward tries to put his arms around Maria. She pushes him away. "Listen Maria, you know we can't take a chance. We can't. It's always been the way."

"Damn it's 'always been the way!' Haven't we learned anything in all these centuries?"

"No!" Terence shouts. "There is no room for debate on this. We must get rid of her as soon as we can. Tonight."

Maria rushes to the window, panting and staring down at the headlights moving in lines, north and south, below her. Outside, the wind stirs the few leaves left on the trees, sending their dried bodies downward to land silently on the concrete and grass. She picks up on the rustle of the leaves, the dryness and the death. They can't truly even be called leaves anymore; all the life is gone.

She presses her head against the cool glass. Darkness envelops the world around her, and she's part of it. Fog has moved in off Lake Michigan and the streetlights glow, as if cauled, in the dim, gray light.

Composing herself with a great show of will, Maria pauses and finally turns to Terence and Edward. "Let's just be done with it, then."

Chapter
Twenty-six

ELISE HAS EVERYTHING packed. One advantage of being poor and depressed is that she hasn't collected much to pack up. Her clothes and the pieces of art she wants to take with her fit inside two suitcases she had stored in the basement when she moved here. She tries to remember how many years ago that was, but it isn't so much the time that confounds her, but the distance. She was a different person back then: young, innocent, with the feeling the world held only promise for her. She could not have predicted the lows to which she would sink. One suitcase, a black nylon thing on rollers, holds paints, brushes, solvents, paper and charcoal pencils. On top of the art supplies is a plastic grocery store bag filled with toiletries (she discarded most of the more lurid make-up, with her whore wardrobe; gone is the heavy black eyeliner, the shadow in vibrant shades of blue and green, the bright red lip gloss). The other suitcase is packed tight with drawings and some of her smaller paintings. The others would just have to be left behind; maybe the next tenant would appreciate them.

She will leave the furniture behind. She is certain that subsequent tenants, regardless of how poor, will quickly haul this stuff out to the trash, where even the garbage pickers will eschew it. The only other furniture she is sorry to leave behind is her drawing board and the stool that goes with it. She has had these since her art school days and they served her well; becoming like an easy chair, something she hardly noticed anymore as she sat and worked.

But a drawing table and stool would be hard to get on the bus. Elise has already called ahead to make sure Greyhound has a late-night trip to Cleveland. She hasn't even bothered to let her parents know she was coming. She will have to assume they would be glad to see her and that their home was always open to her. Elise is certain enough of these facts that she has booked a ticket for the bus, which leaves in three hours, plenty of time for her to catch a southbound Red line train to Harrison Street, then get off, climb up to ground level, and find a city bus to the station. Or maybe she might even splurge on a cab?

Mundane thoughts like these are what keep her from thinking of

Maria. Every once in a while, she has the vague feeling Maria is trying to send her something telepathically. But she has tried her best not to leave her mind open, vulnerable to even the slightest contact from her. Yet there's a slight feeling of anxiety every so often, a signal there is something scratching to get in, just on the periphery of her mind.

Elise knows she is weak, and knows she can't afford to get in contact with Maria in any way, not even through the psychic merging of their thoughts. So, even after she has packed her bags, she continues to keep herself busy: cleaning out closets, emptying what meager food and drink are in the refrigerator, throwing away old letters and keepsakes (she wants to start all over, once she has had a chance to recover under her mother's care), dressing herself in a way she hasn't in a long time. Tonight, she wears a pair of Levis with a hole in the knees and ragged hems, a red University of Wisconsin hooded sweatshirt (she has no connection to the school; she just picked up this particular article of clothing years ago at a thrift store on Halsted Street), and a pair of Asics running shoes. Catching a glimpse of herself, she is almost alarmed at how young she looks in these clothes. She could be a college freshman. The fact is, she isn't all that much older than that, anyway. She says to her reflection, "You still have a lot ahead of you."

She is tempted to cut off her hair, but decides to wait until she is in a clearer frame of mine to make such a drastic change to her appearance.

Now, she sits in front of her window, trying to catch a breeze and keep her mind impermeable. The weather has turned Indian summer, almost hot, with a thick cloak of humidity. Ugly. The warmth has brought out the people of her neighborhood, and they congregate on street corners, laughing, shouting, arguing. Here, the flair of a match. There, the sound of glass breaking. A homeless woman pushes a shopping cart by, its wheels creaking. Wait. Hasn't Elise seen her before? Strains of "Between the Devil and the Deep Blue Sea" fade in, then out again.

Elise closes her eyes. It is in this forced darkness she hears the thrum of a motorcycle engine. It sounds like it's far away, its roar distant, but distinct, just under the sounds of all the other vehicular traffic on the roads surrounding her. The bass thrum of the engine causes her to stiffen and tense.

She backs away from the window, flattening herself against the wall, unable to open her eyes or close her ears as the sound grows louder. Sweat pops out on her forehead. Her hearts beats out an uncomfortable rhythm, staccato. "It's just a motorcycle," she whispers to herself. "It could be anyone."

Sliding down to the floor, she keeps her back against the wall, murmuring "anyone" over and over.

She knows, with certainty, the approaching motorcycle will not be ridden by just anyone. It will be one of them. Somehow, she also doesn't sense that it's Maria drawing near. She's already spoken with Edward. So it must be Terence. She pictures him astride the Harley, his mean/ beautiful chiseled features bearing the stamps of confidence and determination. The image causes her to giggle, but the giggle is something preceding hysteria. There's nothing funny about it. *Maybe none of these creatures even exist*, she tells herself, *and you're just out of your fucking mind.*

"You don't have to answer the door. You don't have to talk." She wishes she had already left for the bus station. She knows she would have had several hours to kill, but at least she wouldn't be as vulnerable. Sure, there are often plenty of scary people milling around in a bus station, especially at night, especially in a city like Chicago, but none of them have the ability to say, with such charm, "I vant to drink your blood."

She giggles again, then stiffens as the roar of the bike engine becomes deafening, then abruptly cuts, leaving silence in its wake. For just one moment, it seems that not only has the engine died down, but also all of the voices and traffic on the street, too. Elise stiffens and resists the urge to creep to the window.

She holds her breath, listening. She hears the creak and slam of the door downstairs (will the landlord never get that lock fixed?), then the slow, heavy footsteps of someone wearing boots, the creak of leather and chains.

In spite of being prepared for a visit for the last fifteen minutes, she screams when the knock on her door sounds. She can barely catch her breath.

Then Terence speaks through the door. His voice is not threatening, but perfectly reasonable and, in his way, friendly. "Elise? Elise, I know you're in there. Please open the door. I just need to talk to you for a minute. Really, I mean you no harm."

Elise lets loose a titter. Terence saying he means her no harm is about as credible as a Christian fundamentalist campaigning for legalizing abortion, or gay marriage.

The knock sounds again. "Just ride it out. Ride it out," she whispers to herself.

A jingle of the doorknob. "Elise? Come on. I'm serious. I need to talk to you. It's important."

Elise stands and backs away from the door, as if she expects it to be broken down and Terence to come flying into the room, fangs bared. She will end up like the poor little girl she heard about on the news, flayed and drained on a beach.

But Terence's soothing voice doesn't match the image. "Look, I wanted just to talk to you and not to all of your neighbors..." He pauses, and she hears footsteps descending the hall stairs. "...Or anyone else who might be passing by, but you give me no choice. Elise, listen: Maria is ill."

Elise runs a hand across her face, her stomach beginning to churn. "Oh yeah, right," she manages to blurt out. "Why should I believe you? I thought you never even got sick; I thought you were immortal."

Terence sighs. "People think lots of things about us that aren't true. We can feel pain. We are capable of ailing." He pauses, and Elise feels her resolve beginning to crumble. Sure, it sounds like malarkey, but what if he is telling the truth? Is she so callous that she can really turn her back on Maria, the only woman to have stirred such feelings of tenderness and need, despite the surreal aspects of their relationship? Terence continues, "I couldn't care less what you do. Maria asked me to come here because she couldn't come herself. She just wants to see you...one last time."

She hears the weight of Terence's head against the door, followed by an exasperated outrush of air. "I would think you'd have the decency, especially since you're the one responsible for her stress. Yes, stress affects us and can make us ill."

Elise's mouth is dry. She shakes her head, disappointed in herself, fearful she has in some way unintentionally harmed Maria, and suspicious that she has been duped, and moves closer to the door.

Elise lets her mind go blank and she tosses her fears and concerns aside. She takes a breath, reaches for the doorknob, turns it, and flings the door open. "Please, please, please. You want me to get down on my knees and beg? Open the door and I will."

"That won't be necessary," she says, resigned.

Terence smiles. There is the satisfied glimmer of an attacker just about to pounce on its stunned prey and Elise shuts her eyes for the briefest of moments.

She jerks her head back. "Why don't you come on inside?" She steps aside to let him enter, believing she is making the most serious mistake of her life, which, when she considers her history, is serious indeed.

Chapter
Twenty-seven

ELISE AND TERENCE attract stares as they walk down her block to Terence's motorcycle. She looks like some preppy college girl in her sweatshirt and jeans (already the sweatshirt is doing just that: making her sweat; but she doesn't have the voice to tell him she wants to go back inside and change. Besides it's always cold inside their house), her long hair hanging loose; step easy (oh, really?) in her running shoes. And Terence, pale, almost albino, in head to toe black leather; there are some freaky characters in this neighborhood, and some potentially lethal ones, but everyone seems to sense that Terence has them all beat. People see him, pause, and then move aside to let them pass, turning their heads to watch them go.

And all the while, Terence simply smiles, confident, cocky, sure of his presence and its effect.

They get to the bike and Elise steps back into the shadows. "I don't know if this is the right thing to do. Are you sure Maria is sick?"

Terence shakes his head, slowly, as if he's disappointed in her, as if she's some animal that can't be made to understand the simplest of concepts. He takes his time to answer her, scanning the streets with his dark eyes, nodding to a couple of guys who slow in their passage to admire the Harley. Then he smiles at her, but his words are tinged with acid. "Listen, honey, I wouldn't be here if it weren't important to Maria. I've seen thousands of pathetic little streetwalkers like you over the years, and, believe me, unless I'm looking for a meal, I wouldn't have even the energy to come after you. Don't think you hold out any fascination for me because you happen to be able to draw some sweet little pictures." He pulls a box of Marlboro Reds from his back pocket and pauses to light one. She's surprised he isn't lighting up the bowl of a pipe or at least a joint. Inside she giggles: perhaps he fears the law. He exhales the smoke through his nostrils and regards her. He shakes his head. "Do what you want, Elise. Go back to your grimy little room. I'll just tell Maria you didn't care enough to come and see if she's all right."

"I..." Elise begins to speak, then realizes she doesn't know what to say. She feels trapped. "What's the matter with her again?" she mumbles, already knowing she will get on the back of the Harley, leaning with Terence into the winds and the curves. God only knows what waits at the other end of the ride.

Terence makes the tip of the cigarette glow bright orange. "She hasn't fed in several days. We're like you in that regard; if we don't nourish ourselves, we get sick. We die."

"I thought you were already dead."

"Don't be stupid. She's despondent, sweetheart, sad. She won't talk. She just stays in bed and stares at the wall. Now, I can't think of anything other than a broken heart that could make Maria depressed. I'm thinking if you just come and talk to her and pat her little head, she might be convinced to take some sustenance, to revive herself. It would be a shame to waste such a long and beautiful life on someone like you." He sizes her up and down, pursing his lips. He blows out a sigh. "Are you coming or not? I'm running out of time."

Maybe I am, too, Elise thinks. But that doesn't stop her from wordlessly climbing on the bike seat behind Terence.

He guns the Harley into roaring, smoking, stinking life and Elise closes her eyes and wraps her arms around him. His broad, leather-clad back feels good, cool, against her face. And just thinking about this simple pleasure blocks out the chorus of voices inside her, all clamoring to tell her the same thing: flee.

But she can't.

They jerk away from the curb, and Terence turns the throttle to make the bike go faster and faster, racing down Sheridan Road, cutting in and out between traffic, ignoring the screeching brakes, blaring horns, and the shouts of profanity. Elise simply keeps her eyes squeezed tight, thinking at least they will be there quickly.

They reach the curve around Loyola University, head east for a minute, and then curve again, heading south. The big old house is only a couple blocks away. Elise finds herself beginning to anticipate, against all logic and reason, seeing Maria again. She imagines her pale and weak, wrapped in thick, heavy cream-colored sheets, her black hair a fan on the pillow. She imagines taking her hand. Elise gives herself the glorious power of being able to make Maria want to live once more.

And how many more lives will that cost?

Elise ignores the thought and opens her eyes just in time to see the big brick house, with its darkened windows, looking so dead against a gray night sky, whiz by.

She tenses, licks her lips, and tries to produce the saliva and voice that will allow her to find words. At last, she manages to scream, "Where are you taking me? The house is back there!"

She leans a bit and sees Terence's sculptured profile betraying nothing. It's as though he hasn't heard her.

"The house is back there," she whimpers. The high-rise apartment buildings are a blur, and at last, they are at Hollywood, which will lead them on to Lake Shore Drive. Terence waits for the light to change, engine idling, the turn signal going *tick, tick, tick.*

Elise knows this is her chance to jump off the bike.

But she can't.

The light goes green and they head south on Lake Shore, faster, faster, heading into a future that's mysterious and dread-inspiring.

What has she let herself in for? She thinks, with longing, of the hominess of a fluorescent-lit bus station, the anticipation of travel, and, on the other hand, the prospect of her parents' surprised and delighted expressions when they open the big oak door and see her waiting outside, curling a strand of her hair and grinning sheepishly at them, the light shining in from the foyer, warm and inviting. Knowing she has forfeited the scene above and all that would follow, Elise hugs Terence tighter and buries her face in the broad expanse of black leather cloaking his back.

Terence bumps the speed up to, what? Eighty? Ninety?

Elise grinds her teeth and feels nothing.

Chapter
Twenty-Eight

Present Day

EVANS MILL WORKS sits, dead and forgotten, south of the Chicago city limits, beyond suburbs like Oak Lawn and Alsip, and drawing near to the industrial Northwest Indiana towns of East Chicago and Gary. The abandoned foundry is the victim of the downsizing of the steel industry in this part of the Midwest and although its buildings still stand, it has become redundant, no longer of use to anyone. Well, almost anyone.

The foundry is made up of six large buildings looming black in the night, great hulks whose smokestacks once shot fire and belched smoke into the sky, clogging it and sending an effluvium of industrial stink out over the waters of Lake Michigan, upon whose shores the foundry rests.

Now the smokestacks are lifeless and the buildings themselves empty structures of rough concrete and crumbling brick with metal roofs. Windows are broken, some boarded over, and some completely cleared of the metal-laced glass that once filled the frames. Those that do retain any glass frame the darkness with shards projecting outward from the windows' sides. They are threatening; more imaginative fancies might liken these windows to the dark mouths of monsters, fangs at the ready to cut, to draw blood from those unwitting enough to draw near.

Inside each building, certain things are constant: the drip of water from the roofs above, the scuffling and squeaking noises of rats, and the smell of mildew and the tang of rusty metal.

The small interior roads of the foundry, which once saw forklift trucks bearing huge cylinders of steel, delivery trucks, and the footsteps of thousands of working men, are now silent and unused, weedy byways of glistening black cinder.

Rusted roofs leak water inside, onto eroding concrete floors, turning back to the soil from whence they came.

Even here, decomposition is almost an organic process.

Evans Mill Works is a place of darkness and silence, dense with shadows. Cold. Not only is it foreboding in its dark quiet, but it almost has the character of something alive, something that waits silently for its prey, blending into the background and then, when that prey is in sight, pounces with lethal certainty.

This is the kind of place where people disappear.

FROM THE SHADOWS, Maria and Edward watch.

Edward is resigned. His face betrays nothing; it's little more than a pair of pale eyes glinting in the darkness, features devoid of expression. He wears black camouflage pants, a black T-shirt, boots, and a black windbreaker. If it weren't for the white of his face, he would vanish into the place where they have positioned themselves: an alcove formed where two industrial buildings meet. There isn't much room for the two of them here, but it's ideal because it conceals them, providing access to a vantage point where they will be able to see Terence's arrival, even though that arrival will have been heralded long before by the bass of his motorcycle engine. But they already accept that his mission may have been unsuccessful; it will be important to see if he has arrived alone. Edward's calm masks a hope Terence will show up with only the wind at his back, disappointment plain on his fine, chiseled features. He will perhaps say something along the lines of, "She was gone. Completely gone. I was able to look inside her apartment and it was bare. Cleaned out."

This is what Edward hoped to hear, even if it meant that Terence would be like a spoiled child, for weeks, who didn't get the present he wanted. Edward had stopped loving this monstrous beauty years ago, almost as soon as he "crossed over." He takes a perverse pleasure in seeing Terence disappointed, in seeing that his charms have failed (although they rarely do). Terence lives to cause misery (unlike Maria and Edward, Terence loves the act of killing and does it more for the pain and suffering he causes than for survival). Edward shakes his head, clearing it of hopes and, mostly, of thought. He wants to be a tool tonight, an automaton, a creature doing simply what must be done. He views their plan as self-defense, even though the person who has the power to harm or even destroy them is benign. It doesn't change anything.

One thing, though: he will not let Terence have the pleasure of feeding on Elise. He will see to that and is certain Maria will support him in ensuring the young woman is given a proper burial (even if it's only beneath weeds, broken pieces of machinery, and scraps of twisted, disintegrating metal).

While Edward appears calm, Maria displays her horror and despair. She is dressed like Edward all in black, but her face is a kabuki mask of anguish. Her eyes are reddened with tears that appear black in the darkness. Her lips are parted with panting sobs. Edward leans close every so often to caution her to be quiet. "She can't know we're here."

"Why?" Maria turns to Edward, mouth in a line, eyebrows

furrowed, betraying both rage and bewilderment. "What difference does it make?"

"You want this to be quick, don't you? It will all be over much faster if she doesn't know we're here, if she doesn't have the chance to ask questions." Edward thinks, but doesn't say: *If she doesn't have a chance to run.*

"How can we..." Maria leaves the question unfinished and turns back to staring out at the night, at the detritus of dead industry, the scraps of metal, the corroded and rusting hulks of machinery. What more is there to say?

They had agreed earlier on this place, here on the south side of the city. The city's skyline, with its lights festooned on towers, practically leans over them in the darkness, at once protective and menacing; a mute giant with a thousand eyes, all glowering. These gleaming towers speak of wealth, commerce, and creativity. Life. They present a bizarre contrast to where Edward and Maria now wait. Here, the buildings seem surreal and distant, something out of fantasy, as if a set designer has placed them against the background of the abandoned factory for effect.

But all they need do to remind themselves of the contrast between what they see in the distance and where they are now is to look down at their feet at the evidence that others have passed through this place, and those trespassers were all bent on mischief, though nothing as horrific as what Edward, Terence, and Maria have planned. At their feet are mashed carcasses of rusting tin cans, discarded rubbers, rat droppings, tiny plastic baggies, and pieces of torn newspaper and advertising flyers, all begrimed with grit and smeared with mud. Maria wonders if others have died here.

Behind them are double doors, the glass long ago boarded up, passage in and out of them dim memory. There was once a padlock and chain, but now the chain hangs down from a door handle, useless. Maria thinks the pitch inside might be a good place to carry out what has to be done. Or, if the kill is so quick that it won't allow even movement into the building, a good place to bring Elise's body; she doesn't think she will have the strength to bury her as she knows Edward will want to do. She can only imagine leaving her there and fleeing as quickly as possible. It's cowardice, she knows, but the thought of looking at Elise, beautiful and lifeless, will tear her apart. She will have to minimize the hurt. The anguish, she reckons, will be nearly unbearable.

She wishes there was a way out, a way to avoid what's coming down the road, like a beast slouching toward them, changing who they are forever. To calm herself, she imagines Elise lying still on the concrete floor, her arms tenderly crossed over her chest, eyelids pulled down to hide the horror reflected in her final vision. Maria tries to delude herself into thinking this odd scene of tranquil repose is serene, as if Elise is only resting before getting up once more and taking up her paintbrush or charcoal stick.

Edward picks up on her thoughts. "And they won't find the body for a long, long time."

"Be quiet," Maria snaps. She sighs and continues to try to think of a way out. She has been trying all day. She has always been clever, always the one the other two turned to for solutions. But she sees no passage out of what they are bound to do.

The darkness around is so palpable it presses in, defying the moonlight and the lights of the city.

The two of them turn outward once more, eyes trained on the darkness, waiting for change, anticipating movement in the still night air.

Edward wraps his arms around Maria and draws her back, close to his chest, his lips on her neck. He lifts his head and says, "I'll make sure we get through this quickly. I can't make it not hurt, but for you, I'll do my best to make sure we don't linger. We can put this behind us."

Maria lifts her hand to Edward's stubbled face. She thinks, "Never," but says nothing.

Distantly, they hear Terence approaching, the great bass thrum of his Harley engine. Maria tenses, pulling away from Edward. She looks back at him and the terror in her eyes is wild, the orbs glinting and sparkling like the crushed cinders of the roads around them, reflecting back the moon. She trembles. "I can't do this."

"Shhh. It's going to be okay."

Maria wants to run. She has never felt so out of control. She wonders, for the thousandth time, if there isn't a way out, if the rules can be bent just this one time. She has never loved anyone with such astonishing depth and abandon, so much it snatches her breath away.

The engine's roar grows louder and Maria cannot avert her eyes from the tear in the chain link fence where they all agreed earlier Terence would enter the foundry. She stares, unable to look away and, at the same time, not wanting to see.

Maria clutches handfuls of Edward's flesh in her hands as she sees Elise, behind Terence on the bike. She looks so tiny behind him. It makes Maria grip even more tightly onto Edward, digging her nails deep into his flesh. It hurts, but Edward doesn't complain; he knows how hard this is. She turns and buries her head in his chest, whimpering. But she can't allow herself even this small comfort. Comfort is for the innocent.

She turns her head back to the blinding light of the motorcycle's headlight and the two dark figures behind it. If she were human, she would see only silhouettes behind the halogen, but her night vision has been acutely honed throughout the centuries and she sees far too much of the woman they are about to kill. The woman she loves... This nightmare image of Elise's approach, Maria knows, will be burned on her retinas for eternity.

Elise is clinging to Terence's back, her dark hair moving like liquid in the air behind her. Something catches in Maria's throat as she sees the terrified look on her lover's face, as she picks up on the scattered hysteria of her thoughts. She lets out a little yelp and then silences herself before Edward has a chance to caution her. She knows that, once Terence roared by their house on Sheridan Road Elise will have grown more and more frightened, terrified, knowing she is about to be delivered to something more awful than she ever imagined.

Maria wants to run out from their hiding place and signal Terence to stop. She wants to take Elise in her arms and bite deeply into the flesh at her throat and continue the process until Elise dies, and then doing what it takes to bring her back, to keep her with her for all time.

But she can't. She thinks of Elise's art. And even though they plan to kill her, living death without her creativity is not an alternative.

There are some things worse than death.

THE RIDE HAS gone so fast. Elise is panting, gasping for air. She feels trapped in the memory of their ride here, how they approached the house the three of them shared...and then passed it. Elise had looked longingly back at its yellow brick façade and remembers, now, how the house seemed benign and innocent, its usually foreboding appearance replaced by her desperate need to be there. She knew that not stopping there was a bad omen; something was going to happen to her, something she might not have the opportunity, much longer, to regret.

Why hadn't she jumped off the back of the bike when she had the chance, where Hollywood Avenue curved into Lake Shore Drive? Why had she remained on the bike, trembling, unable to put enough breath behind words enough to protest, to ask where he was taking her, to find out what was going on? Instead, she remained mute, a docile animal stunned into submission.

She tried to close her mind as they roared south, far too fast, shutting out thoughts of what might await her with the hopes they would crash and she would be sent flying through the night air to crumple like a china doll beside the road. It was a measure of her despair to realize this image was preferable to the mystery of what was waiting for her on the end of this ride.

She couldn't even find the strength to scream, to pound on his back, demanding release, as he pointed the bike south and rode on and on, past Lake Michigan on their left, the towers of downtown on their right, the Museum of Natural History, Soldier Field, Shedd Aquarium, on and on until the city landmarks disappeared, replaced by hulking shadows of housing projects and dying industry. Once they were south of the city, the air seemed colder, and Elise could no longer feel her fingers or toes; they had turned to ice. This sensation was not due to the air temperature.

Could she do it? Could she make her legs work instead of standing, dumb, like a lamb to slaughter? Yes. She can do this. She can run. She will suck in deeply of the air, and set her adrenaline to flowing and she will be impossible to catch... She closed her eyes and thought of nothing until she felt the bike slow after making a turn. Terence was maneuvering the bike through a hole in a rusty chain-link fence. Ahead of her were ruins; the corpse of industry, an abandoned factory and its warehouses. This could come to no good. She tried to steel herself, to endow herself to run once the bike stopped.

But when the bike stops, she is seized with terror. It feels as though her body has become metal, stiff and unyielding. She has the weird sensation that her physical being belongs to someone else and she is only watching from a distance this helpless young woman being taken to carnage and mayhem.

The only thing that continues working is her mind, revving like the engine of the motorcycle only moments ago. Even if she did run, a defeated voice inside her says, where would she go? They are miles from the city now. There may be some people in the looming housing projects to the west of them, but that too is a long journey. Who would hear her even if she could find the voice to scream? And in this area, where screams are commonplace, if someone did hear, would they bother to respond? Would the ghouls that would find her should she run screaming for help be worse than the one she knows? A woman and alone? In her mind, she hears a man's voice: "Can I ask you a question?"

Elise is trapped. She knows it. She shuts down, waiting to be told what to do. She suddenly doesn't even have the energy to wonder what awaits her. If she were not alone with Terence, she might be able to ameliorate her terror by thinking of Maria's love or Edward's concern. But she knows Terence, knows his passion for hurt, and thinks there is little she can do to stop him, whatever it is he has in mind for her. She wishes she could curl into a small ball. She wishes she would wake up, sweating and hurt pounding, from this nightmare.

Terence turns to her. "You can get off the bike, sweetheart."

Elise says nothing; she doesn't move. He pokes her. "Anybody home? I said you can get off. You know: dismount."

Elise manages to swing one leg over and shakily plant both legs on the ground.

Terence laughs. "You look petrified."

"Shouldn't I be?"

"What do you think's going to happen to you?"

Elise finds she cannot swallow. Words are useless, anyway. She can tell from the glint in his eyes and the smirk playing about his lips Terence is enjoying her terror: an owl before it pounces on a mouse. Why give him the satisfaction of playing his little game? Elise stares off into the night, at the dead hulks of industrial buildings around them.

Terence smiles, his teeth glowing in the pitch. When will they morph into fangs? When will he roar like a panther and be upon her, ripping, tearing, making an aura around them of red mist?

She can barely see him and wonders how he seems to be able to see her so clearly, to read the map of emotions limned across her features. It seems useless to talk, but she has to know: "Why are we here?" Elise glances around at the darkness, the pitch so black it seems she can touch it, imagining its feel like velvet. She tenses her muscles, trying to steel them, so he won't have the pleasure of seeing her tremble. "When you came to get me, I...I thought we were going to your house."

"To see Maria?" Terence snickers. "Another lesbian love-fest?" Terence sticks out his tongue, pointing and rotating it. The smile vanishes from his face. "Sorry. I don't provide those kinds of services. Pimp is not on my résumé. I may procure a charming young lady now and then, but not for the naughty purposes you probably have in mind." He giggles, and Elise shivers at the sound of his laugh, the depth of cruelty lurking just beneath the surface.

Elise shakes her head. "That's not what I meant. You said Maria was sick. You told me she needed to see me." She traces a pattern in the dust at her feet with her toe, afraid to look up at his mocking face, afraid to see his pleasure in how easily he had duped her. "Now, I'm wondering what possible reason you could have for bringing me here."

Terence sucks in some breath. "To kill you," he says in a singsong voice. "Are you really so stupid you didn't catch on that I would be bringing you to a remote spot like this for — what? — to party?" Terence reaches in his pocket. "Actually, that's not such a bad idea." He brings out a small pipe; the bowl of dark wood is carved into the shape of a face. In the darkness, Elise can't make out the features.

"Smoke?"

The idea brings her to new heights of terror. She remembers what the pot does, how powerful it is, like another drug completely from the stuff she used to smoke in college. She feels like an animal about to be anaesthetized. She shakes her head. "I'll pass." The words come out in a whisper.

Terence fires up the bowl and immediately the marijuana's pungent aroma fills the air. Elise breathes it in and wonders if she isn't making the wrong choice. If her end here is inevitable, why not make it easier, painless?

And with that thought, she realizes why: because somewhere deep inside, she wants to survive. Even though things look grim, she continues to hold out hope for escape, for Terence to slip up, to look away for an instant, giving her an opportunity to bolt into the darkness. She may even be able to fight him off, however remote the chance for victory. She has no chance of realizing either of these goals should she cloud her mind with the potency of this otherworldly drug.

"Suit yourself." Terence inhales deeply, holds it, then blows the smoke in her face.

Elise holds her breath for a moment, then pushes it outward, hoping she has avoided taking any of the smoke into her lungs.

He takes a couple more hits, then pockets the pipe, and leans in close. She can smell the pot on his breath, but underneath that, a sickening sweet odor, like rotting meat. Elise nearly gags.

Terence smiles, eye glinting. He has an idea. "How about one fuck? Just one fuck, and then I'll let you go. No harm done. No questions asked. You gave it to Maria, why not give it to me?" He touches her shoulder. Her skin crawls and it takes a great act of will not to shrug his hand away. "I'm a much better lover than Maria." The idea is so repulsive it makes her queasy, but she doesn't reject it. She is sure he was lying about "no harm done," but their intimacy and their nudity could make even Terence vulnerable. She could up her chances for escape by at least allowing him to think they're going to have some sort of sexual union.

Couldn't she?

Elise closes her eyes. "Really? You'll let me go?"

Terence giggles. "If you're good."

"Okay." Elise tries to put some breath into her words, but the assent still sounds like a squeak. "Where do you want to do it?"

"Over there. In one of those buildings. I want to bend you over, take you from behind."

Terence saying this makes the phrase "being taken" adopt a whole new meaning.

Elise nods. "I suppose I could stand it, if it means freedom. You wouldn't lie to me, would you?"

"*Moi*? Tell a fib? Never!" Terence isn't even bothering to pretend. Elise hopes his cockiness might make him slip up, allowing her an advantage. Even the smallest leeway could be the road to her salvation. His voice goes deeper and suddenly, he sounds disgusted and impatient. "Can we just fuck?"

"Where?" Elise casts her gaze around.

Terence gestures toward a building in front of them. "Let's make our little love nest over there. I'm sure we can get inside, and even if we can't, there's probably some romantic little nook we can put to good use." Cold, bony fingers encircle her hand, impossibly huge and encompassing. He begins to lead her toward the pocked concrete and crumbling brick of the old buildings. Again, the numbness, bordering on shock, returns. Elise has to remind herself to keep putting one foot in front of the other; she is certain if she doesn't, she will stumble and fall and Terence will just drag her along, like a doll, ripping arm from socket.

They round a corner and Elise can see, even in the shadows, an alcove formed where the two buildings meet. It's even darker inside, which Elise wouldn't have thought possible. She stiffens when she makes out movement, barely perceptible. It's more the sound of rustling than her vision alerting her to the presence of others.

"Come on." He yanks her deeper into the dark. She reaches out, trying to feel her way, and her hand comes in contact with cold flesh. Everything stops. She moves her hand along the familiar face, the terrain of dark hair and whispers, "Maria."

Chapter
Twenty-nine

ELISE DOESN'T KNOW what to think. Her eyes adjust quickly to this even deeper level of darkness. Although they are dim, gray projections of themselves, she sees not only Maria, but also Edward. She puts a hand to a wall for support; her breath comes in short, little gasps.

How could Maria betray her like this? How could Edward, especially after he had advised her to get away? To not be tempted by empty promises?

Equal to the feeling of betrayal is one of panic and terror. She can think of no reason for the three of them to bring her here, so far out of eyesight and earshot of witnesses, other than to kill her. Elise's throat constricts. Her heart stops beating for just a second and then begins to pound irregularly, thumping wildly. The panic of an animal courses through her, pumping up adrenaline, making her sweat. She turns to Maria. "What's happening? How could you do this to me?" she wails, wounded.

Maria says nothing. She simply lowers her gaze to the ground in response.

Edward puts his hand on Maria's shoulder and catches Elise's gaze. It's almost as if he expects sympathy from her. She wants to laugh. Sympathy for Maria because she feels bad they plan to murder her?

When will she wake up from this?

"Maria? What's going on?"

But Maria turns away, shoulders shaking. Elise pivots toward Terence, rage and terror coursing through her, ratcheting up the adrenaline so she feels as though she's on speed.

And she stops.

Terence is smiling. There is something cruel in his closed-lip grin, something predatory. Elise begins to shriek when he opens his mouth to reveal rows of tiny fangs, razor sharp. The fangs glint, even in the darkness, and look surgically sharp.

She shrieks until there is no air, and, gasping, Elise has enough presence of mind, enough of a rush of adrenaline, to turn and sprint away. There is no thought for strategy or cunning. She has become simply a terrified animal, ruled by instinct and self-preservation. She knows these preternatural beings have superhuman speed in their arsenal of evil tricks, but that doesn't stop her from trying to escape. Her lungs rapidly expand and contract, filling with blood and oxygen to match the pumping of Elise's arms and legs. Her heart pumps double-time, sending blood coursing through her veins to nourish at this time of heightened fear. She pounds down through cinder and glass, sending up sprays of dust behind her, eyes wide, searching, searching for escape, never mind how futile the hope. Never mind the odds stacked high against her.

Ahead, she sees the rent in the chain link where she had entered with Terence such a short time ago (yet it seems like forever) and she hurries to clear it. She runs heedlessly north, anywhere to get away. Whatever might await her outside the chain link fence would be preferable to what awaits her here.

At least what is out there is human.

TERENCE STRUGGLES WITH Maria's tight grasp on his arm. "Damn you! Let me go. She's going to get away!" Maria is strong and she holds him tight, hands digging into his biceps like talons.

Edward stands helplessly by, wringing his hands.

Maria whips Terence back against the wall and slams him against it so hard he cannot speak for several seconds. When he gets his voice, he screams at Edward, "Oh you little pussy! I should have known you would just stand there, waiting to be told what to do, too weak to pursue anything yourself." He pauses, then shouts, "Go after her, you idiot! Go after her!"

Maria maintains a tight grip on Terence (under the brute force of her strength, he is like a butterfly pinned to the wall). She allows herself a quick glance back at Edward to see what he's going to do. Edward meets her gaze and doesn't move. Satisfied he will go nowhere, she turns back to Terence.

Maria is panting, and Terence's struggling is beginning to wear her down, but she doesn't want him to see that. She also wants this to be over, because she has her own plans for Elise, and does not want to lose her to the night.

"Now, you listen to me," Maria says, "I need to do this on my own. I don't need you, or Edward's help." A sob hiccups out of her. "I have to be the one. Please."

"It was supposed to be the three of us. I wanted to taste her," Terence hisses, a spoiled child.

"That was never going to happen." Edward jumps into the fray.

"Let me go after her. She'll be easy prey." Terence knows there isn't a human who can outrun their fleet, silent speed. He waits for just a moment, swallows, adding, "I'll bring her back to you." He clenches and unclenches his fists, keeping an eye on the dwindling figure of Elise moving through the night.

Maria shakes her head. "Terence, you've never said an honest thing in your life. Why should I believe you're starting now?"

"What are you talking about?" Terence tries to keep his voice even, to conceal the anxiety and anger.

"Bring her back? Bring her back?" Maria laughs. "She'd be a husk of bone and hair by the time we catch up with you. And you know it. Please..." Maria whispers, frantic, turning her head quickly to ensure Elise is still within view. "I've never asked you for much. You have to let this be mine." Maria searches Terence's eyes for some glimmer of understanding—and finds none.

"Damn it. Listen to me: I'm doing this alone. All of this is my fault...and I love her. I need to do this. My way."

"No!" Terence shouts. "We all share. We always have." There's a little less power left in his fight, but not enough that he can't use Maria's grief to his advantage. He squirms out of her grasp and starts after Elise.

Maria wails, crumbling to her knees, arms outstretched: a plea.

Terence laughs and starts off, covering the ground like a cheetah, feet barely touching the earth. But he feels the pull of something else on his shoulder: hands that feel like iron clamps, ripping him out of the air and slamming him down flat on his back.

Edward stares down. He is breathing heavy and looks at his own hands as if he's never seen them before. He puts a booted foot on Terence's chest. "Let Maria go." He motions for Maria to begin moving forward, to hurry. "After she brings her down, we'll all feed." He glances back at Maria. "Fair enough?"

Maria offers no response. Silently, swiftly, she takes off into the night, covering several feet with each leap. It will take no time at all to catch up with Elise, even though she is but a small dot on the black horizon.

IT IS ONLY minutes before Elise stumbles and falls. Her hands burn as rough concrete rips skin away from her palms. Her lungs burn, too, from the exertion of running. She wants to curl into a ball, to simply close her eyes and let whatever is going to happen, happen. This running, this exertion, she knows, is futile. She has nothing on their strength, their senses, and their determination.

Yet self-preservation, a stubborn instinct, rises up to tug at her, to push her toward life. Her breathing slows down a bit, even though her throat feels scorched. She pulls herself up on her knees and listens.

There is no sound behind her. No echo of footfalls moving rapidly through the night. Could she have gotten away? Is it possible she has eluded them? Elise stands, on shaky, newborn colt legs, and looks around. There is nothing. The night is still, save for a heavy wind off the lake, promising rain. She shivers and hugs herself, cold in spite of the temperature and the heavy, cloying air hanging over her. She pulls her hood up, chasing warmth that's impossible to capture, because her chill comes from inside.

She can't believe it's over, can't bring herself to think maybe they changed their minds and are letting her go. But yet, the silence and their absence tell a different story. She takes a few cautious steps forward, hampered because of a screaming stitch in her side, its hurt brilliant red.

She pauses, wondering which way is north, then west. How can she get back to Lake Shore Drive? She looks up at the half moon, partially hidden by navy blue clouds, and tries to get some bearing on where she is. The lake is east—

She turns around and screams.

Maria stands directly behind her.

Elise closes her eyes, grimacing. She swallows to get some spit going in her dry mouth and then says, "What do you want?"

Maria appears to be contrite; her head is slightly lowered, but not enough to shield the glimmer of her dark eyes, which try to engage Elise's own gaze. Maria implores her. Elise feels she has nothing left to give.

"You want to kill me, right?" Elise blows out a big sigh and considers the sky. "Jesus. Why not just get it over with?" She pulls down the hood of her sweatshirt, pushes a curtain of hair aside, and bares her throat. "Go ahead." Maria's response is silence. Elise lets the hair drop. "Isn't this what you want?" Elise's fear is beginning to be supplanted by a low boiling rage, an anger building slowly into something explosive. "Aren't you going to get rid of me? If you can't have me, no one will. Is that right?"

Maria shakes her head and finally speaks. "What you're saying... What you're saying... I can't grace with a denial. Few things are certain, but you should know by now that I love you." She meets Elise's eyes directly. "I would never harm you."

"Then what the fuck is this all about?" Elise clutches at her side, wishing the burning there would stop. She pulls the hood back up, wishing she could disappear into it.

Maria turns, stops, and looks over her shoulder. "Come with me." She begins walking toward the closest foundry building. "Behind that wall; we can be alone."

Elise laughs, which causes even more pain to shoot through her side. Yet the pain is beginning to ebb. Perhaps she will have the strength to run again. She shakes her head. "No. What kind of idiot do you think I am?"

"You still think I want to hurt you? I couldn't...even if I wanted to. I know I deserve nothing from you, but will you please show me the kindness of a moment alone with you?"

"Why? Why do we have to go over there? Why do we need to be hidden? If you want to say something to me, just say it here."

Maria extends her hand, bone white, and covers Elise's own hand. Elise doesn't pull away at the touch of Maria's cool skin. She tugs. "Please do this for me. I just want us to be out of their sight."

Elise looks back and sees she has not come as far as she thought. She can see two figures in the gloom, Terence and Edward.

"They're watching. Please. I want just a moment alone with you."

Elise follows her into the shadows.

And there, Maria turns to her. "There's one thing I do want from you, my sweet...one small, final thing."

Elise cocks her head, feels the tears, imminent, pooling in her eyes and causing a lump to form in her throat. "What?" she chokes out, barely able to speak. "What? You know I can't—"

"Shhh...just a kiss."

And Elise leans forward. Their mouths meet and Elise grips Maria, cold, against her and hungrily kisses back, not wanting to lose this simple connection of bodies and spirits. She forces herself to break away. "I...I can't"

Maria nods. "I know. I know there is so much you *can't*. And I understand. And I want that for you." She takes one of Elise's fingers in her hand and lifts it. She lowers her head a bit toward the finger and then looks up. "Just a taste?"

And Elise lets her. Just a tiny nip on the end of her finger. She feels Maria draw in the blood. She sees Maria pull her head away, and smile. A drop of crimson adheres to her lower lip.

"Now," she whispers, "this is for you."

TERENCE AND EDWARD watch and wait, listening. The kill shouldn't take long. Within seconds, Maria should emerge from the wall she has taken Elise behind and signal them to come join her. They picture her emerging, but each has a different viewpoint. Terence's mouth waters with anticipation. Edward holds his head in his hands, despair coursing through him, and asks himself why he couldn't have saved her.

When Terence opens his mouth to speak, the night air shatters with a long, piercing wail. The two men look at each other, their eyes meeting, and realize they are on opposite sides for the first time. It's a long, silent stare, yet eloquent. Edward is saying goodbye.

The moment between them is broken. Alarms go off and each is poised to run. They watch as Elise emerges from behind a wall, tendrils of dark hair escaping, tumbling out of her hood, to flow behind her as she begins once more to run.

Terence and Edward exchange one more glance, momentary. The

glance is panicked, with the same question. *Has she wounded Maria? Their Maria? It can't be.*

The figure scrambles north again, at a much faster pace.

"What should we do?" Edward is torn by emotions, desperate to run after Elise and, at the same time, wanting to see her get away. But most of all, he wonders why Maria has not emerged from behind the wall, and is sick to realize perhaps she let herself be wounded by this human.

"What can we do?" Terence spits out a bitter laugh. "We have to get her!"

And Edward watches, helpless, as Terence begins to run after Elise. His speed is superhuman and silent; his feet almost never touch the ground. When he gets within a few feet of Elise's scrambling figure, he leaps high into the sky, almost as if taking flight, and comes down with a thud on her back. Both fall hard into the earth below them.

Edward takes a few cautious steps forward, then freezes when he sees how rage has transformed Terence. They always change when they feed, but this is worse, this is pure animal. Terence's mouth is a grinning rictus of razor-sharp fangs. His fingers have elongated, topped with thick, hoof-like nails as long as daggers. His very body has become longer, a more efficient killer of his prey.

Edward stuffs a fist in his mouth as he watches, in mute horror, what comes next.

Terence sets upon her, rearing back and lifting his clawed hands to come down on her squirming figure. He doesn't allow her even one second to scream as his talons rip through her clothes, then the flesh of her back, yanking out her spine and flinging it, like a snake, behind him. He lowers his growling jowls and begins to tear flesh from bone.

Edward imagines Terence's rage: white-hot, immune to reason, blinding.

Terence bites, claws, and shreds with a terrifying fury.

She has never made a sound. She has never moved.

At last, Terence looks up at the silver light from the moon hidden behind clouds and sends a howl of triumph into the air. The bitch is at last done, dispatched with deadly efficiency.

He wants a trophy. He plunges both hands into the shell of her, tearing and cutting through muscle and bone until he wraps his hands around her heart.

He rips it out, offering it up to the moon.

But the heart is cold, the wounds bloodless, dry.

Something inside Terence closes, like a fist, tight and protective. He drops the cold heart to the ground.

Edward sobs behind him.

Terence turns and sees Edward incapacitated by grief. He knows what's wrong even as he turns back to the still figure beneath him. Her head has turned as he ripped her apart like a lion attacking a gazelle.

He will never forget her face. That face that remains intact, so still and so beautiful.

Maria. Dead at last.

This time, when he sends a strangled cry into the night sky, it is not one of triumph, but of anguish.

ELISE IGNORES THE stitch, ignores the fact there is no more air left in her lungs. She runs on adrenaline alone. Gray light spills over the housing project looming over her, illuminating the broken and boarded-up windows, the gang graffiti, and the rusting guardrails of balconies no one dares to use, except for suicide.

Yet never has a place looked more welcoming. Elise continues to sprint toward it, heart pounding. The first fingers of dawn, magenta-tinted, are creeping over the lake behind her, as the city comes to life.

Elise looks behind her. She will always be looking behind her.

Also from Rick R. Reed

published by
Quest Books

IM

A gay thriller with supernatural overtones, *IM* is the story of a serial killer using a gay hook-up website to prey on young gay men on Chicago's north side. The website's easy and relatively anonymous nature is perfect for a killer.

When the first murder comes to light, the first detective on the scene is Ed Comparetto, one of the police force's only openly gay detectives. He interviews the young man who discovered the body, Timothy Bright, and continues his investigation as the body count begins to rise. But, Comparetto hits a snag when he is abruptly fired from the police force. The cause? Falsifying evidence. It turns out that Timothy Bright has been dead for more than two years, murdered in much the same way as the first victim Ed investigated.

The case becomes a driving force for Comparetto, who finds more and more evidence to support that the person he first spoke to about the murders is really dead. Is he a ghost? Or, is something even more inexplicable and chilling going on? As the murder spree escalates and Comparetto realizes Bright is the culprit, he begins to fear for his own sanity...and his own life. Can Ed race against time and his own doubts to stop the killings before he and his new lover become victims?

ISBN 1-932300-79-6

978-1-932300-79-1

Available at booksellers everywhere.

Coming Next from Rick:

Deadly Vision:
Book One of the Cassandra Chronicles

Deadly Vision is inspired by the mythical seer Cassandra, who was given the gift of prophecy only to be cursed by having no one believe her. Reed's story is about small-town single mom, Cass D'Angelo, whose life changes when a thunderstorm sweeps into her small Ohio River town. Cass must venture out in it to hunt for her son, seven-year-old Max. Lightning strikes a tree near her and a branch crashes onto her head, knocking her unconscious; when Cass awakens a couple days later, she sees into the deepest secrets of those around her. Worse, some teenage girls have gone missing, and Cass can see their grisly fates. She tries to interest law enforcement and the mother of one of the girls in her visions and is rebuffed. The only one who will believe her is the father of the first missing girl. Reluctantly, Cass agrees to help him find his daughter and she does, in a shallow grave by the river.

The discovery opens the door to a whole new life. The police are suspicious. The press wants to make her a celebrity. And the killers are desperate to know how she found their carefully concealed grave. Cass's visions continue, frustrating and terrifying her. She finds an ally in Dani Westwood, a local reporter. The two women begin to probe into the disappearances/murders and start to forge a romance. When Cass's little boy, Max, disappears, Dani and Cass must race against the clock to find him...before it's too late.

Will Cass find her son in time? Will the parents of the other missing girl get closure? Will the killers escape? These are all questions answered by the time the reader comes to the breathtaking conclusion of Deadly Vision: Book One of The Cassandra Chronicles.

Available in January 2008

FORTHCOMING TITLES

published by
Quest Books

Face of the Enemy
by Sandra Barret

Helena 'Dray' Draybeck is a military brat finishing her final year of fighter pilot training at a Terran Military space station. She's cocky about everything except her dismal track record with women. Dray is driven to be a top pilot like her mother, but someone at the space station does not want Dray to succeed.

Jordan Bowers is the daughter of a high-ranking ambassador. She wants a career as far away from politics as possible. As one of the best cadets in the fighter pilot program, Jordan captures Dray's attention in more ways than one. But Jordan won't let anyone get close to her. She hides a terrible secret that could end her own career and turn Dray against her.

When an explosion on their training station turns into a full-fledged attack, Dray and Jordan are put on the fast track to active military duty. But Dray's enemy sabotages her assignment and her chances with Jordan.

The threat of war pits Dray and Jordan against family, questionable allies, and an enemy neither is prepared for. Can they build something more than friendship, or will war and family secrets tear these two women apart?

Face of the Enemy is a stand alone novel set in the Terra/Nova universe, where chip implants and DNA manipulation are commonplace, and bigotry drives an interstellar superpower.

Available November 2007

Land of Entrapment
by Andi Marquette

K.C. Fontero left Albuquerque for Texas in the wake of a bitter break-up, headed for a teaching and research post-doc at the University of Texas, Austin. With a doctorate in sociology and expertise in American white supremacist groups, she's well on her way to an established academic life. But the past has a way of catching up with you and as K.C. spends a summer helping her grandfather on his central Texas farm, her past shows up in the form of her ex, Melissa Crown, an Albuquerque lawyer who left K.C. for another woman three years earlier.

Melissa's younger sister Megan has gone missing—she's hooked up with a man Melissa suspects is part of an underground white supremacist group and Melissa needs K.C.'s help to find her and hopefully bring her out of the movement. K.C. knows she has the knowledge and contacts to track the group. She knows that in the interests of public service, she'd be helping law enforcement, as well. What she doesn't know is how far into her past she'll have to go in order to find not only Megan, but herself as well.

Working to locate the group without alerting members' suspicions, K.C. finds herself drawn to Megan's friend and neighbor, Sage Crandall, a photographer who challenges K.C.'s attempts to keep her heart ensconced in the safety of research and analysis. Confronted with her growing feelings for Sage while unraveling her complicated past with Melissa, K.C. delves into the racist and apocalyptic beliefs of the mysterious group, but the deeper she goes, the greater the danger she faces.

Available September 2008

OTHER QUEST PUBLICATIONS

About the Author

Rick R. Reed's published novels include *IM*, *A Face Without a Heart*, *Penance*, and *Obsessed*. Short fiction has appeared in numerous anthologies, the most horrific of which was collected in *Twisted: Tales of Obsession and Terror*. He lives in Miami with his partner and is at work on another novel. Visit him online at www.rickrreed.com.

VISIT US ONLINE AT
www.regalcrest.biz

At the Regal Crest Website You'll Find

- The latest news about forthcoming titles and new releases

- Our complete backlist of romance, mystery, thriller and adventure titles

- Information about your favorite authors

- Current bestsellers

- Media tearsheets to print and take with you when you shop

Regal Crest titles are available from all progressive booksellers and online at StarCrossed Productions, (www.scp-inc.biz), or at www.amazon.com, www.bamm.com, www.barnesandnoble.com, and many others.

Printed in the U
84486LV00005B

ited States
/142-180/A